CRUSHED

CRUSHED

by

GINNA MORAN

ISBN 978-1-942073-44-4 (soft cover)
ISBN 978-1-942073-45-1 (ebooks)

Cover design by Silver Starlight Designs
Cover images copyright 123RF

For Inquiries Contact:
Sunny Palms Press
9663 Santa Monica Blvd Suite 1158
Beverly Hills, CA 90210, USA
www.sunnypalmspress.com
www.GinnaMoran.com

To Katie, I'd say I'm sorry about the strong emotions this book elicited from you, but I'm not. (Insert maniacal laughter here.) I do hope this dedication makes up for it, though. I appreciate the time and effort you've spent seeking and destroying my errors and for making social media a lot more social. You're awesome! XOXO!

TWENTY-FIVE YEARS AGO

A CRIMSON HAZE shadows my vision as anger rages through me like a fire threatening to burn everything around me to ashes. The bitter, dangerous emotion consuming me keeps me moving forward. It's the only thing that encourages me to succeed in the one thing I want most in life—the destruction of those who've betrayed me by my hands.

I wasn't always like this. I didn't always have this overwhelming hunger for death, for devastation. But then everything changed. Everything always changes. My demonic side started controlling me worse than the man who raised me. My father's obsession with who I should be transformed me from a weak, fragile girl into a blood-thirsty demi-demon. And now it dominates me, controls me. By accepting my heritage as a half-demon, I've inherited the evil that comes with it—the evil that forces me to take deep breaths to stay in control.

The evil burns in a good way, my overwhelming power sizzling under my skin. The faces of the Hunter's Alliance blur as my desire to obliterate them overtakes my soul.

"Calm down," a surly voice begs. "You'll only hurt yourself."

The skin on my wrists stings as I yank at the wired rope binding my hands to the rickety metal chair. My knotted hair falls in my eyes. A scream burns in my throat. I need to get out of here before they discover I've lost control of my demon half—before they try to send my soul to where it belongs.

"You have to let me go before it's too late." My voice comes out as a whisper like the quiet before a storm. A thundering, demonic storm I know is bound to happen if I can't force my demonic half to relax.

Icy fear slithers through my veins. No one can save me. I can't even protect myself. My humanity slowly slips through my fingers. I won't let the alliance do this to me. I trusted them, helped them, and just like my dad said, they've turned their backs on me.

My vision transforms from red to black. A black so dark and devoid of light it feels like I'm being swallowed into a dark cavern of nothingness.

I scream again as I lose control. The demon within me

awakens, and I can't resist its alluring pull any longer. The alliance is going to die.

THE HUNTER'S ACADEMY

MY HANDS TINGLE with electricity. Radiant sparks of light zap from my fingertips with the mere thought of the outcome. I want the energy to flow freely, easily pliable, to strike my opponent. The intensity of my desire increases the voltage until the energy stream glows a blinding white, moving like a placid wave between my palms, growing and swelling until it solidifies.

The power is scary intense yet deliciously intoxicating. It floods from my soul, penetrating the wall protecting my most precious asset. It's raw and unpredictable like a lightning storm and capable of causing death if I will it to.

I thrust the energy ball at Evan. He ducks, avoiding the impact and shock of my power. I sigh at the release, my body thankful for tossing away the energy, which wasn't mine to begin with but my demon father's. Dropping to my knees, I lean forward and press my hands against the shiny wood floor for support.

Evan rushes to my side and lifts me into his arms. Static buzzes in my chocolate-brown hair and wisps cling to his chin stubble. A tiny spark flies as he brushes his lips against my temple. I absorb the heat of his kiss until he gingerly pulls away.

"How does it feel having power of your own?" he asks. It's the same question every time I push the energy from my soul.

"Wrong. I'll never claim this ability as my own. I feel more and more like myself every time I dispel it. I can't wait until it's gone for good."

I flick my fingers, producing tiny flashes of light. They drift to the ground like glittering falling stars until they disintegrate into puffs of smoke. If I wasn't afraid of being vulnerable, I'd release the power all at once just to get it over with.

"But it makes practice more entertaining." Evan's face hovers close to mine for a second, and I expect him to kiss me, but he shifts to set me on my feet instead.

I smirk at his teasing. "I have other ways to keep you entertained, you know." I spin on my heels and break into a jog for the door. My footsteps fall silent as I defy gravity. From all the horrible things Malicevile, my father, put me through, I did get one good thing out of it. I've almost mastered levitation, and I use it so often it's second nature to me.

Evan's scent reaches me before he does. Warm golden amber and heady patchouli circulate through the air, wrapping me in a blanket of goodness. He grabs my hand, intertwining our fingers, to slow me down.

The past month has been utter bliss. I have a place to call home, I never have to worry if Malicevile will show up and try to kidnap me, and I'm actually on a human schedule. It's nice to fall asleep before the sun comes up. The Hunter's Academy is everything I've dreamed of. I'll never figure out why Alana, my guardian, was so against us coming here, but I still see the worry in her eyes sometimes.

Evan steps in front of me, and I stop. "You amaze me." His golden blond hair lies in sweat-dampened clumps around his head from practice. His ocean blue eyes shine with tiny crinkles around the outer corners as he gives me a half grin.

I run my hands up his firm, broad chest before dangling them loosely around his neck. "How so?" Jumping up, I hover inches above the ground to meet his gaze straight on.

"For one, you can kick my ass in a fight. Two, you act like you grew up here in the academy, and three, you never fail to surprise me."

I lean in and kiss him, pulling away quick enough to not draw the attention of the others in the gym. The last thing I need is to be scolded for PDA when I'm training. I miss the old church that my demonic father burned down. At least no one could question my relationships with people there.

It's still hard to believe Evan's my boyfriend when there are so many other girls here that are completely baggage free. But, he chose me, baggage and all. He even helps me carry it, which isn't an easy job—believe me. I've been lugging it around for years.

"Take it outside you two," Hunter Sylvester calls from where he pins down a trainee with a wooden training knife pressed to the boy's chest. "I shouldn't have to remind you that distractions hinder focus."

A warm blush flushes my cheeks. "No, sir, you don't. We're sorry."

"Apology accepted. I don't want to have to ask the Hunter's Alliance to transfer you to another trainer." He helps the boy he's practicing with to his feet.

I let go of Evan's hand. "That's not necessary."

Hunter Sylvester can put in the request all he wants, but the alliance doesn't get involved in demi-demon training. They don't even know how to go about it. We get our training from other demi-demons and just share the facilities. Since they put us out in the field in dangerous situations before they would a human hunter, they're more lenient. We just have to maintain a respectful appearance to prevent animosity on campus. With the motto, *Humans Come First*, it's not a good idea to get on people's bad sides.

Evan smirks at me as I descend to the floor. He slides his arm around my back, grounding me like the tether I desperately need to focus on the present and future.

We turn and stroll together through the vast training room where other students practice combat. It's easy to forget that we're not alone in the world. He guides me into the empty hallway and away from the training room.

Compared to the simplicity of our old church, the Hunter's Academy is like a palace. Gleaming marble floors sparkle with flecks of shimmering minerals embedded in the sleek stone. The lush floor runner matches the burgundy painted walls and bronze-coated crown moldings. Glittering crystal chandeliers dangle from the mirrored ceiling every ten feet.

The stained-glass windows filter colorful light that bounces off every shiny surface—the floors, the ceiling, and even the gold-framed paintings. Round, wooden accent tables hold luscious, blossoming hydrangeas, bringing part of nature inside. And this is only a hallway.

By the luxurious décor of the academy, you'd think that money trees really did exist and the alliance had an orchard of them. I'm still not used to the grandeur of this lifestyle.

Evan pushes open the French doors. It never ceases to amaze me how eclectic the academy really is. Each room tells a story, and with how long the alliance has been around, they have accumulated a lot of possessions.

A young, robust woman happily sits behind a reception counter. Her fiery red hair is braided neatly to the side, hanging limply on her collarbone. She glances from her monitor and smiles warmly with a squint to her muddy-brown eyes. Her shirt is a little snug, and her freckled stomach peeks through the openings of the stressed buttons.

When we reach the counter, I lean on my elbows, resting

my chin on my hands. Evan casually slings his arm around my shoulders, and I watch the woman's eyes trail to his fingers drumming on my arm.

"Good practice, Hunter Evan?" She ignores me completely as she hands Evan the record log to sign us out. I gaze over her tidy desk, scanning for her name plate. Even after a month, I still can't remember her name.

"As always, Sarah." Evan scrawls our names in the out column along with the time. He hands the clipboard back with a friendly smile.

"Who won today?" Sarah leans over her keyboard to give Evan the full effect of her cleavage.

"Cami."

"Any injuries?"

"Just my ego."

Sarah laughs loudly like a hyena after inhaling helium. Flipping her braid over her shoulder, she shows off her protruding collarbone. I roll my eyes and cross my arms. If it wasn't the Hunter's Academy protocol that we answer a series of questions after every practice, I'd have pulled Evan away the moment he set the pen down.

"New powers?"

"Nope."

"Damage?"

"None."

"Angry outbursts?"

"Never."

"That's too bad." Sarah purses her lips, raising a thinly plucked eyebrow at me.

I crack my knuckles together, trying my best to keep a straight face. I'd never let her see that's she getting to me. The last thing I need is for the alliance to consider me unbalanced.

"If you wish to see one, I can arrange it. I just can't promise you'd come out unscathed," I say perkily, like I'm offering a trip to the Magic Kingdom.

Sarah hunkers down in her chair, my ability making it easy for me to tower over her. Evan tugs on the back of my sweatshirt, and I lower to the floor.

"Anything else?" Evan asks, cutting through the thick tension emanating from Sarah's pores. She smells of sweat and white floral perfume.

"That's it. See you later?"

"Same time tomorrow."

Evan grabs my hand and pulls me away from the counter. I beam a smile over my shoulder before jumping onto Evan's back, snuggling my chin in the nook of his neck. He carries me out of the training center and into a neat garden surrounding a stone fountain with a beautiful angel statue blowing a stream of clear water through its trumpet. The heady aroma of roses permeates the air, blending with the fresh, zesty scent of the lemon grove lining the vast property.

He leans forward and picks a white daisy, handing it to me. I put it behind my ear and kiss him, enjoying the time we have together before he leaves for the night.

There are two kinds of people who live at the academy—students and employees. Since Evan graduated two years ago, he's the latter. His job sounds simple: keep demons, demonic minions, and other evildoers away from the academy walls.

If only it were as simple as it sounded. The Hunter's Academy is like a jar of honey to a swarm of flies. Most young creatures and hunters reside at an academy. If a demon were to somehow cross the blessed barrier, it would have the chance to take out the future hunters of the world, giving demons everywhere an advantage. People like Evan prevent that from happening. I can sleep easily knowing that I'm safe, and I know Evan can handle just about any demonic situation...including my father.

"It's not nice leading that poor woman on," I say when we're out of hearing range from the open door. I should be used to the attention Evan gets—most of the halfies get a few extra longing gazes, especially fully trained hunters—but I can't stop the ugly jealousy that tries to force me into acting on my demon half. My brain tells me I'm being ridiculous. Too bad the rest of me doesn't agree. It's the constant inner struggle I have to deal with now that my human façade has been completely cracked by not only my demon dad's presence, but also the fact that I'm around Evan and other demi-demons my entire day.

"I've known Sarah for years. She'd never think it was anything more than me being friendly," Evan says.

"I'm pretty sure she sees the possibility of something more."

Evan grabs my wrist and flips me over his shoulder to face him. I wrap my legs around his waist and look into his startling blue eyes. "She does not. Even if she did, there's nothing for you to worry about. You're the one I want to be serious with."

"I'm not worried about me. I'm worried about her. She'll be heartbroken when she discovers I'm not going to be easy to get rid of. And then she'll start scheduling us at crappy times." I push away from Evan, arching my back until the world turns upside down. He gently eases me lower until my fingers touch the ground, and I'm able to flip back onto my feet. One of these days I'll learn how to do a badass handspring without help to enhance my fighting techniques. I've hit too many walls trying to flip using levitation that it's not worth it at the moment.

"You're the one who is going to get us the bad times if you don't act a little nicer," Evan says. "You know, I love your feistiness, and I get that you're struggling to keep yourself in control, but someone who can electrocute another person with their bare hands is terrifying to humans. Also, you're a showoff, Cami."

I turn away, covering my heated cheeks as he slaps me with a reality check. I didn't realize I was showing off until Evan mentioned something. I'm proud of my abilities and use them every chance I get. It's not that I'm purposely being a showoff. The more I practice, the more natural they feel. If I don't use them, I forget how. I'm only a beginner. I can't hit a start button and wait for them to magically manifest.

"Ouch. That hurts, especially coming from the boy who

parades around wearing a layer of demon blood after the end of his shift to show how successful his hunt was." I try to sound like I'm teasing, but his words do sting.

He pouts his bottom lip before pulling me closer. "I didn't mean it in a bad way. I just meant that not everyone is okay with us halfies. Subtlety gets you a long way in the alliance. Remember, humans come first." Evan spits out the Hunter's Alliance motto as if it leaves a bitter taste in his mouth.

I get his point. Not every human hunter appreciates us or is as unbiased as Alana, David, and Cadence. But isn't that how it is with everyone? The world, human or supernatural, will always have issues with each other. It's how we deal with the differences that matter. The alliance has been kind to me, has taken me in, and that counts for something. They could've easily turned their back on me completely when I managed to survive confronting Malicevile.

I skip in front of him, walking backward to face him. Poking his chest, I say, "You're right. Flaunting my curse can be unsettling. Even for me." I shove my hands into the pockets of my track pants, suppressing the sudden chill icing my bones.

Evan pulls me into a hug, stopping me from walking, and breathes softly into my hair. "You're not cursed. If you were, do you think I'd still be hanging around?"

"Yes, actually. You can't resist a date with danger."

"No. I can't resist a date with you."

I stay wrapped in his arms without saying a word. It's hard to believe any of this is real. I've been waiting so long for my life to turn around. And now that it has, I'm not sure how to enjoy it. All I can think is that something bad is bound to happen.

I stare at our elongated shadows stretching across the cobblestone path. The blazing sun sits low in the sky, and I imagine the demons slowly waking up, preparing for the evening on the other side of these protective walls.

Then I remember Evan will be out there, too.

"We should get going," I say. "You have a long night ahead of you."

CONFLICTED

"ARE YOU KIDDING me?" I read over the content glaring at me from the computer screen.

After my slow, agonizing recovery from the power-overload and injuries inflicted on me by Malicevile, I've finally been able to attend class again. The academy isn't exactly what I expected. Along with combat and weaponry classes, there is actual studying involved, too. I'm enrolled in a little bit of everything until I decide what I want to do with my life. Sometimes, I really feel like having a desk job—other times, I feel like conquering armies of demons. But now, I just want the day to be over with.

"When are you going to stop being surprised?" Alana asks,

peeking her head in from the kitchen doorway.

"When there's nothing more to be surprised about."

My assignment for the night is to scour the internet for mythical creatures and compare my list with the one created by the Hunter's Alliance. The list is quite long: zombies, witches, vampires, fairies, banshees, mermaids, elves, pixies, and trolls. Plus, the ones I've dealt with, demons, werewolves, and angels. There are more creatures in the Veiled Realm than I could've ever imagined.

Alana chuckles. "So, never."

It's nice not having to be protected day and night, but I do miss her constant company. Alana has given up hunting to take on a research position in the archives. I never thought I'd see the day where she would sit behind a desk, but I think she does it for me. She's the only family I have, and she'd never do anything to jeopardize her own life unless it was for me. That's something she doesn't have to do here. She gets to enjoy a long needed vacation after being on her own for so long.

"Most likely. Will I ever get to meet any other creatures?" I ask, thinking about all the things I still need to learn about. I'm sure I encountered some other creatures in Desertville with Cadence, but I'll never know for sure.

"Only if they allow it. Personally, I've met only halfies and werewolves."

"I bet I could sniff one out," I say with a laugh.

"You'll have to tell me if you do."

The landline rings, interrupting our conversation. Alana returns to the kitchen to answer it. Tired of staring at the monitor, I put the computer into sleep mode and click off the screen.

The alliance assigned apartment is nicer than anything we've previously lived in. The plump, forest green carpet leaves a small bounce in my step when I'm not levitating. Large framed photographs of city skylines—places I wish to travel to after I graduate—decorate the cream colored walls. A cluster of our family photos lines a section of the wall nearest the front door, giving the place a personal touch. Sitting in front of a deep-seated, tan couch rests a black coffee table with no space to even set a cup on since it's littered with all of David's deteriorating ancient books.

On the wall across from the couch hangs a flat screen television above the fake fireplace; a layer of dust coats the screen. I'm so used to not having a television, so I forget it's even there. A tall bookshelf is shoved in the corner nearest the hallway with all kinds of books neatly arranged in alphabetical order. On the other side of the hallway entrance is an area considered the workstation. A laptop computer rests on a creaky folding table I use as a desk.

A heavy curtained, sliding glass door leads to a quaint cement patio with two plastic lawn chairs that face the sprawling lawns designed for community activities. It's not as luxurious as the rest of the academy, but I'm so happy to call this place home.

"Cami," Alana says, appearing in the doorway again. "It's Dylan. Do you want me to take a message?"

She asks the same question every time he calls like one of these days I'll finally tell her that I don't want to talk to him. So far, times with Dylan only get awkward when he thinks something is wrong with me. He knows his boundaries, and he understands that he was never a choice to make—not with his absence. "No, that's okay. I'll take it in my room."

I pad down the hallway to my bedroom and flounce on my brand new bed before reaching for the phone on my night table. Pressing the receiver to my ear, I listen for Alana to hang up her line. One of these days I'll ask her for another cell phone. I've broken too many to expect her to just buy one for me.

"Can I come in?" Dylan asks before I have the chance to greet him.

I hang up the phone without answering him and walk to my bedroom window, pushing my sheer pink curtains aside. Dylan stands on the other side of the glass, his dark eyebrows peaked in amusement. He's wearing a hooded sweatshirt, covering his messy black curls.

As I slide the window open, Dylan pops the screen off. I offer my hand to let him in. His chocolate eyes never waver from mine as I step backward to give him room.

"We have a front door," I say, moving back to my bed.

"I know, but Alana doesn't like me much."

I don't disagree. Alana blames Dylan for dragging me into the world she worked so hard to protect me from. She thinks if he would've kept his mouth shut, we'd still be living inconspicuously away from all this. I don't see it that way, though. Dylan helped me discover the truth about my heritage. He was there for me when I was beaten and broken, not physically, but spiritually. He helped me grow and led me to Evan. The good he brought to my life outweighs the bad, and I wouldn't change anything.

Pulling the chair away from my desk, Dylan meanders across the room with it to sit next to me without invading my space. He's wearing his usual dark washed jeans that hug his hips perfectly, his flat stomach peeking from under his sweatshirt as he raises his arms to pull off his hoodie. I stare at my hands, self-conscious of the attraction I still have for him even though I've rejected him for Evan.

"She'll get over it," I say a little too late as a response to his comment, my mind clearly wandering as his apple scent wafts over me. I lean against my pillow, lifting my eyes to the corkboard hanging crookedly on my pale purple walls. It was my attempt to personalize my room, pinning photos, magazine clippings, and sticky notes, among other things, to it.

"And until she does, I'm going to use the window." Dylan runs his fingers through his hair, pushing the loose strands from his eyes. "That way she doesn't have to pretend to be nice to me."

I cover my smirk with my hand. You would think it would be easy for a demon hunter and a nephilim to get along, fighting on the same side, but Dylan and Alana are an exception. They only tolerate each other at best. Most times, Alana is blatantly obvious in her unfounded—at least to me—distrust.

I nudge his arm with my closed hand. "I'll let her know you said that. She'll be happy to know you've thought of her."

"Could you also let her know that the alliance requests the honor of both of your presences tomorrow after your first class?"

My joking mood turns serious fast. "And I thought you came to hang out. I should've known it would be business." I sit up and sling my legs off the bed. As I move to stand up, Dylan grabs my wrists to keep me in place.

"I didn't have to come over here to tell you that. I came because I wanted to see you." Dylan's crisp scent washes over me, wiping away all traces of my annoyance.

A tiny spark escapes my hands, and I tug away and shove them into my pockets before I fall back onto my bed. Dylan either didn't notice, or he's pretending the sparks didn't happen as he shifts to pick up a photo of me and Evan from my night table. It's my favorite photo, where I'm full of smiles right after my release from the infirmary. Cadence had taken it right outside this apartment when I was told this was to be our place.

I reach out to snatch the photo from him, but he sets it back down before I touch it. "He makes you happy," Dylan says softly. It's not a question, and I'm not sure if he is talking to me or himself. He's never really asked me about Evan, but he knew that we were more than friends—our similar heritage sparked something indescribable between us. It was an instant attraction. I just felt like we belonged together. It was clear to almost everyone without even having to say a word.

I lean forward and place my hand on Dylan's knee. It feels weird that I have this need to comfort him. He lost his chance the moment he stepped out of my life. He even said it was for the best. Now he's just going to have to accept it. No amount of dream walking or kind words will change my mind. He'll only ever be my friend.

"What does the alliance want?" I ask, changing the subject. It's moments like these that make me wonder why I don't tell Alana to just take a message. Something keeps Dylan in my life, though—like my soul wants his protection. It's deeper than what's on the surface.

The shadows clouding Dylan's eyes melt away as quickly as they came. I breathe a sigh in relief. I didn't want to have to ask him to go.

"I'm not sure. I bet they're just trying to get to know you better. It's not often that they get a demi-demon who is prone to getting in danger as much as you. They only have your best interests in mind," Dylan says.

"Why's that?" I've told the alliance everything they need to know about my past for their records. There isn't much more to tell that they don't already know. I'm the spawn of a demon, I've acquired my father's power, and I survived everything he has thrown at me because I have people who care enough about me to protect me and nothing more. If that isn't good enough, then I don't know what is.

"To make sure you never have to fight for your soul like that ever again." I'm pretty sure that's not the reason for the alliance's interest and stems purely from Dylan's own need to protect me. He said it himself the first time we met—he sees my vulnerability and wanted to help me. But I don't show that same vulnerability anymore. Hell, I don't think I need his protection, either.

I bite my tongue before I can argue. I want to tell him it's something else because before I came to the academy, they abandoned me and everyone I loved to die. If they cared about my soul, they would've sent in reinforcements to help or even showed some concern about whether I made it through the night with Malicevile hunting me down. They didn't want to get involved because I'm not human. To them, I'm not worth saving unless I can benefit their cause, which now they see I can.

"How sweet of them." My words drip with sarcasm. "And I thought they believed I didn't even have one."

"They'd be stupid to think you didn't. Yours shines as bright as the sun. It's very hard to miss even to the untrained human eye," Dylan says. I glimpse the outline of his translucent wings before they turn invisible again.

Staring at my hands expectantly, I wait to see the glow of my soul that Dylan spoke of. Small sparks erupt from my fingertips again, and I fist my hands. The power might come from my soul, but it's a parasite, a foreign substance attached to my being—the evil left behind by my father.

"Don't look so sad, Cami." Dylan moves from the chair, and I feel the bed shift beneath me. I refuse to look at him. I will not get lost in his fathomless eyes. I don't need his comfort anymore. "It'll go away."

Oily darkness seeps into my heart, my inner demon outraged at the mere thought of losing an ounce of power. Who am I kidding? I *am* my inner demon. It isn't a separate part of me no matter how much I want it to be. I'm conflicted. I might hate the power sizzling in my core, but my soul refuses to give it up. It's intoxicating and liberating being able to use it at will.

I swallow the bitter emotions before I lose control. "I think you should go."

I don't want Dylan to know how much I still struggle with the shadows threatening to consume me. My father did something to me the day he burned the church to the ground. He tilted the balance between my human and demon half. Only Alana and Evan know what he did to me and what I'm capable of. I'm not willing to share it with anyone else. Not Cadence, not David, and especially not Dylan. But if I don't stay calm, I could easily be swept away in dark red rage, and Dylan would surely find out because he would be standing directly in its path.

A soft breeze caresses my hair as his wing brushes against me. "Will you be okay?"

"Yes. Please, just go."

Dylan frowns but doesn't argue. His lips are feather light against my cheek before he stands up and walks to the window. He pushes open the curtains and slips outside. I watch as he adjusts the screen and our gazes meet.

"You know you can tell me anything," he whispers.

I shake my head so subtly that I'm not sure he saw. His sad smile darkens his eyes before he disappears into the night, leaving me alone with my troubled thoughts.

NOT A MONSTER

"I'LL MEET YOU in the courtyard at five minutes to ten," Alana says, slinging a tote bag filled with old files and paperwork over her shoulder. She probably spent all night reviewing the work the alliance has her doing now.

"Sounds good," I say.

David sits at the dining table, drinking from a mug of coffee while reading the alliance-issued newspaper. He yawns and shakes his head to stay awake long enough to kiss Alana goodbye. After the night shift with Evan, he looks exhausted.

Alana kisses David on the forehead before giving me a hug. She pats my back before slipping out the front door.

Evan strolls into the room, his bare chest gleaming with shower steam, sending my heart racing. I imagine running my fingers across the curves of his stomach muscles for a moment before sipping my orange juice and setting the glass on the counter.

He brushes his hand over his damp hair, slicking it back on his head. As he waltzes closer, he pulls a black T-shirt over his head and then leans down to greet me with a kiss.

"Ready?" he asks.

My backpack hangs from my fingertips, and he takes it off my hands so I can shrug into my leather jacket. I'm the only one in my small class who wears one, but I feel naked and vulnerable without it most days. I hate to admit it has become my security blanket, and I can't explain why it eases my tight nerves.

Once I'm ready, I wave to David, who shuffles down the hallway before closing the door. I follow Evan out of the apartment.

Taking our time, we meander down a cement path toward the academy's cafeteria. Leafy oak trees shade the marigold-lined pathways. It's like walking through a magical garden where everything moves and glitters with life. The tall, red brick buildings scattered about have bronze-plated placards named after long ago hunters who originally founded the academy. We pass a large dormitory bustling with activity as the other students start their mornings.

Evan yawns and wraps his arm around my waist. He leans

into me, and I levitate slightly, bearing his weight. The subtle change in my height goes unnoticed as long as I keep my feet moving.

"You know, you can go straight to bed when you get home," I say, breaking the comfortable silence.

"And miss seeing you? Sleep can wait."

I roll my eyes as I laugh. We stroll up the cement steps that lead into the gigantic cafeteria. Evan opens the heavy door for me, and I step into the crowded room.

White lace tablecloths decorate cedar tables that are pushed together in four long rows. Matching benches have enough room for ten people to sit. Morning light filters through the curtains of the huge windows, lighting the cafeteria in a soft, warm glow. The only windowless wall has a huge floor to ceiling mural of an angel flying over a sunlit ocean. The place is beautiful in its amazing simplicity.

Evan turns toward the line of students and faculty members waiting to get breakfast. "Go ahead and find us a seat." With David working the nightshift, he never cooks breakfast for us anymore.

Lowering to the floor, I glance around the room. I spot a shining head of deep purple hair and head in that direction. Other students gawk at me, like they're still seeing me for the first time. I plop down across from Cadence at the end of a table. She smiles, showing off her perfectly straight teeth, and I smile right back at my best friend.

"I'll never get over how many cute boys live here," she says, winking at a brown-haired boy across the way. He blushes, caught by surprise that Cadence has shown him attention, before lowering his gaze to his plate of food.

"I know, huh," I say, watching Evan pick up three plates before balancing one on his arm and the other two in his hands.

She rolls her eyes. "He doesn't count."

"He does to me."

"Ugh, I miss single Cami."

"Me too." A warm pair of hands covers my eyes, but I'd know that scent anywhere. Dylan squeezes my shoulders before moving around the table to slide in next to Cadence. The entire female population sighs when Dylan flashes me a smile. He's the only nephilim living on campus, and seems to know everyone because he helps the alliance leaders with who knows what—he claims he's passing along messages, but I think it's more than that. I don't bother to ask. I'm used to not getting straightforward answers.

Cadence punches him in the arm harder than I expect her to, and he moves with the motion. She flips her purple hair over her shoulder, sending a whiff of her coconut shampoo in my direction.

"You know I'm single, Angel Boy," Cadence says jokingly, batting her thick black lashes.

I nod at the brown-haired boy still gazing longingly at Cadence. "Not for long."

Cadence blows him a kiss this time, and I swear the boy is about to pass out. Her attention can be quite overwhelming. I adore her confidence and carefree attitude, and of course, her kickass moves and chic style. She's the kind of demon hunter you would see in a movie. Her beauty is all natural, pure human—not enhanced by angel or demon blood.

"Find someone you like?" Evan sets down two plates filled with every breakfast food you could imagine. I steal a blueberry muffin before Cadence can reach it and rip it in half to give her a piece.

"I did, actually. Do any of you know his name?" she asks. She nibbles the muffin, careful not to smear her deep plum lipstick.

"He's in my defensive combat class," I offer. "I can find out who he is later."

"Perfect!" Cadence waggles her brows. "You're a babe."

"She is, isn't she?" Evan wraps an arm around my shoulders and kisses my cheek. I squeeze his fingers and look up so he can kiss me on the lips. "Have fun," he adds, whispering into my ear. He always takes his breakfast to go, which is probably for the best since he attracts just as much attention as Dylan.

I release his fingers. "See you later."

I gaze at him as he maneuvers around the tables before he exits. Dylan watches me watch him, and I smirk. I wish he wouldn't stare at me like I'm the only one in the room. It makes me antsy to finish eating and leave.

"Hello? Earth to Cami," Cadence says, waving her fingers at me. "Distracted much lately?"

I take a deep breath, shrugging my shoulders. I wouldn't be

like this if Dylan weren't here. His presence screams for my attention, and it takes everything in me not to give it to him.

"Blame him." I tilt my head towards Dylan. "He delivered a message last night that has me on edge."

"Oh, jeez. Again? What did you do this time that you have to go in front of the alliance?" Cadence swats my hand. "Electrocute a teacher? Levitate in front of the human hunters? Wait. Please tell me you didn't call a werewolf a dog."

I stare at Cadence, startled. "Dylan said it was probably to get to know me more."

She raises her eyebrows. "Yeah, right. I know they have everything they need to know. My dad's a leader, remember?" She taps her finger on her cheek. "Maybe too much PDA. No, they'd bring in Evan for that."

"You're scaring her," Dylan says. "I'm sure Cami has been on her best behavior."

I sigh. "What he said. Where do you even get these ideas, Cadence?"

She shrugs. "People like to speculate. You sure you didn't show off or something?"

I cover my face with my hands. She thinks I'm a showoff, too. Ugh. What's the point of being the spawn of a demon if I can't demonstrate my abilities every once in a while? It's the least I deserve with Hell wanting to keep me toasty.

I let her words sink in for a minute, and then yesterday's practice flashes through my mind. "I might've threatened to unleash my anger on the training center attendant." Embarrassment blossoms heat up my collarbone remembering the jealousy that got the best of me.

Cadence brings her hand to her lips to hide her gaping mouth. "Cami, you didn't? Poor Sarah. What did she ever do to you?"

Dylan chuckles at Cadence's dramatics. I just feel guilty. Students gawk from nearby tables in our direction, leaning closer to hear our conversation. It's not usual for trainees to sit with mentors and other faculty members, even if Cadence and Dylan are basically the same age I am.

I reach out and squeeze Cadence's arm. "Can you keep it down? I was just joking with her...sort of. I didn't think she'd go to the alliance."

"So, you've electrocuted one of your teachers?" Dylan breaks in, flashing an amused smile.

"No. I don't know where Cadence got that. She has a wild imagination," I say defending myself. "I've never levitated in front of the humans outside of the training center, either. Well, at least not noticeably."

"But you *have* called a werewolf a dog," Cadence says, laughing.

"He shouldn't have said I smelled like a demon," I retort.

My chest tightens as I think about what I'm going to say to the alliance if Cadence is right. I'm sure they don't take threats lightly, even if I was joking. I'm going to owe Sarah a giant, heartfelt apology. She just annoyed me with her sweetness. I'm going to blame my demon half for the jealousy that snuck up on me. It doesn't help that I sometimes forget that not everyone is like my friends. People are terrified of demons, even demi-demons, and I can't blame them. I'm afraid of them, too.

Sensing my fear, Dylan reaches across the table and gently rests his hand on mine. When our skin touches, something within me stirs and a small pulse of power ripples from me to him. He blinks a few times as I accidentally shock him. Mortified, I try to jerk my hand away, but he then covers it with his other hand, holding my hand between both of his.

This whole situation has me on edge. I'm usually not so out of control with my power. It's like the demon within me is trying to keep others away. It's the only thing I can think of.

When Cadence glances at our hands, I jerk away from Dylan. A million questions raise her eyebrows, and I know she'll corner me later. I wish Evan had stayed for breakfast. I could use his hand holding to give me some extra strength instead of making me feel out of control and bare.

Clearing my throat, I ask, "You can't go ask the leaders what it's about? You're the one who delivered the message to me." I can't let the silence draw out. Silence is a terrible thing when it comes to thinking things through.

"Afraid not. You're worrying too much for something that's probably nothing." Dylan takes an apple slice from my plate and pops it into his mouth.

"Will they expel me?" I have a million scenarios crossing my mind. I can't help the dozens of questions I want to pummel messenger boy with. My heartbeat quickens when Cadence looks at Dylan for his answer.

"No. Don't be ridiculous," Dylan says. "If this is the case, you'll be forgiven if you're truly remorseful. You obviously didn't shock Sarah. Situations like these are dealt with carefully. Since you're new here and don't know the rules, they'll be lenient."

"I deserve whatever they do. I let Sarah get to me, and I shouldn't have. But it's not like I would've obliterated her. I'm not a monster." Why do I have to convince myself this more than anyone? If she really did anger me, would I have lashed out? Would Evan have been able to stop me? I feel like running home and hiding in my room for the rest of my life. What if I do lose control? I couldn't live with being me after that. *Stupid demon dad.* This is his fault.

"You don't sound so sure of yourself," Dylan says.

"Really, Angel Boy?" Cadence asks, slapping his arm. The sound resonates loud enough to draw attention to us from people at other tables.

Dylan's dark gaze holds me in its intensity, like he's searching my soul for something that I can't even see. He's doing his angel thing again—trying to break down the walls I've lined with steel. They're not meant to keep others out, though. They're meant to keep my demon half imprisoned within me.

My face reddens. "Whatever, Dylan. It doesn't matter. If you don't drop it, you're going to be the one I obliterate."

My words come out louder than I mean to say them, and the boy who Cadence was flirting with sinks lower in his seat.

He cringes when I smack my hand on the table and sparks fly, but only I notice them.

Cadence fakes a loud laugh. "She's joking," she says over her shoulder.

I guess I'm not the only one who questions whether or not I'm a monster.

Dylan smirks. "Is this how you treated poor Sarah?"

Cadence smacks him again. I'd think he'd move by now, but all he does is smile as he rubs his arm. Probably because he deserves it. The room quiets a notch, and I hunker down on the bench to avoid feeling like an animal trapped in a cage at the zoo.

I roll my eyes without responding.

A few more students stare in my direction, and I wish I'd just grabbed a bowl of cereal at the apartment. Word travels fast here. Now instead of being the poor, clueless demi-demon who thought she was human because she was raised by them, I'll be the demi-demon who has it out for the training room receptionist.

Unwilling to sit here under the watchful eyes of half the campus, I slide from the bench and stand. "Thanks for ruining my breakfast. I'll see you guys later."

I ignore the dozens of eyes peering at my back as I rush across the dining hall and to the door. Next time, I'll be sure to sit somewhere close to the exit.

Sunlight wraps around me when I burst from the double doors. Plopping down on the bottom step, I cradle my head in my hands and suck in a deep breath. I refuse to cry, but the stress is overwhelming.

Dylan's apple and rain scent reaches me before his shadow falls over me. "Cami, I'm sorry. Everyone knows we were joking."

I can't decide whether I should knock him down the stairs or allow him to sit next to me.

Heaving a sigh, I say, "You sure about that? I saw what you were doing in there."

"Doing? Joking around like a friend?" He doesn't sit next to me. Instead, he leaps the few stairs to the pathway so he faces me.

I consider bolting away, but where would I go? Class doesn't start for another thirty minutes, and there's absolutely no way I'm going back into the dining hall even though I should. I left my stupid backpack on the floor under the table. Home is starting to sound pretty good, but then Evan would know something was wrong, and he doesn't even know about the meeting.

I throw my hands up as I hop to my feet. "No, you were pulling that angelic crap, studying my soul or whatever it is you do. You have to stop that. I'm half demon, not broken."

He rubs the back of his neck. "I was just making sure you were okay."

Shaking my head, I push past him. "Try asking."

"So you can lie to me?" He falls in step with me as I stroll away from the dining hall. "You don't think I know that you've changed since first meeting you, but I do, Cami. That bastard of a demon father did more than try to break you."

When I last faced my father as I watched the church burn to the ground, it was like he poked the beast that hid itself so well under my skin. Maybe that was his intent to begin with. He realized he was losing, so he took it upon himself to unleash the darkness he'd passed down to me. He's silently waiting for me to fail here—he said it himself in the letter he sent to try to break me. And now, I fear everything he said is coming true. If the alliance figures out that the demon within me begs to break free, they'll send me away.

I stop in my tracks, averting my eyes to the sky. "Will you stop bugging me if I tell you what's really going on?"

His wings blink into view for a quick second, creating a soft breeze that blows my hair from my face. "I can't promise anything, love." It's the first time he's called me that since I arrived at the academy. He usually saves the sweet talk for when he visits my dreams.

"Dylan..."

His dark eyes smile though his mouth doesn't. "What? I'm your friend, Cami. Can't I care about you?"

"Isn't there a rule or something against that? It can't be normal for a nephilim to befriend a demi-demon." I smile as I say it, because it does seem ridiculous, all things considered.

He tilts his head back, his black curls falling away from his eyes, and laughs. "Now you're just trying to change the subject. Deflecting me like you deflect others' abilities."

He's got me there. "So."

"I want to help you with whatever you need. It's my job, you know. To watch out for you and all." He lightly pushes my shoulder as he says it, all thought of what happened in the dining hall in the recesses of my mind.

"And I thought you were my friend. I hope this job pays well," I say, sarcasm lining my words.

His face grows serious as he holds me in his gaze. "That's not what I meant."

"Mmm-hmm." I grin as I push past him to head through campus. "Come on, Angel Boy. Why don't you walk me to class?"

He slides up next to me, gently locking his fingers around my wrist. "I have a better idea."

For being half angel, he sure likes to break the rules. Maybe that's why he does it, because he can get away with it.

"And what's that?"

"There's someone I want you to meet."

VULNERABLE

DYLAN GUIDES ME along the perimeter of campus, following the four foot fence that separates the campus from the lemon groves. His arm brushes against mine, but I keep my hands in my pockets. Nerves tighten my stomach as I think about the possibility of getting in trouble. It's bad enough that I'm ditching class. Now I'm about to head into a restricted area. And for what? To meet someone who'll probably judge me like everyone else.

"No offense, Dylan, but this is a strange place to meet someone. What are they even doing out here?" I stop when he does. His scent of dewy apples drifts over me when he stops to look down at me. I levitate a few inches to match his height while placing my hands on my hips.

"She lives here," he says, flashing his wings behind him before he flies a few feet into the air to hop over the fence without climbing it.

"Who? One of your girlfriends?" I ask. I can't help it. Cadence said that nephilim tend to attract lots of girls. And Dylan's hot. *Not like you should care...*I shake the thoughts from my head. Negative emotions tend to be harder for me to control these days. I've never been the jealous type before; at least I didn't think I was. And it's getting on my nerves.

"She's definitely not my girlfriend," he says, motioning for me to jump the fence.

Bending my knees, I launch up into the air and levitate over the fence. Dylan takes my hand, pulling me back to earth. The soft dirt mutes the sound of my boots hitting the ground, and I peer around the outskirts of the lemon grove.

Dylan walks deeper into the grove, weaving in and out of the trees. The scent of nature wraps around us—the smell of dirt when it rains, the greenness of the leaves in the trees, even the woody scent of the trunks.

Dylan stops in place and brings his finger to his lips, stopping me from saying anything. A moment later, a lemon propels through the air, heading straight for me. Dylan jerks out his arm and catches it before it can smack into my chest.

I clench and unclench my fingers, sending sparks shooting from my fingertips. Another lemon zooms through the air, and

I dodge it. The last thing I expected was to be pummeled by flying fruit.

A tree branch snaps from my right, and I hold up my arm, preparing to send an energy ball in the direction of the sound.

Dylan knocks my hand down, jumping about a foot when I shock him. "What are you doing?" he asks as he shakes out his hand.

"We're being attacked," I say, peering around the grove for whoever is trying to hurt us.

"They're just lemons," he says. "You can't just unleash your power on everything you think is a threat. You have to control yourself."

I frown. "That's easier said than done," I snap. "You try living with all this evil swirling within you, just waiting for you to crack so it can escape."

"So, that's what's wrong." He doesn't ask because it's obvious. "Have you told anyone?"

"Just Alana and Evan."

He gives one quick nod. "Good. Don't tell anyone else."

His words make me uneasy. Tears prickle in the corners of my eyes. How can I control something so powerful? Even now that I'm out of harm's way—out of my father's reach—he's still going to be the cause of my undoing.

A small cry sounds out from the trees, drawing my attention away from Dylan. The voice, soft and musical like the wind blowing through a wind chime, grows louder as the rest of nature seems to quiet. The chirping birds no longer even whistle their songs.

Sprinkles of water drip on my face even though there aren't any clouds in the crystalline sky, and a new scent, like nature embodied—fresh-cut grass, blooming gardenias, the sun, the wind, the crisp night—trickles through the overpowering scent of lemon.

"Your friend is so, so sad, Nephilim," a girl says as she strolls from the trees. She saunters up to me, stopping only an inch away. I don't move as her nose nearly touches mine. Tears sparkle in her eyes like they're mixed with glitter. "Make her stop."

"I wish I could, Annabelle," Dylan says.

My mouth falls agape when I take in the breathtaking girl before me. Her curly auburn hair is entwined with small tendrils of ivy. Lily of the valley flowers hang from her pointed ears, seeming to magically hover in place. Her lips are painted raspberry red, striking against her creamed coffee complexion. Her eyes, like shimmering pools in the sunlight, shift through the colors of the rainbow with every subtle movement. Her delicate nose points upward, and an adorable dimple peeks from her chin. She looks timeless in a simple slip dress made out of the most fascinating material. It flows around her ankles even with her lack of movement. I'm tempted to reach out and caress it.

"Annabelle?" I ask.

The girl steps away and smiles. "The nephilim named me. You like it?"

I continue to gape at her in fascination. She exudes pure goodness like she's untouched by the evils of the world. I wonder what that would be like.

"It's beautiful," I say, eyeing Dylan in my peripheral vision. "I'm Cami."

Annabelle's tears dry on her cheeks in the wind. It's strange to have this girl cry for me because I'm sad. She doesn't even know me. "Why were you sad, Cami?" she asks, dancing around me like a child who can't stand still for a moment.

I shrug. "It just happens sometimes."

"Is it because of the darkness?" she asks.

I scrunch my brows. "What do you know about that?"

She spins again while pulling a strand of ivy from her hair. She stops for a moment to fashion a crown on my head. It takes everything in me not to yank it off. A few jasmine flowers bloom from the palm of her hand before she pokes their stems through the curls in my hair.

When she tugs at my jacket, I yank myself away, holding my palms out at her. She gasps as a spark unintentionally bursts over my skin. I rub my hands together, snuffing it out.

"I'm sorry," I say. "I didn't mean—"

"The darkness will steal your light away," Annabelle says. "You can't let it."

She says the words like she knows everything about me. I turn to Dylan, who watches us with curious eyes. He doesn't say anything, though. He lets Annabelle continue to dance around me.

"I don't think I can stop it," I finally say after a moment. "It's who I am."

Annabelle stops dancing in front of me. She turns to look at Dylan. "You can't bring her back here. She shouldn't be in these walls."

I step back in surprise. "It's not like I want to be half demon."

She touches her finger to her lips for a second. Then, her eyes light up and she unfastens a necklace from around her neck. She hands it to Dylan before saying, "If she's being honest, then that will help her."

"What is it?" I ask.

Annabelle doesn't look at me. She acts like I'm not even here.

"A sun stone," Dylan says as he steps up to me to place the necklace around my neck. An opaque stone, sparkling yellow and orange in the soft sunlight that trickles through the trees, warms the skin on my chest where it rests. "I was hoping Annabelle would part with it."

"So, we came here for a necklace?" I ask.

He shakes his head. "I brought you here to meet Annabelle. She's a forest nymph—Mother Nature at her finest—and she told me everything I needed to know."

I grimace. "Hasn't anyone ever told you it's not nice to use someone?"

Dylan closes the distance between us. I avert my eyes in search of Annabelle, but she's already gone.

"Look at me, Cami," Dylan says, nearly whispering the words.

"Dylan, stop. You can't do this," I say, putting some distance between us. I don't know what I'm angrier about—the fact that he made me ditch class to come out here to have some forest nymph tell me things I already knew or how he's trying to get under my skin all over again, like I'm somehow his business.

"Why are you so afraid to let your guard down with me?" he asks.

I spin away. "I don't have to answer that. This was a mistake. Clearly I'm still susceptible to your angelic charms."

He rubs his hands over his face. "My charms? I'm not doing anything. That's all you."

"Me?" I fling out my arms, sending a small ball of energy directly at him.

He ducks just in time before it hits him. My eyes widen, my mouth dropping open as I realize I nearly electrocuted him. I'm too on edge—too vulnerable. My inner demon preys on my moments of weakness.

"I—" My mouth snaps shut as Dylan meets me with worried eyes.

He pushes to his feet before dusting the dirt off his dark jeans. "It's okay, love. While that would've been uncomfortable, I'm a fast healer. It'd take a lot to hurt me."

That's beside the point. It doesn't matter if he can withstand my power—I shouldn't have lost so much control that I accidentally unleashed it. "I have to go, Dylan. I'm really sorry."

I half-run, half-levitate from the lemon grove in the direction of campus.

"Cami!"

Instead of looking back, I do what I do best. I keep running.

BETTER ALLY THAN ENEMY

WHEN I REACH the main path, I slow down. I don't want to look like a lunatic running across campus. I already draw enough attention as it is. The campus buzzes with life as students sit at picnic tables, enjoying having class outside.

I take a shortcut through the manicured lawn, heading straight for the Hunter's Alliance Assembly Hall named after the famous alliance member Robert Kissinger, a man I've never heard of.

I hop over the hardy hydrangea bushes bordering the walkway that leads to the stone steps of the grand entrance. Ignoring the gaping stares from the students and faculty members,

I focus solely on Alana's tired expression. Her sunny blond hair is pulled back into a neat ponytail at the nape of her neck. Her gray eyes narrow, and her lips press together when she spots me. Her hands rest on her hips, and I don't know who I should be more afraid of—her or the alliance.

"I know I'm late. I had an incident. I'll tell you later." The words rush from my lips before she has a chance to say anything. I grab her hand and fly into the building, nearly knocking over Evan in the process. His hands grab my shoulders, steadying me.

"What are you doing here?" I ask, though I don't complain. Instead, I hug him, sucking in his warm amber scent to clear my head.

"You do realize that the first person the faculty calls is me when you miss a class?" He peers into my eyes. I expect him to ask where I was, but instead he asks, "Why didn't you tell me you had a meeting with the leaders?"

"It wasn't intentional. I just found out last night while you were on patrol."

"Cami, Evan. Save it for later. We're late," Alana says, tugging me away.

I wave to Evan. "I'll see you at home!"

Ignoring the call from the receptionist, Alana pushes through the oak doors that lead to the assembly room. I've only been here once before when I was released from the infirmary. Its vaulted ceilings display an angelic mural with blue skies and gold-lined clouds. Portraits of old, long-past alliance leaders hang on the deep brown walls. A mahogany table is situated near the far back wall with enough hardback chairs to fit ten people. Only three of the chairs are filled. Two men in sophisticated dark suits and a woman wearing chic jeans and a cardigan sweater gape at me as I stop short, pulling away from Alana. I nearly trip over my own feet as I skid on the smooth floor.

I slink forward, half-smiling, and drop into a chair placed directly before the alliance. Alana sits quietly on a black leather couch adjacent to me.

"Time is of the essence, Ms. Anders," the rounder of the two men says. The placard in front of him says Clark Stephens, and I vaguely remember him from my orientation to the academy. His dark brown hair is cropped short, making his ears look larger. His boyish features hide behind a face full of stubble, though his round, flat nose looks like it's been broken a couple of times, giving an edge to his soft features.

"I know, I know. I'm sorry. I lost track of time." I fold my hands in my lap to keep them from trembling.

"That's interesting," the woman says. She tucks a strand of her highlighted, dirty blond hair behind her ear. She narrows her burgundy-colored lips together. "I was told you were missing from your morning class after running out on breakfast. Would you like to explain yourself?"

I run my hands nervously over my head, feeling the flowers and ivy vine. Cringing, I say, "It's a long story I don't want to get in to. I won't miss class again." I don't want to tell them about Dylan introducing me to Annabelle. I don't even know if the leaders are aware that a forest nymph hangs out in the lemon grove.

"Secrets are frowned upon," the woman says.

"That's enough, Raya." I would recognize Cadence's father anywhere. They look alike. His honey brown eyes tilt up like Cadence's and shine with a friendliness only the father of a best friend could show. His hair is parted neatly to the side, hanging slightly on his forehead, and he smiles. "I'm sure Cami will fill out the proper paperwork to excuse her absence from her classes. We have more dire things to discuss."

My heart sinks. I was hoping they would've forgotten why they summoned me, but they haven't.

"Mr. Dubois, am I in trouble?" I ask. "I can explain—"

"Why would you think that?" he says. "And how many times do I have to tell you, call me Aston, please."

Because I threatened your precious Sarah. "Because I've been summoned."

"No. Your presence was requested. It wasn't an order," Aston says. I could zap Dylan again for this. I was freaking out because apparently he sucks at relaying messages.

"Then why does it feel like I'm on trial?"

Clark scrunches his eyebrows. "If you were on trial, you'd be in front of all the alliance leaders."

My lips form the shape of an O. I lean back in relief. I'm not in trouble—they just want to get to know me more. I glance at Alana, who hasn't said a single word, and she shrugs her shoulders.

"Okay, then. Why am I here?"

"You received a letter in the mail yesterday," Clark answers.

He pulls a small red envelope from his breast pocket and slides it to the edge of the table. I lean forward to grab it but hesitate. It reeks of cinnamon and clove, the same scent of my father. I force my fingers to work and pick it up.

"You didn't open it?" This is bad. Probably catastrophic. My palms sweat and the envelope crinkles between my fingers. My breath quickens. I want to scream my lungs off and throw the stinking letter into a fire. Four pairs of eyes study me, gauging my reaction. I don't do anything. I don't eagerly open the letter or throw it away. I just clutch it for dear life. I'm terrified to open it. What if it's been bewitched?

"No. This isn't a prison, and the letter is addressed to you, left right outside the walls. Do you know who it's from?" Raya asks.

"My demonic father," I answer honestly. I can't hide everything from the alliance. They're the ones protecting my life. "It smells just like him."

"So, the werewolf was right," Clark says. "He said it was covered with demon stink."

"Yeah, he was," I confirm.

Folding the envelope in half, I shove it into my pocket. I refuse to read it in front of the leaders. They said it themselves, it's *my* letter. I need to read it privately because I'm not sure what it says or how I'll react. I won't let them see my struggle with the demon within me, threatening to consume my soul. If they ever witness one of my outbursts, I'm sure they'll immediately lock me up. I won't risk it.

Surprise peaks Raya's brows. "You're not going to read it?"

"No, not now. Sorry to waste your time. If it says anything important, I'll fill out the proper forms and let you know. Now, if you'll please excuse me, I need to go. I'm not feeling well."

"Let us help you, Cami," Aston says. "This has to be troubling to you." He sounds sincere, but the grimaces on the other two leaders' faces says they're more annoyed than anything.

"It is, but I just need a moment. I don't really want to read it right now. I promise to fill out the forms." I don't wait for them to release me. Instead, I stand up and move as quickly as I can to the door. I tune out their pleas, pull the door open, and make my escape.

⁂

I burst through the apartment door and trip over my backpack that Cadence must've dropped off. Before I slam to the ground, I stop an inch away. Levitation rocks in moments like these. I push on the invisible barrier and stand before Evan can swoop down to help me up. When I get to my feet, I tug his hand and pull him toward his bedroom. I'm overwhelmed in a good way by his delicious scent that seems to linger on everything he touches.

He sits on the edge of his bed before me and pats the spot next to him. I slide onto his bed, curling up against him with my legs flung over his. The fear from receiving another letter from Malicevile melts away as he holds me and kisses my hair before moving to my cheek and then to my lips.

"So, are you going to tell me what happened this morning?" Evan brushes his fingers over my hair.

I turn to look at my reflection in his wall mirror. I've forgotten about my hair. People probably think I'm weird with the sudden desire to make myself up with pieces of nature.

I laugh at myself, though I find Annabelle's short makeover to actually look pretty good on me. The ivy vine remains in place, the perfect crown, and fragrant jasmine flowers cling to my curls as my hair spills over my shoulders. I look like Annabelle, like I'm a forest nymph, and I feel good about it. I'd take being a forest nymph over a demi-demon any day.

I bring my eyes away from my reflection. I rehash my morning to Evan, leaving out most of my conversation with Dylan, though I do mention that I accidentally shocked him a few times. "And then during the meeting, the alliance leaders gave me this." I hold up the envelope.

"Are you okay?" He looks me up and down and touches his warm finger to my cheek.

"Yes...no. I don't know. I'm scared."

"About what the forest nymph said, Dylan, or the letter?"

"Dylan is as scary as a baby duck, Evan. He's just trying to be all angelic with his power or whatever toward me."

He snaps his head back as he laughs. If I were Evan, I'd probably be uncontrollably jealous, but if he ever is, he hides it well. Evan has more control than I can ever hope for. I'd be okay if I was even half as good as him. "No wonder you shocked him. I bet the leaders put him up to it."

I frown. "I don't think so. He's my friend." I can't imagine Dylan would lie to me. I know he has a save-Cami-complex. "It doesn't matter anyway. I can handle Dylan." I pull the envelope from Malicevile from my pocket. "It's this I can't handle."

"You haven't opened it," he says, taking it from me.

"I wanted you to read it with me," I say.

Using his finger, Evan breaks the seal of the envelope and pulls out a sheet of cream-colored paper. Malicevile's insignia is stamped at the top, and I touch the lightning bolt zinging through a triangle. It's handwritten in slanted script.

Dearest Camilla,

I hope you are enjoying your stay at the academy. They'll put you in better shape for when you finally join me. I know we've had a bad start and that you hate me. I know you'll never be by my side if I continue to torment you. So, I'm writing this to tell you that I'm waving a white flag. I'm going to leave you alone because you will come around on your own. That is your only fate. You can pretend all you want that you're human, but you're not. I can show you the world. I can show you how to control the power that will consume you if you let it. I make a better ally than enemy. Give it some thought.

Best,

M

Malicevile has written his number on the bottom of the letter, and my soul shakes at the thought of calling him. I crumple the letter into a ball and throw it at the wall. It's a trap. He wants me to let my guard down. He hasn't given up. He'll never give up.

Tears glitter on my eyelashes, and I carefully dab them away. Evan holds me closely, rubbing his hand down my back.

"It's going to be okay. This is good news."

"I'm not so sure of that," I say. I'm not sure of anything anymore.

DANGEROUS

MY LOOPY HANDWRITING covers the form I have to submit to the Hunter's Alliance regarding the letter from my father. I'm not sure how I feel about them seeing it. My demonic relationship with him is personal in a way, now that I hold some of his power within me, and I don't want them to think we're on friendly terms. It wouldn't look good on my part.

I refuse to attach the letter, and for my best interest, I exclude the part about my fate being with him and his obvious interest in me contacting him. The alliance would have a field day with that, and people getting involved on my behalf would surely get hurt. The results were catastrophic the last time my friends tried to intervene.

I absently play with the yellow stone fastened around my neck. It pulsates with heat and calms my fragile nerves; it's almost like having a piece of the sun over my heart. Annabelle was right about it keeping the darkness away. I already feel more in control.

I sign the bottom of the form and slide it into an envelope. It would be easier if the alliance would let me just shoot them an email, but they have a protocol that everyone, even me, must follow. It maintains their strong foundation, keeping every little detail in order.

I pick up the envelope and head to Evan's room. He sleeps sprawled out across his bed on his stomach with his face in the pillow.

My light footsteps cause him to flip over and smile. There's no sneaking up on him unless I levitate, but sneaking up on a demon hunter is the worst possible idea unless I brace myself for an attack, even here in the safety of the academy.

Like two oceans, his eyes hold my stare, and I can't stop my heart from racing. He runs his hand over his golden hair before rubbing his scruffy cheeks. His muscular arms flex when he leans on his elbows, the definition shadowed by the soft glow of the lamp on his bedside table.

"Want to go on a walk with me?" I say, reaching my arms out to pull him to his feet.

"Always." He scoops me into his arms, carrying me over the threshold of his room and into the hallway.

After a moment, he flips me onto his back and then tugs the envelope out of my hand so I can hold on. I rest my chin on his shoulder, concentrating on levitating so he doesn't bear all my weight, though I doubt it bothers him. I've seen him drop hunters twice my size in training.

"I can carry you without your help, you know," Evan says.

I laugh into the nape of his neck. "I'm not so sure about that."

He reaches his arm behind him and grabs my leg. I squeal and push away from him, floating higher in the air. My head hits the low ceiling in the hallway, and Evan laughs as he yanks me back into his arms before kissing me on the lips.

He strolls forward, refusing to stop kissing me. The setting sun beats down on my back as we exit the apartment. We missed practice today because I didn't want to wake him after his lack of sleep. I never made it back to class either.

Evan trips over a small solar light stuck into the ground on the side of the pathway. He shifts sideways before crushing me, and we land on the soft grass.

I jump to my feet before he can grab me again and dash across the lawn toward the assembly hall. Evan runs behind me and catches up before I'm even halfway there, tackling me back to the ground. I laugh as he pulls me closer by my ankles and leans down to kiss me again.

"Come on," I say, breaking away. "The secretary will be locking up soon, and I don't want to risk running into an alliance member tomorrow."

He helps me to my feet. "Good call."

The fiery glow of the fading sunset lights the brick building in front of us. The stone steps sparkle in the light as I take them two at a time. Evan waits at the bottom while I rush inside to find the secretary packing up her things.

I wave the envelope in my hand, and she nods to a small tray marked 'inbox.' I drop it in and turn quickly away before anyone catches me and tries to start a conversation. I don't want anyone taking away my time with Evan.

"You're in a hurry." Dylan hovers in the doorway to the meeting room. A small dimple flashes on his cheek as he gives me a warm smile.

"Yeah," I say, turning to walk away. I'm not in the mood to deal with him. Not after this afternoon.

"Please, wait. You've been ignoring my calls. I went by your apartment but you weren't in your room. We should talk."

I can't help but pause because he sounds so sincere. His eyes are so earnest, so caring. He might not be the boy I care so deeply for, but he doesn't deserve the backlash of my attitude toward the alliance.

"I'm sorry. I have a lot on my mind." I brush my dark hair out of my eyes. "Malicevile sent me a letter, you know."

"Don't let that demon get to you. That's what he wants," Dylan says, squeezing my shoulder. "He'll try to push you over the edge until you have no one to go to except him." It's like he's read the letter himself, though it's impossible.

"I wouldn't even do that if he was the last person on earth.

I'd rather be alone." I glare at the floor. "Please, stop worrying about me. I'm fine."

"You're not." Dylan grabs my arm and gazes into my eyes. "Let me help you."

I pull out of his grip. "I don't want you to get hurt, Dylan. I'm dangerous to be around. Even here."

Dylan scrunches his eyebrows. "Not to me."

I puff a breath of air through my lips. "Evan is waiting outside. I have to go." I turn and walk away with a heavy heart.

⁓ ℓℓ ⁓

Evan holds my hand as I walk on the fence separating the campus from the lemon grove. I hop from picket to picket barely touching the tips of my toes to the fence. Without levitation, I would end up face first in the dirt because I'm highly uncoordinated on my feet. That's why Evan holds my hand. There have been too many occasions where my ability decided to just stop working no matter how often I use it.

"You seem tense," Evan says, breaking the comfortable silence between us.

"It's nothing really. I ran into Dylan when I was submitting my paperwork. I know he knows about how Mal's power is changing me for the worst. I don't want this to get out. I have it under control."

"You're not changing, you're adjusting. I know what it's like being part demon, remember? You know we have a choice to be good."

"I don't know if that's true in my case." I want to believe

Evan, I really do, but he doesn't feel what I'm going through. Being demi-demon is who he is. My demon half feels separate yet attached, like a parasite getting its life force from its host, possessing it and ultimately destined to take over unless it's extracted. My human half isn't strong enough to kill my inner demon, and I'm afraid of what it will do to me.

"It is, Cami." Evan stops walking and turns to look up at me. "We all have a choice. You just have to know your options."

"And what are my options? Stay here and let the alliance rule my life or leave and let Malicevile? I don't like either. I want to live my life without people telling me what to do or who to be."

"You can. You're not a prisoner. Once you finish your training, we can leave. We can go anywhere you want, and you'll be strong enough to not have to worry about Malicevile all the time. We can destroy him and send him back to Hell."

I open my mouth to argue, to say Malicevile can't be destroyed, when I hear a small, tinkling giggle. I jump from the top of the fence into the grove, leaving Evan in confusion. I hear him jump the fence, but I continue to walk deeper into the grove.

"What are you—"

"Shh!" I hiss, waving my hand toward the trees. It's darker without the glow of the stadium lights shining throughout campus. It actually feels like night.

The laughter continues, and I follow the melodious sound

with Evan trailing behind me. A flame bursts in his palm to help light our way. The small flame casts shadows around us, turning the grove eerie in its soft light like a haunted forest.

"Watch out!" the girlish voice screams, and I duck in time to watch a large branch collide into Evan. He falls backward into the dirt and prepares to throw a fireball.

"Don't!" I hop to my feet to block Evan from getting a good aim. "It's only Annabelle. She doesn't know you."

I turn away from Evan and glance around for signs of the forest nymph. The empty grove is quiet, apart from Evan's heavy breathing. I glimpse movement near the wall and head in that direction.

"It's okay, Annabelle. Evan's my boyfriend. He won't hurt you. You can come out now."

A small figure steps out from behind a tree. Annabelle glows within the darkness. Her auburn hair shines like a flame against her pearlescent light brown skin. Flowers bloom from the intricate braids framing her head, and she is as beautiful as I remember.

"I told you not to come back." She skips through the dark grove.

Wrapping her slender arms around me, she kisses both of my cheeks, surprising me. After releasing me, she takes a step back and places her hands on her hips.

"I'm sorry. I heard you laugh and wanted to talk some more." The Veiled Realm would be a lot more bearable if more people were like Annabelle.

Annabelle's gaze flickers to Evan. She twirls around him, kissing both of his cheeks as well. He blushes and steps back shoving his hands into his pockets.

"I like him. He makes you happier than the nephilim." Annabelle slides a daisy behind his ear before he can protest. "You make Cami happy," she says to Evan. "Which makes me happy. I don't like sad people."

Evan flashes an amused smile at me. "She makes me happy, too. She's like my own personal golden ray of sunshine."

"That's impossible." Annabelle's smiling expression turns serious as she knits her brows together. "Her darkness will snuff out your light. But the sun stone should help some."

The smile falls from my lips. Her honesty is enough to smack me with my own reality. Maybe Evan will finally believe that part of me is out of control, and if I don't keep it in check, I'll be lost.

I turn to Evan. "See, I'm not crazy."

Annabelle twirls around me before touching the stone over my heart. "You know yourself best."

Evan doesn't speak as he stares into the distance at nothing in particular. I wish he would say something, but Annabelle doesn't leave much room for argument. She knows things that no one else does. She's in tune with everything around her— nature, animals, and even people.

The lull in conversation makes me fidget. I play with the sleeve of my jacket while rocking on my heels. I wish Evan would look at me. It's like he's starting to put a wall around himself. Maybe he's even a little afraid. I wouldn't blame him.

I take his hand, but he doesn't take his eyes away from the wall he's staring at. The wind picks up, and I'm not sure if its nature or Annabelle doing it, but the stench swirling around me makes my heart fall. Cinnamon and clove intrude the fresh, zesty scent of the lemon grove and fear creeps into me.

Annabelle's eyes widen when she turns her attention to where Evan is staring. "Run!" she screams before disappearing into the darkness of the lemon grove.

I'm paralyzed. I can't get my feet to move. All I can do is wait for my father to appear to take my soul. I knew his letter was too good to be true.

His voice reaches me before I can see him. "It's so good to see you, my precious Camilla."

All I can do is brace myself for what's to come.

BLOOD BOUND

MY MOUTH GOES dry, and I can't find my voice. Malicevile hovers into view on the other side of the tall brick wall. He leans on his elbows on the top, looking quite comfortable. I expect the wall to explode as the blessed barrier repels my demonic father, but nothing happens.

His flawless features take me aback. I only remember the evil lurking in his eyes before now. His dark hair looks silvery in the moonlight, and his intense green eyes flash a mesmerizing red reflection that sends a shiver through me. The last time I saw him, his eyes looked like they wanted to kill me. Today, they look almost normal despite his cat-like pupils. He's like an angel in disguise with his Roman nose and strong jaw, and it's hard to see past his charm. Under his good looks lies a demon of the worst kind—a demon who I am blood bound to.

"You know, daughter. I didn't want to have to come here. You could've saved me the trouble had you just called." Malicevile's hypnotic voice coaxes me closer. I shake my head, concentrating on keeping calm. Darkness clings to the edges of my soul, threatening to consume it if I let it take over.

"Cami, get behind me," Evan whispers. He places his hands on my shoulders to move me, but I'm cemented into the ground by my will to never back down.

"Don't worry Daughter's boyfriend. I have no intentions of hurting her. Even if I did, these holy barriers would never allow it. I only want to talk." Malicevile rests his head on the palms of his hands. "I advise that you listen to what I have to say."

"I'm listening." The words come out weak, barely audible. I'm not even sure I said them.

Malicevile's emerald eyes darken. "Good. Since you decided you would rather have a professional education instead of learning from the best, all I ask is that you be very, very careful what you reveal to these humans. They do not have your best interests in mind like I do. They only see you as another pawn in their little game of demon hunting."

"You're lying. To care about me would mean you have an ounce of humanity within you. I know for a fact you don't, Mal." He's trying to manipulate me to turn my back on the alliance. I know it.

"Silly child. Humanity has nothing to do with our bond. My blood runs through your veins. My power through your soul. My interest lies in that you are a piece of me, and I can't risk humans destroying you," Malicevile says. "Can't you see they've already turned our kind against us? They send you out to kill your own kin."

Anger rushes over me. "You killed my only family. You showed me what side I should be on. I look forward to sending demons back where they came from. Especially you."

"There is so much I have to explain." His smooth voice gets under my skin.

Explain? Like he deserves the time to give me an explanation for tormenting me, for hurting my family, for ruining my life. I hate how human he sounds.

I sneer. "Save it. I'm done with your evil mind games."

Evan pulls at my hand, drawing my attention to him. He's been so silent that I almost forgot he was here. "Don't fall for his manipulation. He's trying to plant doubt in your head."

Malicevile scoffs. "I'm not planting anything that isn't already there. It's time to wake up, Camilla. I might've ascended from Hell, but I'm not going back to serve as a minion to my father."

Fear grips my heart. "You belong with the devil."

"Lucifer is your uncle, dear. See how the humans have tainted you? You think I'm lying? Look how the alliance protects their precious nephilim while sending you into battle. You are half of the creature they seek to destroy. What do you think will happen when their silly war is over? They'll hunt you next."

My chest tightens, and I can't breathe. The edges of my vision darken as the threads holding my consciousness threaten to snap. I can't process anything he's saying. Not because it's absurd but because it feels true. It makes sense. The Hunter's Alliance does believe that *Humans Come First* after all.

He raises his hand, creating sparks when he touches the holy barrier. "I'm not telling you this so you'll come running into my arms," he continues. "I'm telling you this so you can watch out for your safety. It's my responsibility as your father to take care of you." He points at Evan. "You should take care of her as well."

I burst out laughing.

Malicevile tilts his head to the side and stares at me seriously, which makes me laugh even harder. He sounds so diplomatic and caring. It sounds ridiculous coming from his mouth. I never thought I'd laugh in the face of evil, but this is insane. He appears to be sincere...it's unimaginable that what he's telling me could possibly be true.

"Take care of me?" My voice rises in pitch, the words coming out as a squeak. "You have no right to even think that you can come in and act like my father. My dad is dead. You murdered him!"

Evan wraps his arms around me from behind. Laughter spills from my mouth as tears blur my eyes. I'm hysterical. This entire situation leaves me utterly confused and vulnerable. My hands shake uncontrollably, and my knees buckle. The only thing holding me together is Evan.

"Even if you're right, how can you even think I'd trust you? You took everything from me!" Anger tightens my chest. "And for what? So you could run in and play Daddy Demon? Did you honestly believe that I would be so easy to break? That I'd come running to you to pick up the pieces that you broke in the first place? I *hate* you." My vision turns red, the dark crimson color shadowing everything in my sight. I'm losing control.

"Cami, calm down," Evan whispers. "Please, calm down. We need to go."

"Not until I'm finished." I yank my arm free from Evan's grip.

"Listen to your boyfriend, Camilla." Malicevile's brows lower, concern masking his smooth expression.

I squeeze my hands into fists. My nails bite into the skin of my palms. I imagine a soothing light surrounding me, and the soft touch of an angel's wings. The sun stone rests heavily on my neck, and I grab it, willing its power to banish the darkness threatening to consume me.

"Good girl," Malicevile says.

Praising me like a puppy gets under my skin. I refuse to look at him. I know the moment my eyes meet with his, it's over. I won't be able to control my inner demon any longer. "What have you done to me?" I whisper. My heart aches. The pain of being in his presence is a lot to bear.

"When I knew you wouldn't stop fighting until one of us was dead, I gave you the power you needed to survive being in the presence of our enemies. Of course, that has some side effects," Malicevile says.

Evan pulls me farther back. "Seriously, Cami. We need to go. Someone may come looking for us. Talking to a demon would get us thrown out of here. It's what he wants."

I nod my head in surrender and let him drag me with him. I can't gain anything conversing with my demonic dad. It riles my emotions and puts my sanity in danger.

I can't help glancing at Malicevile one last time before the grove becomes dense with lemon trees. "What kind of side effects?" I ask, already sensing that what he has to say is devastating.

"The power is only temporary...and there is a chance that your soul has become unbalanced."

I scream. Tears burn in my eyes, clouding my vision. My throat burns as I force my mouth to close. My stomach heaves as I fall to the ground, clawing my fingers into the soft soil, grasping for something solid to hold onto.

Malicevile altered my soul with his power. He added to the demon taint already flowing in my blood. He wasn't trying to help me. He was trying to turn me into a monster.

I feel the weight of Evan's hand grab my shoulder. I swing my arm behind me and knock him away. I stare at the dark soil, watching it transform from brown to red as my anger escalates. I push to my feet and tilt my head up to stare at Malicevile. His usual intense green eyes have gone blacker than the night.

My chest tightens, and my heart hammers against my ribs.

The world narrows to where he is all I can focus on. Fiery heat flows through my veins like my blood has transformed into molten lava. I want nothing more this very moment than to see him suffer for what he has done to me.

My boots pound against the dirt as I run toward the wall between us. It might as well be protecting him from me and not the other way around. I toss an energy ball at his face, and it collides with the protective barrier in a waterfall of glittering sparks, lighting the night sky.

I growl in rage and throw another one. No matter how hard I try, my power will not penetrate the invisible barrier separating us. I need to get on the other side of the wall.

My body becomes weightless as I lose gravity and push off into the air. Gathering all the electricity I can manage into my palms, I levitate higher, inches away from my demonic father hovering midair. He's close enough to touch if I stretched out my arm.

The tiny pinpricks of fear turn into huge, boiling bubbles of rage as I glare into his sadistic, evil eyes. The world blurs and morphs into a fiery pit of red. I can't stop the darkness begging me to let go of my humanity.

A part of my soul dies as I lose control.

Swinging my arm, I push it through the protective barrier. I release the power from my fingertips, but they sputter out. Something yanks my leg, pulling me away from my revenge.

"Let go of me. I want out of here!" I scream and vault toward the wall again.

I'm forced to the ground as someone presses their body weight into my chest. I thrash and fight, never taking my eyes from Malicevile, hovering just out of reach. A beautiful smile plasters across his face, mocking me, urging me to try. I punch the person holding me down, forcing them to fall backward. I swivel my legs free and use the person's chest to launch into the air.

My feet touch the wall, and I reach out and grab Malicevile's face in my hands. My nails scratch the smooth skin of his cheeks, and he smiles. I release a stream of energy and watch his dark hair lift with static. His mouth is moving like he's talking to me, but I don't hear the words. The world is silent and red and as dark as the tainted power lining the edges of my soul.

Malicevile's hot hands grab my wrists. I flinch and yank my hands in an attempt to free them. Energy flows from me to him, and he pushes it back into me like a never-ending cycle.

My breath becomes shallow as I struggle to keep the power constantly flowing, but he pushes it into me faster than I can release it. My legs become limp as my levitation fails, my concentration locked on keeping the demonic energy out of me.

My wrists ache as Malicevile dangles me from the top of the wall. He holds me just out of reach, and I'm unable to transfer the power.

The world blurs as he releases me, and I fall hard to the dirt. A shadow blocks Malicevile from my view, holding my hands above my head. I kick and wiggle, struggling to get my hands back on Malicevile. The person holding me down flips me onto my stomach, and I jerk my neck up to the wall. Malicevile is gone.

"Help me! She's lost control!" The voice sounds so far away like a whisper on the breeze.

My face presses hard into the ground, and I cough and spit as dirt goes into my mouth. I struggle to get up, but the weight of another body keeps me down. Something heavy slams into the back of my head and stars burst in my vision.

I close my eyes in surrender, my body going limp. There is no use fighting any longer. Malicevile is gone. I didn't get my revenge.

I let the fog clouding my mind take control, and then all is dark.

※

"Cami, why did you do that?" Dylan asks.

We're sitting on a bench in a luscious garden. Vibrant lavender-colored roses bloom on leafy bushes. The blossoms are abnormally large, the size of a dinner plate. A stone fountain gurgles with foamy, blue water, cascading down a pile of crystal rocks. Sun sparkles from the sky, engulfing us in a halo of mesmerizing light. I'm in a world that resembles what I imagine Heaven to look like.

"Do what?" I ask, unsure of what he wants to hear.

"You could've gotten yourself killed going after Malicevile like that. I almost lost you."

"To lose me, you'd have to have me in the first place," I

say. Dylan just doesn't understand that I'm with Evan, that I will never be with him.

"That's not the point. I just want to know why."

I glare at the flowers, like the pretty blossoms were what wronged me. "I wanted to hurt him like he hurt me."

"Well, you didn't hurt him. You only hurt yourself...and Evan."

My heart falls.

Dylan takes my hands into his and squeezes them. Tears line my eyes, threatening to escape. *What have I done?* I only wanted to go after Malicevile, but I let myself lose control. I released my inner demon and it clouded my thinking. And now, Evan is hurt. I could've killed him because of my anger.

"What have I done?" My chest heaves with sorrow. "I don't deserve him. I'm only going to bring him down with me."

"It's okay, Cami. Evan is fine. He's only a little bruised, nothing more than usual when he's training or in the field."

"This is different. He wasn't injured on the job or during practice. I injured him because I lost control."

"He forgives you. He knew it wasn't really you."

I groan into my hands. "He shouldn't. What I did is un-forgiveable. How can I be with him if there is a possibility this could happen again? It isn't fair to him."

Dylan pulls me against him. His glorious, iridescent wings wrap around me, soothing my aching heart. He lifts my chin, and I look into his chocolate-brown eyes. The light shines so brightly within them that mine probably look like inky pools of darkness.

"I'm not the best person to give you advice on this matter. You know how I feel about you. But what I can do is help you if you let me. I don't think you can handle this on your own. Your soul isn't as bright as it used to be when I first met you. But I can fix it. You know I'd do anything for you."

I half smile, my heart not in it. "You are too good to me. Even after everything."

"You're still the same girl I met on the bus."

"I don't think so."

"You're right. This you is better."

I lean against Dylan, soaking in the light shining around us. He kisses my forehead, and we sit in silence, enjoying the peacefulness around us.

"Can we stay here awhile? This place is nice," I say.

"As long as you want, love. This is your dream."

ABOUT TO FALL

I SIT UP in a cozy bed in a room with creamy yellow walls. Black-framed landscape photographs accent one wall, and adjacent to it are floor-to-ceiling white bookshelves brimming with books of all shapes and sizes. On the bedside table, a digital alarm clock sits next to a crystal reading lamp that casts a low glow through the room. I've never been here before, but it smells faintly familiar, like an apple orchard in a rainstorm. This must be Dylan's room.

I lean on my elbows and the rough sheets beneath me crunch and send black flakes of charred fabric around me. I grimace in confusion, wondering why the mattress under me is burned. Turning over, I dangle my feet off the edge of the bed. My knees shake as I find my footing, but my legs can't handle the sudden weight, and I fall back onto the bed with a thump.

The door cracks open, and Dylan peeks his head in. "Good morning, love. How are you feeling?" He clicks the door closed behind him.

"Horrible. It feels like I journeyed through Hell with Dante and Virgil."

He pads forward in socked feet and sits next to me on the bed. Brushing his fingers through the crisp fabric, he says, "You had a rough night."

"I'm sorry about that. Why am I here and not at home? Where's Evan? Who knows about this?" The questions fly from my mouth as quickly as I think them. I haven't felt this confused in a long time.

"Evan asked me to look after you. He had to go to the infirmary...and Alana couldn't take care of you without the risk of electrocution. I heal quite quickly, faster than demi-demons, so the only thing damaged is the bed," he says softly.

My heart sinks into my stomach. *Please, let Evan be okay...* I don't know what I'll do if I find him seriously injured because of me. I can't live with the thought.

"Only Evan, Alana, and I know what happened—and well, Annabelle. She's the one who brought me to you," he continues.

I blow out a long breath until my lungs are emptied of all air, and then I slowly take a calming breath. "Please, take me to the infirmary. I need to be with Evan."

"I don't know if that's a good idea." Dylan places his hand on mine, and instead of making me feel better like it should, it only makes me feel worse. It's like he's keeping vital information from me.

I knock his hand away. "Just take me!" Tears run down my cheeks as I begin to hyperventilate.

Dylan pulls me to him, embracing me. "Okay, okay. But you have to calm down. Here, take my hands."

I grasp his fingers. His cool skin steams against my hot hands. He uses our interlocked fingers to tilt my chin up, and I look him in the eyes. My heartbeat slows, and I catch my breath. The pain and heartache numbs the longer I stare into his fathomless, chocolate-brown eyes. I study his features—his smooth cheeks and peek-a-boo dimple, the way his black hair curls on his forehead, his perfect smile. He wears all black and seems too dark and brooding today to be angelic, yet I see the angel in him—his sheer, iridescent wings wrap around me in feather softness, almost like they're not really there. He shines with pure, ethereal light.

"That's much better, love. Now we can go."

I'm too weak to walk, and Dylan insists that I might freak the newer students out if I levitate the entire way, so I reluctantly accept his help, burying my face in his neck as he carries me. It isn't cute or romantic, more pathetic than anything. I'm a demi-demon who can't even stand on her two feet, being carried by a nephilim. It's embarrassing.

I feel ridiculous in Dylan's hooded sweatshirt and track pants that cover my feet, but it's better than my shredded jeans and T-shirt. My hair, a mess of brown tangles, flies around my head in the lingering static from my father's power.

I have the worst headache ever, like I've been hit in the head with a boulder, but Dylan swears he only hit me with a rock to knock me out just long enough to get me out of the grove. He should've used a boulder, though. I deserved to have some sense knocked into me.

The infirmary is all the way across campus from Dylan's apartment. He lives in the section for singles, a couple of doors down from Cadence, while I live in the family units that are spacious with multiple bedrooms. The majority of the apartments in my complex are empty. The hunting business is not really family-oriented. Most hunters are here because they have nowhere else to go.

I pull my hood over my head before Dylan carries me through the lobby. It's buzzing with life, most hunters just off from the night shift. I don't want anyone to recognize me because gossip flies fast in such a small community. The last thing I need is to have rumors flying around that Demon Girl was caught being carried by Angel Boy from his apartment.

"You can look up now. No one's around," Dylan whispers.

I tilt my head up and stare at the sun shining through soft, white clouds. The lemon-scented air mingles with Dylan's irresistible apple and rain scent.

"You'll tell me if someone is coming, right?" I ask, glancing at his sunlit face.

"You shouldn't worry so much about someone seeing you. We've all had bad nights," he says, catching my eyes.

"Not like I have. I'm a hot mess," I say.

Dylan furrows his brows, shadowing his shining eyes.

"And don't judge me. Girls are allowed to be vain. You, on the other hand, probably never have to worry about anything," I add, brushing his black curls behind his ear.

"I worry about you." Dylan's voice lowers in something that sounds like concern.

I can't help the sinking feeling in my stomach. It bothers me more than it should that Dylan cares about me, and I've nothing to offer in return except for my friendship. I'm not even good at that. This would be much easier if we'd gone our separate ways, but fate brought us together for some unknown reason. I can't—I won't change my mind about Evan, though. I've fallen hard for him.

"Dylan..." I can't seem to form a response.

"Cami, please. You can tell me not to worry a thousand times, and I'll still continue to. I care about you whether you want me to or not—and that won't change. Ever."

"Just stop. I can't handle this right now. It's too much. I'm just going to break your heart."

Dylan halts in his tracks and peers into my eyes. I've never seen him look at me this seriously before. His eyes shadow with sorrow, a sadness so heartbreaking that tears blur my vision.

"I know that!" The sudden rise in his voice startles me.

He's never raised his voice at me before, and I breakdown, letting the tears flow freely. "I've known since the minute you came here, bruised and broken, barely hanging onto your life. When I peered into your soul that day to help ease the pain Malicevile caused you, all I saw was Evan."

My mouth falls open at his revelation. It takes a dozen deep breaths to compose myself. I want to scream at him and be angry for his intrusion. But I can't. He means more to me than he thinks, just not in the way he wants to. My heart might belong to Evan, but Dylan is still the boy in my dreams. I feel selfish for needing him so much, for wanting to be in his company, and for dangling him along a road that might lead to a dark place—a place an angel will never belong.

"I—I don't know what to say," I stammer. "I did everything in my power to get in touch with you before I found out who I was. I even called here. You never even tried to find me. All you did was haunt my dreams. It wasn't enough."

Dylan only nods. He closes his eyes for a long moment and begins to walk again. I bury my face in his shirt to hide the bitter emotions threatening to weaken me. The silence between us is tense, thick with all our unsaid thoughts.

We reach the infirmary doors, and he stops. "I'm sorry," he whispers into my hair. "If I could go back, I'd change everything. I regret not trying harder to convince you to come with me. I would've told you the truth. I didn't mean to let you slip so easily through my fingers."

Tears burn my eyes. I let him get too close to me when I

shouldn't have. I've done nothing but caused him pain and grief. He's my angel, and I've let him down.

But he's not mine. The thought lingers. He isn't my angel— I lost the right to call him that when I chose Evan. The truth scares me. Part of me doesn't really want to let Dylan go. He can be cryptic, mysterious, downright enraging even, but I can't picture my life without him. He's too close to my heart to easily discard. And it bothers me. I shouldn't think this way. If it came down to losing Evan or Dylan, both would devastate me, but the thought of losing Evan terrifies me more than anything. If there was such a thing as a soul mate, Evan would be mine.

"But you did. The past is the past, and we can't change it. I wouldn't want to. We can only live in the here and now and hope we survive." I wipe the tears from my eyes. "Now, please, take me inside. I need to see Evan."

Dylan pushes through the doors to the infirmary and strides past the nurse's station. He carries me down a narrow, white hallway with red painted doors lining both sides. The doors are numbered with small plastic envelopes dangling from the handles with name tags.

The infirmary reeks of blood and pain, an odd smell for such a clean and sterile environment. Dylan slows as we reach a door at the end of the hallway. The tag on the door reads Evan Whiteshaw. My heart skips a beat as Dylan gently knocks and turns the knob.

I close my eyes, fearing the worst case scenario. What if Evan is broken from head to toe? What if he's angry at me?

What if he wants to break up with me? I'd be lost without him, but a tiny part of me wishes he would. He'd be safer without me. Everyone I know would be safer without me.

Excited laughter slows the hammering in my chest. I peek through my eyelashes to see Cadence sitting next to a sprawled out Evan on the fluffy hospital bed. It's not the cot-like hospital beds I've seen before. The bed is twice the size of a twin bed with large pillows. The comforter is a deep, gorgeous green accenting the cream-colored walls. The top of the bed is inclined so that Evan and Cadence are sitting up.

I swallow hard and finally look at Evan. His damp hair glistens in the soft glow of the tableside light. A blue shadow circles his left eye, trailing over his cheek down to his jaw. He's wearing a simple black T-shirt, and a blanket covers his legs. His hands rest in his lap, white bandages twining around his hands and wrists. I'm relieved to see that a black eye and some bandages seem to be the extent of the damage I've done, yet I'm mortified to have been his attacker in the first place.

I point at the bandages. "What are those?"

"Burns."

I blink a few times. "You can't be burned."

"Not by fire. These are from the high voltage electricity that was radiating from you."

I squeeze my eyes shut, forcing the tears to stay where they are. I had thought maybe I'd scratched him. But electrocution? He could've died.

"I'm so, so sorry. What have I done?"

"Bring her here," Evan says.

Dylan gently sets me into Evan's lap. He wraps his arms around me, careful not to use his hands. I bury my face into his chest. My hands tremble, and my stomach heaves. I don't think I can hold it together for another minute.

Evan holds me. "I'm okay, Cami. I'll heal. You can't blame yourself."

How can I not? Words are lost to me. I know if I try to speak, I'll break down into a blubbery, crying mess. The fight last night, my conversation with Dylan, seeing the harm I've done to Evan—everything has left me on the edge of a cliff about to fall. I'm not at risk of releasing my inner demon, but I'm on the brink of hopelessness and sadness, the same grief I felt when I lost my parents.

Cadence rests a comforting hand on my arm, setting me off. Tears spill from my eyes, soaking Evan's shirt. I watch Dylan leave through my blurry vision and sob harder when the door clicks closed. I've never felt so miserable. Cadence rubs my arm while Evan brushes my sticky hair from my eyes, neither of them saying anything.

I gasp and hiccup through my tears, unable to stop. My head throbs, and my heart aches. My body hurts like I'm bruised to my very soul.

Evan brushes his lips against my forehead, using the tips of his bandaged fingers to lift my chin. His eyes shadow with a sorrow that mirrors my own. He leans forward and kisses my tear-stained cheeks and lastly my lips.

"Shhh," he whispers. "I'm really okay."

I nod. He sounds so calm and collected, even after everything. I could handle if he were pissed at me, maybe even disappointed. But this? I don't deserve his understanding, his kindness. I don't deserve him at all.

"I—I'm so s-sorry," I stammer. I can't apologize enough. "My f-father turned me into a m-monster."

"You're not a monster. He is. You're nothing like him." Evan swipes the tears from my eyes. "I'm just glad I was there to stop him. I'd do anything for you. I love you, Cami."

I suck in a small breath as his words sink in. We've talked about how connected we feel, how much we care for each other, but this is the first time he's actually said that he loves me.

I can't find my voice to say it back, but I rest my head on his chest, holding him tighter. It takes me a while to compose myself, and when I finally do, I remain quiet. The moment has passed.

Cadence stays silent, continuing to rub my arm. I'm completely exhausted. I can't even move my lips to talk. I close my heavy eyelids and listen to the rhythmic beating of Evan's heart until it's the only thing left I hear.

THE DEMON'S DAUGHTER

"I LOOK RIDICULOUS," I say, loosely dangling my arms around Cadence's neck. She suggested a pretend piggyback ride so Dylan wouldn't have to come back to carry me. She could carry my weight if she wanted to, but we both agreed that there was no point to show off. She melts enough hearts as it is.

"People give each other piggybacks all the time. Would you prefer me to cradle you like a baby? No one will think anything of it, except maybe how strong and badass I am." Cadence laughs and spins around, blurring the sky and lawn into one.

"People do not. They give little kids rides. And if you spin again, I'm going to quit levitating to see how strong you really are," I say.

The world comes to a halt, and I shake the dizziness away. Cadence turns her head to glare at me, and I smile for the first time all morning.

The nurse in the infirmary asked us to leave an hour after I fell asleep in Evan's arms. She explained that he needed his rest and that we could come back in the evening to walk him home. Thankfully, he only had minor injuries from my attack.

"My place or yours?" Cadence asks.

"Yours. I'm still not ready to face Alana." I pull my hood up to hide from the kids staring at us as we pass through the quad.

"She'll understand just like I do," Cadence says. "But, next time you better be the one to tell me what's going on. I almost went crazy when no one would tell me where you and Evan were. I thought you had run off together without asking me to join you."

"I'd never do that. I'm sorry for not telling you. There has been a lot going on—a lot of bad things. I didn't want you to get wrapped up in it."

"Friends are supposed to get wrapped up in it. They either help you or go crazy with you. That's what friends are for."

"I'll have to work on it. You're the closest friend I've had since Alana, and she doesn't really count."

"Good."

Cadence enters through the double doors leading into her apartment complex. She strides through the lobby and to the elevator that takes us to her floor. We enter and the doors slide shut, locking us in the tiny space with slow music blasting through the speakers in the ceiling.

When the doors ding open, I glance at Cadence's apartment that is directly in front of us. She lets me levitate through the door, and it looks like she got more stuff than the last time I was here, which wasn't even a few days ago. A sleek, black leather couch and loveseat are positioned in an L-shape in the center of the room. A flat screen television hangs on a vibrant purple wall with small shelves on each side of it. Small framed photos scatter across the side tables and the mantel over the electric fireplace. Onyx-colored drapes cover the sliding glass door that leads to a balcony. The room is clean and tidy, and screams of Cadence's taste, chic yet badass.

Levitating to the couch, I ease my sore body onto it. I bend my knees to my chest, finally gaining enough strength to move around. Cadence kicks off her boots and pads into the open kitchen to make us something to eat.

"Now that we're officially alone, spill," Cadence says, plopping a frozen dinner into the microwave. "You spent the night at Dylan's and most of the morning, and he carried you all the way to the infirmary. Also, you're wearing his clothes. What happened?"

The way Cadence says it isn't accusatory, more curious. Coming from anyone other than her, I'd start yelling about them making bad assumptions. She just wants the details.

"I didn't know I was at Dylan's until I woke up. He was

nice enough to let me fry his bed, and decent enough not to force me to walk around with my ass mooning the entire school. He carried me for the same reason you did. I'm ridiculously weak. Nothing else happened," I say, replaying my morning in my mind.

"I don't care about what you did. I want to know what you two talked about. You can't tell me you were that upset because Evan isn't immune to your electricity."

"Yes, actually I am, among other things. I'm disappointed in myself for finding my breaking point and that I lashed out at my boyfriend who risked his wellbeing to save me." I hold my knees. "And because Dylan made me feel like crap for things that weren't meant to be."

"Can you blame him? He's so obviously in love with you, and you've chosen his friend instead. I'd do everything I could to win you over if some other girl came in and knocked me from the bestie position. It's like ten times more devastating when your love is rejected." Cadence brings two plates with small black trays filled with orangey noodles.

"I couldn't reject someone who wasn't there." My voice rises in pitch. "You know how hard I tried. Why are you standing up for him?"

"I'm not. I just feel bad for Angel Boy. He's fighting a losing battle, yet he's so persistent. It's romantic in a way."

"Annoying, you mean. I'm happy with being his friend one minute, then guilty the next because of our friendship. He's so caring, so sweet, and I hate that he's all those things to me. I hate that I desperately want him to stay around, and that I have such a strong connection to him. And I hate that I've allowed myself to feel this way. In the end, if it came down to who I couldn't live without, I'd pick Evan—not Dylan. I'm scared that if I don't put a stop to his unrelenting hope that I'll change my mind, he'll get hurt and not just his feelings."

Cadence gapes at me. She sets her plate on the coffee table and leans her elbows on her knees, resting her head in her palms. Her deep purple hair falls in her eyes, and she intently stares at the space between us.

"Well, crap. I'd hate to be you, Cami," she says.

I'm glad that I'm not the only one who agrees. "Right? I have enough on my plate as it is. I don't have time to worry about this. Besides Evan's and Dylan's concern for me, Malicevile swears he needs to protect me, too. I guess since force wasn't all that effective, he's now trying to be all fatherly." I shake my hair into my face to cover me like a veil, like it'll somehow hide me from the world. "All I want is to graduate and go to college, not be a demon's daughter or an angel's girlfriend. I'm happy with Evan. He's the most human even with his fire power."

"Wait a minute. What is Malicevile trying to protect you from?" Cadence asks.

"From this," I say, waving my hands around. "From the alliance, from this school…I don't know. Maybe even from myself. He claims that's why he gave me some of his power, because he can't be here to protect me."

"Don't get upset, but what he's trying to do makes perfect sense. I've been involved with the alliance long enough to know that they're only concerned about humans. Nephilim are lucky to have good grace on their side," Cadence says.

"I'm glad I'm not the only one who sees his reasoning. It's his motives that scare me. Why would he make the effort to protect me if I'm being trained to kill him?" I ask.

"I don't know. It's something we'll have to find out."

"I was afraid you'd say that." The last thing I need right now is to bond with my dad. It unnerves me that I've grown used to calling him that instead of what he really is—a demon. "How do you suppose we do that?"

"We can break into the research center, or we can break you out of here so you can ask Malicevile yourself."

"Breaking and entering it is."

<hr>

I'm extremely nervous as I follow Cadence out of her apartment. My hair is still damp from the shower, and I'm wearing a ridiculously short dress that I might never return to Cadence because of how good I look in it—even if it isn't breaking and entering attire. My legs have gained most of their strength back, so I'm able to walk somewhat normally.

My palms sweat and anxiety tightens my chest. I've never broken the law before, especially one of the alliance's laws. I don't know how they punish criminals—I don't really want to know. Cadence has assured me that if we're caught her dad would pull some strings and get us a lighter punishment. I pray she's right.

The Yvette Donovan Research Center is on the opposite side of the courtyard, in between the family apartments and the training center. It's a small, red brick building the size of a two-bedroom house. It's open to the entire academy, with the exception of certain files that they keep under lock and key. Malicevile's is one of them. It could hinder the academy if someone decided to steal it and return it to him or destroy it. It has classified information the alliance needs to keep him under control. Unfortunately, that's the file I need to get my hands on. Who knows what else I'll find in the process. I could definitely use the opportunity to take and destroy my own file.

Our biggest advantage in attempting to steal the file is that Alana works in the research center, giving us an excuse to visit. I would ask Alana to steal it for me, but I don't want her getting in trouble, or worse, kicked out. She might be my official guardian, but the alliance could claim her unfit, and I could end up in someone else's hands—someone who doesn't care so much about me. If that happened, we'd be fugitives.

"This should be easy," Cadence says.

"Isn't that what most people say before things get difficult, and they end up getting caught?" I ask.

"Sure, but I know this will be easy. Ben Carter is on duty, and he has a thing for brunettes."

"But you're not brunette," I say, eyeing Cadence's purple hair. I glance down at the skimpy dress Cadence gave me to wear. She was planning to use me as the distraction the entire time.

She beams a dazzling smile and winks at me. "What can I say? You're quite seductive with your demonic charm. Humans tend to find you irresistible."

"Yeah, yeah," I say. "You have charms of your own."

I inhale a long breath, ignoring the sinking feeling in my stomach. We'll be in and out of the research center in a matter of minutes. We've only come for one measly file that will never be missed. I should have a right to look at it in the first place. Malicevile is *my* father.

Cadence holds out her arm, stopping me in place. The placard above the door reads Yvette Donovan, named for one of the first successful researchers to capture a demon on film. My demonology professor dedicated an hour to studying the blurry images. For being one of the highest ranking demon academies in the United States, I was surprised to discover that most students have never encountered a demon in their lives. A small percentage of them had to see the alliance's psychologist afterward. If they knew that my demon daddy likes to visit and write letters, they'd probably have heart attacks. I like to keep my personal life under wraps though.

"So, it's your job to distract Ben while I sneak in and grab the file. If things go wrong, run. I'll take the blame. It'll look better that way," Cadence says.

I nod and follow behind her as she pulls the door open. A wave of cool air engulfs us, blasting from the air conditioning unit stationed in the corner window. The simple room has light brown carpet with matching walls, resembling the inside of a cardboard box. Large canvases hang on the wall with portraits of gorgeous women and handsome men. The paintings are titled "Demons in Disguise," and I study each face, afraid of seeing Malicevile's.

A rickety table sits in the middle of the room with a husky man in his mid-twenties typing away on a keyboard. The monitor of his computer looks like a plastic box, ancient when it comes to modern technology. It doesn't surprise me though. The alliance still keeps actual paper files. They may have a fancy website for communication, but I don't think they trust the internet. Demons like my father can easily persuade a tech genius to hack the system. The alliance's filing habits make sense.

"Can I help you?" the man asks. His name plate reads 'Ben Carter,' just as I suspected.

I beam a huge smile and bat my eyelashes without saying a word. I saunter closer to the table, twisting a strand of my dark hair around my index finger. Cadence moves to the wall and pretends to be interested in the demon portraits.

"I'm not sure," I say, leaning on the table. "I'm researching different jobs around here for when I graduate. I don't think I could survive a demon attack. What do you do...Mr. Carter?" I pick up his name plate and run my fingers over the letters.

He smiles widely, and cute dimples flash on his cheeks. He runs his hand over his frazzled, dark brown hair. His eyes crinkle mischievously, their hazel color shining brightly. He smoothes his plain, white collared shirt before leaning on his elbows.

He straightens his shoulders. "I keep track of the demon documentation."

I bite my lip to keep from laughing. He says it like he has the most dangerous job in the world. I feign interest, thinking about all the ways I could kick his ass if he moves an inch closer.

"That is so cool!" I squeal. I sound completely fake, but Ben doesn't seem to notice. "I bet you've seen a million scary demons."

He shrugs. "They're not that scary."

I bet Ben has never come across a demon in his life, unless he is just trying to impress me. People have desk jobs in the academy for one of three reasons: They didn't cut it as a hunter; they were a hunter, but the alliance needed their intelligence more, or they've retired. I honestly think Ben here falls into category number one, or he'd be in the back and not playing receptionist.

"Whatever! They so are." I glance over my shoulder to see the room empty. Cadence's plan worked perfectly. "I heard about this girl who was hunted for three years! She, like, almost died."

Waggling his finger, he motions me to lean closer. He stretches his neck, his lips inches from my ear. His hot breath smells like spearmint gum, and it tickles my hair.

"I know her guardian. If you want my opinion, she's quite incompetent. Any good hunter would've been able to kill one stupid demon," he says.

My mouth drops open. I try to swallow my pride to keep my cover, but this jerk has no idea what he's talking about. I pull away and stand erect. Narrowing my eyes, I say, "Like you've ever killed a demon."

The smile vanishes from Ben's face.

"I have!" His voice startles me as it booms through the room. "I've killed plenty of demons."

I roll my eyes. "Liar. You're nothing but a weak, scared human who hides behind people like that hunter you've called incompetent."

"Take that back!" He snatches my arm, gripping it in his fingers.

"Make me," I whisper.

Ben raises his hand to slap me, a move that utterly surprises me. I duck before he can make contact and sucker punch him in the nose. He screams, covering his face with his hand. As he stands up, he knocks the table over, the computer smashing to the ground. Things keep getting worse and worse. My anger gets the best of me.

He rushes toward me, forcing me to levitate back before he can attack. I can't believe such a small insult set this man off. No wonder he's not in the field. I was wrong about there being only three reasons a person isn't a hunter. Number four would be because Ben would probably shove his partner into a demon to save himself.

Before he can get his hands on me, I kick him in the stomach, knocking him back into the wall. Energy crackles in my palm as he spits a few curse words in my direction, demeaning me for being only half human.

I flick my hand out and zap him with a low voltage amount of electricity to get him to shut up. It knocks him out, and he slides to the floor.

My eyes widen in horror as I stare at the mess I've created. If only I could've controlled myself I wouldn't be in so much trouble. I can't believe I attacked a defenseless man. Why couldn't I just walk away? I had to try to prove a point when he talked badly about Alana. This is far worse than my empty threat toward Sarah. *Oh, God.*

I lean against the wall and slowly slide to the floor. Cadence should be out any minute, if I'm lucky.

I panic when I spot the camera blinking in the corner. "Cadence!" I yell. "Hurry."

Cadence appears in the doorway at the same time as the front door flies open. She disappears as blinding light pours into the room. I squint through the light to see a massive silhouette stepping into the room.

"Don't move," a man says, charging forward.

I cover my face with my hands.

When the door closes, I watch the man pull a walkie-talkie from his belt. "We need medical attention in Yvette Donovan, stat."

The man checks Ben first before strutting to me. Grabbing me by my wrists, he hoists me from the ground and spins me so my back faces him. Cold metal sears my skin as he snaps hand-cuffs in place.

As much as panic grips at me, tears don't pour from my eyes. I hate that all I can think about is how mad I am that I was caught and how Ben totally deserved it. "I'm sorry. I didn't mean it," I say even though I totally did mean it.

The man shoves his hand into my back, pushing me forward. I have no choice except to walk out of the research center with my head bowed in shame. My heart threatens to smash through my ribcage to leap on the ground in front of us. My good name will be ruined the moment I'm paraded across campus for everyone to see. I'll forever be known as the demon's daughter.

PURGATORY

SWEAT DRIPS DOWN my forehead as I stare at the cement cell the alliance locked me in. An impenetrable metal door blocks my only way out, and if someone doesn't let me out soon, I'll have to use the nasty stainless steel toilet near the cot I don't feel like sitting on. I'm pretty sure hours have gone by, but I can't really tell. No one has come to tell me what's going on, and I'm afraid no one ever will. I'll surely die here.

My dry throat burns as I think about a cold glass of water that I doubt will be offered to me anytime soon. The sweltering air, filtered by a single vent, nearly suffocates me. The alliance couldn't possibly lock me up forever without hearing my side of the story. *Could they?*

Is it possible that I don't have the same rights as the humans we are trained to protect? Fear nudges my heart. The alliance doesn't follow human law. They do as they see fit. If they think I should be locked up forever, they won't hesitate to do it.

I shuffle to the cot and force myself to lie back and stare at the gray ceiling. I wonder how Evan is doing. He would've been released by now. I wish I could explain what happened. I hate this uncertainty.

An alarm rings loudly through the cell, startling me, and I fly off the cot. The door swings open, and a girl my age saunters in. Her dark hair rests on top of her head in a messy bun. Her tight fitting jeans show off her curves while an off-the-shoulder top allows a Hunter's Alliance tattooed symbol to peek out over her shoulder. The X with the sun and moon looks identical to those plastered on safe houses. Her black eyes shine in the fluorescent lighting as she steps closer, her stiletto heels tapping the cement floor in loud clicks. She offers me a small smile.

She sets a tray of food and a water bottle on the edge of the cot and surprises me by sitting down. "Crappy place, huh?" She crosses her legs before leaning back on her arms.

"I've been in worse places," I say, trying to keep from crying in front of this stranger.

"I know. Dylan told me all about you. He's the one who sent me here. I'm Katie, by the way." She holds out her hand, and I cautiously shake it.

"Cami," I say. I stare at the beautiful girl. She sounds familiar, but I can't place her anywhere. I'm pretty sure I've never met her before.

"Well, I hope this helps. The alliance will be ready for you sooner or later." She taps the tray and pushes to her feet and then saunters to the door. "Oh, I almost forgot. Dylan told me to tell you to get some sleep." She winks and taps on the door three quick times. Translucent wings unfurl from her back for a split second before they disappear as the door buzzes open. Just as fast as she came, she's gone, and I'm left alone once more.

Until she mentioned it, the last thing on my mind has been sleep. I didn't even think about how Dylan can visit my dreams. I still don't fully accept that it's really him and not my imagination. But sleep might be my only reprieve from this tiny cell, and I'll do anything to stop myself from going crazy. I also need to know if Cadence managed to steal my dad's file. If she didn't, this whole thing would be worthless. I couldn't blame anyone but myself though. I let Ben get to me, and now the whole alliance and academy probably thinks I'm some uncontrollable monster. *Maybe I am.*

I close my eyes and start counting, hoping to force myself to fall asleep. This cot is stupidly uncomfortable, purposely trying to prevent me from my dreams. It has an inch of padding and no pillow. I twist and turn, finally growing tired of the silence.

My eyelids become heavy as I breathe in and out slowly. Listening to my heart rhythmically beating, I find comfort in knowing I'm still alive. I could've been dead a long time ago.

After a long while, I finally give up and open my eyes. But I'm no longer in the cement cell. I'm sitting on a wooden bench in a sweetly fragranced garden. The sun shines above me in a crystalline sky. Water, gurgling from a marble fountain, creates a melodic sound as water falls from the trumpet blown by the angel statue stationed on a circular pedestal in the middle. Vibrant lavender-colored roses bloom on long stems, and the citrusy scent of the lemon grove wafts through the air. This is a much nicer place than the cell I'm imprisoned in. I would die happy if I never have to leave.

"What have you gotten yourself into?" Dylan materializes in front of me. His translucent wings expand out, flapping gently behind him. He looks so sad—so lost. I want to get up and run to him, but I don't. I refuse to lead him on anymore.

"I didn't mean to hurt Ben," I whisper, staring at my hands. "He provoked me. He tried to hit me, and I lost it. I was angry and scared. He called Alana incompetent, and I—I don't know what else to say. I didn't mean to hurt him."

"Did he hurt you?" Dylan reaches out and touches my chin so I have to look into his gloomy eyes, now lined with anger. "If he hurt you I'll—"

"You'll what?" I cut him off. I don't want him to do anything stupid. "Beat him up? Get him kicked out? He's been punished enough."

"But the alliance is going to punish you! Even if it wasn't your fault, you attacked a human using your demonic powers. This is bad, Cami. I don't think I can even help you."

"I was protecting myself. This isn't fair!"

"I know, love." Dylan cups my face. "You would've been okay if you had just punched him. Zapping him is what got you in this mess."

My heart sinks. I wouldn't be sleeping in a prison cell if I would've stuck to human combat. Since I used my father's gift, I'll now have to face whatever punishment the alliance throws at me. Malicevile was wrong to think I could use it to protect myself here. I'm worse off.

"What's going to happen to me?" I ask.

"I can't say, Cami, but I'll do everything in my power to make sure you aren't thrown to the werewolves."

I swallow hard. *Please, be a figure of speech.* Werewolves scare me to death since my run in with them in Desertville.

I cover my face with my hands, holding my frail sanity together. "You're so good to me, you know. I don't know what I'd do without you."

"You would enjoy the roses," Dylan says, smiling.

"That's not what I meant," I say.

"I know."

He shifts from foot to foot, and I pat the empty seat next to me. When he sits down, I snuggle next to him, letting him put his arm around me. *This is only a dream.*

It feels wrong to be sad in such a peaceful, happy place. I wish I could make things better between the two of us. If only we could have a fresh start. But, I wouldn't change anything I've been through. I've learned too much and have experienced invaluable things. I couldn't imagine my life any different. I'd go through Hell all over again to end up where I am right now. Well, not including the imprisonment. I'd change that in a heartbeat.

We sit together for what seems like forever. Time is hard to track here. The sun always shines, and I never have to worry about anything bad happening. Dylan ensures I have a peaceful rest.

"Dylan?" I ask. Everyone I love flashes through my mind, reminding me I can't stay here forever.

"Yes, love?" He wraps his feathery wings around us in a blanket of pure, mesmerizing light.

"What would happen if I asked you to let me stay here? I'm afraid to wake up."

"It would be like being in a coma. Life would continue to move on without you." He stares intensely at me, gauging my reaction. "You don't want that, Cami. That isn't how you should live your life."

Wouldn't it be better for me if I stayed here? I would never have to worry about anything again. I could live the rest of my life in this beautiful dream world without fear. The more I think about it, the more I want to. I don't want to go back.

I hide my eyes by shifting my head against his chest. "You don't know what I want."

Dylan twines our fingers together, pressing his palm against mine. The heat between us is electrifying. Together, we could supply enough energy to power an entire town.

"As much as I'd love to spend the rest of eternity with you, just like this, we can't. You'll be missed. What about Alana and David? Cadence? What about Evan? You don't want to be without him. I know how much he means to you."

I know he's right. I miss Evan already. I miss my whole family. It seems like years have passed. My heart aches thinking about the hell I've put them through these last few days, and I know Alana and Evan are losing their minds over my arrest.

I answer his questions with a deep sigh. What difference does it really make, though? My life is in the hands of the alliance. What scares me most is that Malicevile might be right about needing to protect me from them. I barely shocked Ben Carter, and now I'm stuck in a cement cell.

I'd hate to think what would've happened if I'd accidentally killed him. The alliance would probably euthanize me like a rabid dog. Being demi-demon is like being entirely demon in their eyes. I lost my human rights the moment I arrived—the moment Alana decided that we needed to stop running.

"Why do you have to be so reasonable? Life is about spontaneity, about living. I have a hard time living in this world. I'm too good for the bad guys and too evil for the good guys. I'm sick of living in Purgatory and tired of having to worry about my life and who's out to get me." The words fly from my mouth, and I can't hold anything back.

"The only things I want to worry about are school dances, going to college...normal stuff," I continue. "I bet the academy doesn't even have prom. I was really looking forward to going to prom this year, but no. School dances consist of combat training and sweatpants—not dancing and glittery gowns. I hate this." I didn't realize until this very moment how much I want to be normal. I've been so concerned about surviving through another night that I've never really thought about all that I've missed out on.

Dylan presses his warm lips to my cheek. He lingers, his warm breath tickling my skin. His apple orchard and rainwater scent comforts me. I could be near him forever if my heart would allow it.

"I wish I could make all those things possible. I'd do anything to make you happy," he whispers into my ear. "I mean it."

"Dylan, please," I whisper. "Don't do this. You shouldn't be so concerned about me. There's nothing I can offer you in return."

"I'm not asking for anything," he says.

"Neither am I." My heart breaks as guilt consumes me for not wanting the same thing he does.

"You might not admit to it out loud, but I know my feelings for you are not unrequited. I can see it in your eyes. You just don't want to accept the possibility that we have a connection that goes soul deep."

Tears rim my eyes, knowing that what he says is true. Dylan and I share an invisible bond that I don't know how to break. I'd give anything to rid my mind of the confusion I feel when I'm around him. I hate how he makes me doubt myself.

"I have accepted it, okay? I've known since the moment you flashed your wings that there was something unbreakable between us. But I'm in love with Evan."

Dylan bows his head in defeat. I think I've finally made him understand that we'll never be together. We can never be together. He's an angel, and I'm a demon. Our human sides aren't strong enough to overpower the differences in our species. Dylan is pure—good by default. I'm, well, I'm not so good. My demon half won't ever let me forget that. Angels and demons aren't meant to be together. That's why they are on opposing teams. There isn't a middle ground where we could live happily ever after, even if we could balance each other out.

I pull away from him to give myself the space I need. "You've known that I'm in love with him. You're just making things harder on yourself."

"Denying my feelings for you is what's hard. This, admitting my love, is easy. I have the right to be in love with you even if you don't want me to be. I'm not going to deny how I feel about you, Cami. I love you to my very soul. I'm not asking you to love me back. It's just—I know I'd regret it if I didn't let you know."

This dream feels like it is turning into a nightmare, yet I still can't find the will to ask for him to leave. His confession has almost made me forget what lies ahead of me.

I pull my knees to my chin and rest my head on them. I can't find the right words to respond to Dylan, so I just stare at my bare legs. I watch him from my peripheral vision. His chocolate-brown eyes shadow with something other than sadness. It's like the shadows on my soul reflect in his eyes, and he can feel everything I feel—the hurt, the pain, the guilt.

My body trembles as I hold back my tears. I'm emotionally exhausted. If I think about Dylan any longer, I'm sure that I'll reach my breaking point. I can handle demons after my soul, the punishment I'm sure I'm going to have to endure from the alliance, and even being a demon's daughter. What I can't handle is the heartache I put my angel through. It's devastating.

The trembling in my knees shakes the bench, and I even feel the ground shifting under us. Black fog swirls through the air, blocking the precious rays of sunshine. The stones crack under my feet, startling me. It's like an earthquake rolls through my dream, threatening to smash this world to pieces.

The bench groans, and one of the legs snap. I pull Dylan to his feet before we topple over. The rose bushes fall sideways, their roots unable to keep them stable in my quaking world. I can't keep the world in focus.

"What's happening?" I frantically glance around.

"Don't be afraid," Dylan says. "All you have to do is wake up."

"No. Not yet!" I yell. "I'm not ready!"

The thickening fog wraps around Dylan, ripping him from my fingertips. My stomach heaves as the shaking intensifies. The ground cracks, and I jump to the side, afraid of falling into the dark crevice. The shiny cobblestone path disintegrates beneath my feet, causing me to lose my balance. I try to levitate but nothing happens. My powers don't work here.

The earth rips out from under me, and I cling for dear life to the edge before my fingers give out. Dylan is gone, and I'm all alone. I concentrate on the sound of my heartbeat as I plummet into utter darkness.

ACT HUMAN

"GET UP."

The earthquake follows me into the real world as I open my eyes. A muscular man in black slacks and a matching black dress shirt with the Hunter's Alliance insignia printed on the breast pocket shakes my shoulders. I'm disoriented and confused, staring at the stark walls and toilet.

I sit up and smack the man's hands from my shoulders. Usually when someone opens their eyes, it means they're awake, right? The man steps back and glares at me. His thick eyebrows knit together, creating deep creases in his forehead.

"You have a visitor," he says.

He struts to the door, and it buzzes open. Alana steps in and rushes to me. She flings her arms around me, hugging me in a death grip. The man leaves the cell, locking Alana in with me.

Her pale gray eyes shine with tears, and I pat the cot for her to sit down. Her light blond hair is a mess, flying in all directions, and she's still wearing the lab coat she has to wear to work.

"Tell me exactly what happened." Alana's voice cracks, sounding hoarse like she's been screaming.

"I was at the research center, you know, doing research, and the receptionist guy, Ben Carter, called you incompetent which made me say some not-so-nice things and he—he was going to hit me!" My voice comes out louder than I want it to. "So, I punched him, but he kept coming after me, and then I zapped him. I didn't know what to do. He was trying to hurt me. I couldn't let him."

Alana squeezes me again without saying anything.

"What's going to happen to me? Are they going to sentence me to death or something? I'm scared." Tears escape my eyes and drip down my cheeks.

"No, the alliance wouldn't do that. Something like that could start a war between creatures and hunters, but I can't say you won't be punished," Alana whispers, like she's afraid we're being listened to.

"They're going to keep me locked up, aren't they?" Fear ices my blood. I'd go crazy in here.

Her solemn expression doesn't change. "If they think you're unstable and at risk of hurting another human again, then they might."

"I'm not! When are they going to ask me what happened? I have rights." I release a long, loud wail, hoping someone besides Alana will hear me. I'm afraid if I stay in here any longer, I'll turn into a raging lunatic.

Alana winces. "Calm down, Cami. David and Evan are with the alliance right now. We'll sort this mess out." She leans forward and presses her lips to my ear. "Tell me the truth about why you were at the research center. I need to know these things. I know I don't have the right to press you about secrets, and I know things have changed between us, but please, trust me. I can help you."

I shake my head and lift my chin to the guard. I can't risk saying anything incriminating in a cell. I don't know if this place is bugged, or if the guard outside my door has super hearing. Evan has had a right to be suspicious of the alliance, and his reason for making sure I don't use my powers in front of humans is rational. I'm going to have to keep my guard up until I'm able to leave the academy for good.

"Okay. I understand." She clasps my hands for a moment before pulling away.

Being trapped in a fiery church doesn't even compare to being locked up in a cement cell. I would rather face Malicevile every day than this. Before, I was okay with dying to save my friends. I don't want to die now, not without good reason. If the alliance decides to never release me, it's tempting to call on Daddy Demon for reinforcement, because then his theory would be right. This isn't exactly the protection I thought I needed.

I sigh. "Have you seen Cadence? How's she taking this?" I ask, changing the subject. I need to know if she was successful in pilfering the file. It feels like I've been in here for weeks; I've missed so much.

"Hard. She hasn't said one word since she called her father for help and he denied her. She's waiting in the lobby for me. I'm the only one allowed to visit you besides the staff because I'm your guardian."

"If her dad doesn't help me, I'm going to be fed to the sharks. I know it. Do I even get a lawyer? A police report? A trial? Anything?"

She straightens her shoulders. "David is defending you. You might be able to give a statement if he succeeds in making a case. He has to convince the alliance you deserve to be heard."

"You've got to be kidding me, Alana. You should be there instead. You know me better." I tug at my dark, messy hair. "Don't get me wrong, David is great about getting his point across, but I trust you the most with my life, more than any-one—even Evan."

"It's better this way, trust me. I'm in no condition to de-fend you right now. You might not be able to tell, but I'm an emotional wreck. I'd screw everything up." Tears shine in Ala-na's eyes, and I know she's right. She's more effective using actions than words and would rather knock someone out than argue her point across to protect me. That's what makes her the best bodyguard against demons.

"Let's hope so. If I have to stay in here, I'm going to go insane. I can't live my life like a caged animal. I'd rather die. Better yet, I'd rather sell my soul for a free pass." I look at the cold floor as the words escape my lips. I'm ashamed to admit that it's true. Malicevile may scare me to death, and he most likely has ulterior motives, but he wouldn't do this to me. With him, I'd have some rights...*I think.*

"Please, don't talk like that. Not yet. You've been in here less than a day, and the alliance hasn't even convicted you of anything. Think of this as detention," Alana says.

"You try thinking of this cell as detention when you're the one not allowed to leave." I cover my mouth with my hand in shock. Alana doesn't deserve the attitude I'm giving her. "I'm sorry. I'm freaking out."

Alana is about to respond when the door buzzes open and the guard barges in. Alana nods her head at him before standing up to leave. I knew it was too good to be true to think she could stay a little while longer.

"Keep your chin up, Cami." Alana pats my shoulder. She kisses the top of my head before leaving in front of the guard. The door slams shut, and I'm alone once more.

***

The hours drag on. I can't sleep. I can't eat. I can't do anything except pace restlessly around my cell. It's just big enough that I can get the exercise I need to prevent me from feeling claustrophobic. I've pulled the thin mattress from the cot and leaned it against the wall to use as a makeshift punching bag.

My knuckles burn as I continuously practice my jabs in smooth, consistent repetition. My hand combat is still not even close to being as good as Cadence's and Alana's. With all this free time, I've realized that I'm now reliant on my demonic abilities. If I'm going to stay out of trouble, I need to act like I used to only a month ago—I need to act human.

It's scary to think that I have to actually think about acting like a human, when part of me is and always will be. Learning about my heritage and my father will never take that away from me even if I tend to forget about it. I think that's where the alliance is flawed. How am I, or any other demi-demon or creature for that matter, supposed to remember what being human is if the alliance doesn't treat or see me as human? What use is it to act like everyone else if I can never be like everyone else? My life blows.

I give up on exercising and decide to sit cross-legged on the floor. I hover midair and close my eyes in meditation. Listening to the rhythmic beating of my heart, I breathe in sync with it. I'm about to finally find utter peacefulness when I hear voices yelling on the other side of the door. It sounds like someone is losing an argument. I hope it's my guard.

The door buzzes open, and Evan rushes into my cell. My heart flutters in my chest, and I breathe in his seductive scent, filling my lungs with his smell. His hands are still bandaged and his black eye has gotten darker, but he is the best thing I've seen all day.

We don't speak.

I press my lips to his and kiss him like it's our first kiss all over again. His arms hold me tightly, and he lifts me off my feet. I twine my legs around his waist, craving for him to turn around and carry me out of here, but I can smell the guard hovering in the doorway. He's been here as long as I have and is in desperate need of a shower.

"I should be furious with you," he whispers into my hair. "I leave you alone for a couple of hours and look what mess you've gotten yourself into."

"I'm angry enough for both of us," I whisper against his cheek. "How did you get them to let you in?"

"He didn't have a choice. I'm here to pick you up. You're being released under supervision, and I got dibs on the first shift."

"How? Isn't it more practical to assign someone who doesn't give a crap about me?"

"There aren't enough hunters to spare, and since I can't work in my condition, I get to play babysitter, which is fine by me. I'd do it anyways."

"For how long?" I'd hate to have someone by my side day and night. A girl needs her privacy.

"Not long. Just until your punishment hearing later today. You've been let out early to attend classes."

School was the last thing on my mind. I didn't expect my

early release to be due to school instead of good behavior. I guess it's the first part of my punishment. At least I have Evan to keep me company. He can also keep the gossip mongrels at bay.

I stare down at my dress, which is more fitting for a night out. "Damn. Do I have time to change and shower? I don't even know how long I've been locked up." I glance around the husky guard, but I only see a bare, white wall.

"I'm to escort you directly to class," he says. Sympathy and love shine in his eyes, and I can see that it bothers him that he has to treat me like a threat to the academy's community.

"Don't worry about it. I'll survive. I'm just glad to get out of here. We can at least take advantage of the time we can spend together. Maybe you can be my partner in combat. I need better competition."

Evan smiles as he sets me on my feet. "Yeah, we can teach your classmates a thing or two about hunting. It's good to be able to show off every once and a while."

"Then what are we waiting for? I'm dying for a little fresh air," I say, jumping onto Evan's back. I rest my chin on his shoulder and wink at the guard as we exit the cell and enter the real world.

LOOKS CAN BE DECEIVING

THE SETUP OF the classrooms seems to be more of an after-thought compared to the rest of the campus. For being named the Hunter's Academy, there are fewer students than there are actual hunters. Five small warehouses make up the learning facility, odd-looking against the beautiful stone work of the other buildings. The buildings are situated just northeast of the dormitory, far enough out of the way that visitors don't see the buildings unless they seek them out. The atmosphere on this part of campus is more similar to a small business district without the packed parking lots. The classrooms within the warehouses are perfect for more intensive training though, with only a handful of desks for actual bookwork. Everything taught in the academy is more hands on.

I ignore the gaping stares as Evan jogs me past the dormitory. If word got out that I electrocuted some dude, I'm sure I've been permanently marked as trouble. If it hasn't, I must look ridiculous, being seen more often than not riding on people's backs. They've probably marked me as lazy, which I couldn't care less about.

My heart slides into my stomach when I spot the purple hair of a girl sitting on the cement steps of my first class. Cadence rests her head on her folded hands, peering through the bustling students, most likely looking out for me.

I wave, and her smile lights up like the sun peeking through a cloudy sky. She jumps to her feet to meet us halfway. Before Evan has the chance to put me down, I fly off his back, knocking Cadence to the soft ground in the biggest bear hug. She laughs, hopping to her feet and then helps me up.

"You don't listen, do you? I told you to run if anything happened. And what did you do? You got caught and thrown in jail for a day and a half. At least it wasn't for nothing," Cadence says.

"Really? You got it? What does it say?" I ask, dying to get a look at the file the alliance has kept on my father.

"I didn't look at it. I think you should be the one to do that. It's your life and your demonic heritage. I'd rather you read it for yourself than hear it from me." Cadence kicks the soft ground with her boot.

Coming up from behind me, Evan slides his arms around my neck. He breathes softly in my ear, and I lean into him, taking comfort in the confidence and strength emanating from him.

"Why is it that every time you have a brilliant idea, Cami is always the one getting injured, kidnapped, or locked up?" Evan asks Cadence. I can't tell if he's serious or joking. He sounds a little bit of both.

"Because she lacks the finesse and grace that I have." She bats her long lashes before lightly punching me in the arm. "Or because no one cares enough about me to try any of those things."

"That's a good thing," I say. "You do *not* want to receive the attention I do."

Cadence laughs, lifting my mood with the sound of her charming voice. "Whatever you say, babe. I wouldn't complain about all the attention." She winks at Evan, and he kisses my cheek, causing Cadence to roll her eyes.

I sigh. "If only I could pick and choose the attention." I shrug my shoulders and watch my peers begin to enter Building Two, where my first class takes place.

"That would be nice," she says. "We better get inside. Don't want you to be late on the day of your hearing. The alliance is crazy if they think you'd be left alone anyways."

I scrunch my brows and walk ahead with Evan and Cadence trailing behind me. They stand at the back of the open room when I take a seat on my usual yoga mat positioned in the front row. Every class begins with some sort of warm up. They expect us to be as nimble as possible for combat. I'll be able to do the splits by the end of the semester, with a few more weeks of practice.

Hunter Miller scrawls on the whiteboard, declaring that today's lesson will be getting to know your opponent. There are ten students in this class, a mixture of humans and creatures. It's a way to understand different species fighting techniques and also a way to prepare for dirty tactics that demons seem to fancy during combat, like using nails and teeth.

Being a demi-demon puts me in a good position for battle. I've been restricted from using electricity because the power isn't technically mine, so I must use what I was born with unless another demi-demon student uses their ability on me. I'm allowed to absorb powers for short periods of time. The human students have a different sort of advantage because they are able to use daggers, clubs, whips, and all sorts of other weapons. All those weapons are dangerous but can't be used at a distance unless they have awesome throwing skills, which I haven't seen yet. I'm hoping one of my classes will eventually cover knife throwing. Only real hunters ever get their hands on guns, but they're not enough to kill a demon.

"It's nice to see you back, Cami," Hunter Miller says. She flips her curly, black hair over her shoulder and smirks. I've missed two days of school, and I bet all my teachers will have the same smug reaction.

"I wasn't sure I was going to be able to make it, but here I am with my backup," I say, refusing to let her get to me.

"I see that. I've been looking for guest fighters for a while now. It's nice of you to have volunteered to be here, Hunter Whiteshaw and Hunter Dubois." Calling Cadence and Evan by their titles is weird, but it's a sign of respect in a formal setting. Students get in trouble for using first names in the classroom, but we're free to do so everywhere else. It's a strange role, but with the variance in ages between students and teachers, it helps set the professionals apart.

"Always a pleasure," Cadence says, winking at a small cluster of boys gawking at her from their mats. "I can't wait to teach your class a thing or two."

Evan chuckles without adding his own comment. It surprises me how quiet he is when he's around strangers. I don't really see him as the brooding, mysterious type. At least not with me. I wonder if the academy has something to do with it. He's been uncomfortable with the entire situation since we moved here.

"If you two will stand up here, I'd love to demonstrate how to get to know your opponents without any fighting demonstrations," Hunter Miller says.

Cadence saunters to the front of the room, and Evan casually strolls behind her. Like me, Cadence is in a black dress with combat boots. I'd never have worn this dress to class if I'd been able to change. But Cadence is a different story. She is the fashionista of the hunters and can fight in anything, which is an advantage in my book. Her dark purple hair is braided down her back, with a faux black flower pinned behind her ear. Her honey brown eyes shine bright against the dark contrast of her heavy eyeliner. I bet half the boys in the room have already fantasized about kissing her plum lips.

Evan wears a simple button-down shirt and jeans. His blond hair is neatly brushed out of his aqua eyes. He looks absolutely normal. But behind his eyes and easygoing smile lies a predator most don't know exists. He's lethal, strong, and a great fighter. I'm excited to see if the class's observations about my best friends are correct.

Hunter Miller holds a marker in her hand, ready to write on the whiteboard. "I want everyone to imagine the classroom is an alley in the middle of Los Angeles. It's dark and you're alone. At the end of the alley, Hunter Dubois is blocking your path. She's demon-tainted, and the only way past her is to fight. How do you fight what you're unsure of? Let's start with clothing. What does Hunter Dubois's clothing say about her combat skills?"

A boy with a shaved head raises his hand. I should really learn people's names if I'm going to fit in. "Yes, Sebastian," Hunter Miller says.

"Her dress says one of two things. She's either a demi-demon with the ability to heal quickly, or she is stupid and a terrible fighter."

Cadence smirks, raising a single eyebrow. Nothing anyone says will get to her. Hunter Miller writes a less offensive description on the board.

"Her combat boots lead me to believe she's a great kicker," a red headed girl says.

"Her entire ensemble confuses me," a boy, whose name I think is Adam, says. "She's hot and scary. I don't know what to expect."

I laugh out loud. Adam shrugs his shoulders, unfazed.

"This is good," Hunter Miller says. "We all know looks can be deceiving. "Now, Hunter Dubois, can you explain to the class why you have chosen to wear a dress instead of more appropriate hunting attire?"

"Sure. I like to look good while I destroy demons. Just because I'm a hunter, doesn't mean I have to be a fashion victim. I can fight wearing anything. I'm *that* good," she boasts, which gets her a dramatic eye roll from Hunter Miller.

"I bet you've never faced off with more than a lower level demon," Sebastian quips.

I fist my hands. "She's fought more demons than you could ever imagine. She fought my demon father alone, so I could run. That's more than you'll be able to say about your entire career."

"That's amazing!" the girl next to me squeals. "Do you tutor? I'm looking for someone to train me who understands my needs."

Cadence laughs. "We can arrange something after class." Cadence can be a great role model when she's not breaking into buildings or on quests to find her soul mate. I have a strong feeling she will become more involved in the academy. It'll be good for her.

"Thank you for your participation, Hunter Dubois," Hunter Miller says. "Now, let's move on to Hunter Whiteshaw. What do you get from him?"

"He's easy to take out," a boy says from behind me. "Those bandages aren't very threatening."

I wince, the reminder of what I've done to Evan being made a joke. "I'd like to see you try," I snap. He wouldn't be joking if he faced him in a real-life situation.

"Why do you say that, Cami? Tell us from a visual perspective," Hunter Miller says.

"See the way he fists his hands through the bandages. It shows that he is ready to fight at any moment. Also, look at his belt. There isn't a weapon, which means he doesn't need one," I say. "If you look at Hunter Dubois, you can see her dagger in a hip holster."

"His dagger could be hidden on his leg, under his jeans," Sebastian argues.

"Everyone knows hunters only put their backup weapons there. Well, at least I *thought* everyone did. If he doesn't have a holster within reach, he won't have one there either." I brush my hair behind my ear in frustration. I really hope Sebastian doesn't decide to work in the field because he'd never survive.

Evan grins at me, enjoying my need to defend him. He loves when people underestimate him so he can prove to them how powerful he really is.

I'm surprised the non-human students haven't spoken up

yet. Most have been born with a sixth sense to identify another creature, unless they want to see where this goes. I have to admit that it feels good to prove the humans here wrong when they're so self-assured, and I bet others agree with me.

"I want to close this discussion with one last question," Hunter Miller interjects. "Hunter Whiteshaw, would you please give us a demonstration? I think Sebastian needs to be enlightened. Oh, and class, please feel free to protect him if you want."

Evan nods his head and clasps his hands together. Smoke sizzles from his fingers as the bandages catch fire. Sebastian's eyes widen as a ball of fire bursts in Evan's hands. Evan pitches the fire, aiming for Sebastian, and the class goes utterly silent as the ball zooms for the cocky boy. He scrambles on his mat, trying to get away, screaming as the fire closes in on him. I reach out, snatching the fire seconds before it collides with Sebastian, holding the fireball tenderly in my fingers.

Sebastian slumps forward in tears, and I can't help pitying him. I would love to say that Hunter Miller's decision was wrong, allowing Evan to do that to the poor boy, but I think he learned an important lesson today—one that I've known for quite some time now. Looks can be deceiving.

I snuff the flame out and pat Sebastian's back, comforting him. There are mixed emotions emanating in the room—some frightened, some smug, some pitiful like me.

"I think that will conclude our learning portion of class today," Hunter Miller says. "I hope you've all gained an important lesson. Now, grab a partner. It's time to fight."

When the hour ends, she dismisses us from class. Evan smacks Sebastian on the back as he passes by. The boy composes himself, not allowing his fear to consume him. "You know, Cami is a great defensive fighter. I bet she'd be willing to teach you a thing or two."

Sebastian nods, and we leave him standing there, shocked and awestruck. Cadence brings a first-aid kit to put new bandages on Evan's hands before we head to my next class.

I just hope this day ends quickly so I can learn what's going to happen in my life.

GUILTY

I COUNT THE seconds ticking away in my last class of the day. I've managed to survive human combat, distance combat, weaponry, and demonology without getting into trouble. The Hunter's Alliance must have kept my incident under wraps because none of my classmates have mentioned anything to me, and I haven't heard them gossiping about me either.

It seems that only my teachers know what happened. My creature teachers were kind and almost happy to see me, where my human teachers looked like they wanted to ban me from attending class. I've never seen such a rift in moral standards or opinions within the alliance before.

My last class of the day is my favorite. It's a fairly new class that's been added to the curriculum to help appease those who believe the alliance is discriminating. The class is Species Awareness and can be taken only by half and non-humans. Cadence wasn't even allowed to participate, forcing her to find something else to do besides follow me around. There are secrets that creatures of the Veiled Realm pass down through generations—secrets that can never be known by humans.

Today's topic covers endangered species that have almost been wiped out by the alliance and demons. According to legend, the number of witches left is miniscule. They were hunted by the alliance for centuries because of demon association. As it turns out, the two species are not connected. The last surviving witches remain in hiding, living in the human world, posing as humans or demi-demons. I wonder if I could detect a witch like I can other species, but I'd first have to know what they smell like, which can be tricky.

"If the alliance is capable of taking out an entire species, shouldn't we be going into hiding like the witches? I think it's a good idea to follow their example," a girl named Ella says. She's only a quarter demon but still can kick anyone's butt if she wants to.

"We'd rather be on their side than against them," Hunter Garcia says. "It's also improbable if you think about it. The alliance gives us a safe place to live, allows us to use our strengths freely, and does a good job at keeping the human world from knowing about us. We need them as much as they need us."

"I could survive outside of the alliance," Ella says. "I'm barely even demon."

"Not to the alliance," I quip.

"To the rest of the world," she retorts.

"And everyone else in this room. You could say I grew up human, but the moment my demon side was revealed I was automatically marked a demon. I've never had specialized training until now. I didn't even know that other species existed. I can pretend all I want that I'm human, but I'm not. Like you, I'll never be. I wouldn't change anything, though. I am who I am, and I accept it. You should, too," I say.

Ella opens and shuts her mouth but doesn't say anything. I wish I could agree with her logic, but I can't. Not anymore. The only way I can survive in this world, living a semi-normal life, is to learn to live with myself and with what life has dealt me—good and bad.

Hunter Garcia nods her head with a smile, and her short, red-streaked hair bounces against her dark skin. Her smile fades as quickly as it came, her hazel eyes darkening when there's a loud knock at the door.

A man wearing all black, with the exception of the bright yellow Hunter's Alliance insignia embroidered on his breast pocket, steps into the room, dangling a shiny pair of metal handcuffs from his hand. His military cropped hair makes his rugged features more intimidating than if his hair was a little longer. His caramel-colored eyes shine in the fluorescent lighting before focusing on me.

"Hunter Garcia, I'm here to collect Ms. Anders," the man says.

"You can't wait five minutes for my class to finish, Sam?" Hunter Garcia says.

Sam winces, embarrassed by the lack of respect Hunter Garcia shows him in front of her class. "I don't like waiting." His deep voice carries a threatening note to it. He turns to me. "It's now or never, Anders. Unless you like being locked up."

My heartbeat quickens. I'm mortified that Sam has interrupted my class to take me to my hearing, when Evan was going to take me straight there after class was over. Now, gossip is sure to spread and everyone will find out what I've done to Ben.

"I'm coming," I say, my voice low.

I shuffle to the door with my head bowed, refusing to look at my classmates. Evan rushes to my side, squeezing my hand. Sam grabs my shoulders, spinning me around to face my class before cuffing my hands behind my back.

"Is that really necessary?" Anger lines Evan's voice. "She's been without them all day."

"I have a right to transport her in any way I feel necessary." Sam grins as he spins me back around. "As for the rest of you, hurt a human and you'll end up just like her."

Embarrassment crawls up my neck, reddening my face. If I wasn't afraid of the consequences I already face, I'd punch him in his smug smile. I'm not a criminal. *Not that they know of, at least. Cadence was the one who took the file.*

Evan follows next to me with his arm around my waist to

help hide the handcuffs. It makes the walk to the assembly hall less painful with him by my side. If Evan wasn't demi-demon, I'm sure Sam would've protested his accompanying me. I stroll forward with my head held high. I refuse to let this get to me.

Sam reaches out to pull me up the steps when Evan's heavy hand swipes his away. I smile my thanks and take the first step slowly.

"You don't have the right to lay your hands on her. She hasn't been convicted. If she is, and you try that again, you'll be sitting behind a desk answering phones for the rest of your career, Samuel." Evan's glare doesn't waver from Sam's until we enter the foreboding, brick building.

I press my lips together to keep the smile from my face. It wouldn't be one of my better ideas to laugh at the man in charge of bringing me in. Who knows what lies he'll tell? I'm sure Hunter Garcia will be getting a phone call later.

Evan guides me to a tan sofa that faces the bright, ethereal mural painted on the wall. With my back to the lobby, I can't see what's going on. I take comfort in the fake clouded sky with sunny silhouettes of glorious angels. The details are fuzzy, letting me imagine the angels how I think they should be. I imagine Dylan among them, shining the brightest like the sun. Small flecks of gold leaf accents glitter from the wall. It's an amazing sight that shouldn't be kept secret, but it will never make it into the human world. The Hunter's Alliance can be quite stingy.

"I'm going to announce your arrival," Evan whispers in my ear. I nod my head but continue to stare at the mural.

I'm left alone with disgruntled Sam for what seems like eternity. He whistles what sounds like a death march under his breath, and I'm becoming extremely nervous. No wonder they have this guy in the academy. I don't think he could function in the human world without being arrested himself—or attacked and killed by a lower level demon.

"I don't know why good looks are wasted on the evil," Sam mumbles. I catch him gawking down my dress and tug it as high as I can manage without revealing my thighs. I burn him a dirty look before turning my eyes back to the mural.

My heart lifts when I hear familiar voices behind me. "I'm checking in as Cami Anders's representative," David says. I resist the urge to turn around and beg for him to save me.

If David is here, Alana isn't far behind him. She would never abandon me—ever. The smell of apple orchards and rain storms hits me before I hear his voice. Dylan has a quiet conversation with David and Alana, but it's too low for me to catch anything.

Warm hands rest on my shoulders, and I glance up to see Evan's liquid blue eyes staring down at me. He kisses my forehead, lingering for a moment. His scent is rawer than Dylan's, warmer, sexier.

"Please, uncuff her," Evan says to Sam. "I'll be taking over from here. Her representative has requested her presence before the hearing."

Sam grumbles to himself as I stand up and turn around so he can remove the handcuffs. I cringe as his plump fingers squeeze my wrists before he yanks the cuffs from me.

"Thanks," I whisper as Evan leads me down a narrow hallway to an unmarked door. He knocks twice before pushing it open, revealing a small room with a square, wooden table and bench seats.

David sits at the table with his hands folded on the tabletop. He stands up to greet me, giving me a big bear hug before motioning me to sit across from him. Evan remains at the door, guaranteeing no one will barge in without notice.

"Oh, God, David. I'm so sorry to have put you through this." Tears threaten to spill from my eyes. "I don't know how to thank you."

"You're a part of my family now. I'd never leave you hanging," David says, grabbing my hand. "As you already know, I'm not one to sugarcoat things. What you've done is unacceptable in the alliance's eyes, and you will be punished. What you tell them will determine your punishment, so I need you to do your best to act concerned, remorseful, and constantly apologize. Waterworks are not beneficial, so try your best to hold yourself together. Lastly, tell it like it is. Throw that bastard under the bus, even if whatever you say is embarrassing."

David rubs his beard and smiles. "I'm not going to let them lock you up again. I promise," he adds.

"I know. I promise to never get into this situation again, either," I say.

David doesn't pressure me to tell him the truth about what happened and why I was in the research center to begin with.

He only cares about me getting the minimum punishment possible. I love his faith in me and how he treats me like an adult. He's very rational and helps me find my own way out of crummy situations. He truly believes I can protect myself and gives me credit, even if I feel it's sometimes undeserved.

"Do you have any questions?" David asks.

I mull the event over and over again in my mind. I wish Cadence were here so I could ask her what to do. The last thing I want is to get her involved in my problems, though. All she asked me to do was distract Ben, not knock him out. If our lives were switched, I know she wouldn't bring me into this mess either.

"Will Ben be present? Do you know where he stands on demi-demons?" I finally ask. I'm screwed if he is anything like Sam.

"No. He's already given his statement. As for your other question, I believe he's neutral. He's dated a couple of creatures before," David says. Relief floods through me. I still have a fighting chance as being seen as innocent.

A quick knock on the door prevents me from saying any more. Evan quietly opens it, nods, then quickly shuts it with a thud. "They're ready for you, Cami," he says.

I bite my lip. I don't think I'll ever be ready for this. Not in this lifetime or the next. I grip the table and push to my feet. David follows suit, coming to my side before draping a heavy arm across my shoulders in a hug.

Evan allows us to exit first and follows behind as David

guides me down an elaborate hall I've never been down before. Ornate gold fixtures hang from the ceiling showering us in a glittering waterfall of light. The sunny yellow walls make the walk less miserable. We stop in front of a wide set of double doors where a hunter poses fiercely in her all-black uniform. She pulls both doors open, revealing a dark auditorium with a line of floor lights leading to the spotlight-lit stage.

A small crowd takes up the first three rows, and I recognize my teachers among other hunters. Alana and Cadence sit front and center, and my heart jumps with excitement when I see a familiar brunette woman in perfect makeup next to them.

I haven't seen Jacie Hallowitz since the day before the church burned down. I want to run and hug her, but with the given circumstances, I doubt I could even get away with a wave without breaking my remorseful appearance.

Dylan sits in the third row next to his friend Katie, my first visitor in jail. She taps his shoulder and our eyes meet for a brief second before I glance back to the stage. For being a formal sentence, I expected to see all ten alliance leaders present, but again, I'm face-to-face with Cadence's father Aston, Clark, and Raya.

Evan breaks off down the first row of seating and finds a place next to Jacie. David climbs the stage steps before me and motions for me to sit in the metal chair directly in front of the leaders before taking a seat off to the side.

I take a deep breath, calming the butterflies beating their razor sharp wings in my stomach. I lift my chin high, refusing to look at the crowd here to witness the announcement of my punishment. *It'll be okay. It'll be okay.* I chant the words over and over again in my head, begging them to be true.

Aston clears his throat, settling the murmuring crowd. He stands up, rubbing his clean shaven face. "Camilla Anders, you have been found guilty of injuring a human with your demonic abilities. Do you know what that means?"

I lick my lips. My mouth is drier than a desert, sticking my words in my throat. I swallow hard, nodding. "Yes, Leader Dubois. It means I'm in more trouble than a demon getting trapped in the sunrise with Alana knowing its location."

PUNISHMENT

"THIS IS A serious offense!" Clark's voice booms through the auditorium, and the crowd falls silent from their sudden laughter.

I sigh. I was trying to be truthful, not funny, but it does make me feel better that people are still able to joke about it—the creatures can at least.

"I'm sorry, Leader Stephens, it won't happen again. I understand my actions were a very serious offense, and I'm here to face the consequences," I say, my voice barely louder than a whisper.

"Under normal circumstances, the presence of all alliance

members is required for sentencing, but months would've gone by, and we didn't feel it necessary since this was your first offense," Raya says. "We've brought together your soon-to-be fellow hunters to guarantee a fair hearing as well. The only thing we require of you is to answer a couple of questions before the proper punishment is determined."

My stomach drops. I could've been left to rot in that small cell for months. A simple warning would be suitable enough. I've really learned my lesson, but apparently there will always be more to learn.

I nod my head, folding my hands in my lap. Aston opens a file in front of him and flips through a couple of pages. "Is that my file?" I ask. "Can I see it?"

The audience gasps. If I don't stop saying the first thing that pops into my mind, they're going to kick me out of here before we've even begun. But seeing my file just out of my reach is too irresistible to let go. I'm more curious to see what the alliance has said about me than Malicevile. I believe I have a right to know what it says. It is *my* file anyways.

"You can request that a copy be sent to your apartment later," Aston answers. "Please, hold the rest of your questions until the end."

"Yes, sir," I say. "My apologies."

"Good. Now that everything is clear, let's get started so we can get out of here and on with our lives," Raya says.

Wanting to rush things can't be good. It almost guarantees that my punishment has been predetermined. They're only allowing me to speak to ease the minds of the creatures and not necessarily to give me a fair chance. I hope that my age, naivety, and new student status will benefit me. I can't even imagine what kind of punishment they have in store. I hope they don't believe in torture or other inhumane methods. Just because I'm technically not a purebred human, doesn't mean that I deserve to be treated harshly.

"Since we've heard Hunter Carter's story, our questions are going to be based on what he told us. First, Ms. Anders, what were you doing in the research center?" Clark asks.

I concentrate on the rhythmic sound of my heartbeat, calming my frail nerves. "I wanted to waste time before Hunter Whiteshaw was released from the infirmary. I decided to stop by and see what kind of jobs could be a possibility in my future. You see, I don't see myself being in the field. I believe I'd be better at something...safer."

"Are you aware that one year of field work is mandatory from all graduates, Ms. Anders?" Clark asks.

"Yes, sir. I just figured I'd get ahead of myself. I've killed three lower level demons and helped Hunter Whiteshaw kill a soul sucker, so I've never had any questions about field work. No one has ever taught me anything else. I thought I'd teach myself." The lies come so easily it scares me. I've never even rehearsed what I was going to say, and the words come out perfectly, convincingly. Cadence is probably laughing to herself.

"On this self-teaching expedition of yours, what led to your conversation with Hunter Carter?" Raya asks, taking over for

Clark.

"Well, I thought he was cute," I blurt. *Oh, crap! Why did I say that? Evan is sitting only feet away. Ben Carter is so-o-o not my type.* My cheeks heat in embarrassment as the crowd chuckles in unison. "I never expected it to end badly."

"Why did it end badly?" Raya asks.

"He was bragging about how demons weren't scary, and I argued that they were. Then, Alana was brought up, and he pretty much called her a bad hunter. I said something that hurt his ego, and he went off on me. He tried to slap me, so I punched him. Then he went wild, and I couldn't protect myself. I didn't mean to electrocute him. I was only trying to get away. I'm so sorry. It was wrong, and I accept the consequences for my actions." The reason why I was at the research center might be a lie, but the rest is the truth. I just hope they believe me.

"To ease your mind, Hunter Carter admitted to handling the situation inappropriately. He has offered a formal apology to you and your guardian Hunter O'Neil. But unfortunately, rules are meant to keep the peace in the community and using demonic abilities is not something taken lightly," Raya says.

"You're sentenced to seven days of local demonic combat cleanup effective tomorrow at four o'clock in the morning. Please report to the front gate five minutes prior for instructions."

My mouth drops open. That's not exactly the punishment I was expecting. I'm not sure whether I should be relieved, scared, or grossed out. Seven days isn't long at all—it could've been worse. The fact that I'll be forced to leave campus is unsettling with Malicevile prowling around, and I'm almost certain the alliance is aware of that. They could be secretly setting up for my death. It would be so easy to call it an accident.

By the loud murmur of the crowd, I'm not the only one concerned. Alana stands up, crosses her arms and shouts, "You've got to be kidding me! You're putting my charge in danger!"

"And the academy!" Hunter Garcia adds from the last row. "If she steps one foot off campus, demons will flock from everywhere to try and nab her to up their rank. We don't have enough active hunters to fight them off. You're signing our death sentence!"

I stand up, gripping the arm of the chair for support. If I don't step in soon, the hunters will start a riot, and I'm sure the alliance will find some way to blame that on me, too. I turn, facing the crowd. The mass of hunters, so engrossed in their own arguments, don't notice I've moved.

I levitate three feet from the stage, and yell, "Enough! I've heard enough. Just stop. I have something to say."

All eyes look up at me. Now that I have everyone's attention, I'm not sure what I'm going to say. I lower back to the stage, placing my hands on my hips.

"A wise hunter once said I was a plenty capable demi-demon." I turn, briefly smiling at David. "He turned out to be right. The alliance would never make a decision that would hinder and hurt what they've put so much time into creating. It's okay to question their reasons, but you have to trust them. And trust me. I would never agree to do anything that would risk the lives of my family—and you, all of you, are my family. So, alliance leaders, I fully accept the terms of your punishment."

The auditorium falls silent. I guess my speech wasn't convincing enough to earn the crowd's applause. I shuffle my feet, returning to my chair. Clark looks pleased, Aston seems thoughtful, and Raya appears to be bored out of her mind and ready to leave. It doesn't really matter that the crowd isn't happy, but at least I think I've won the alliance over. They will no longer consider me a threat to their precious society.

"That's a wise decision you've made, Ms. Anders," Aston says, smirking. "You are free to go."

David guides me to the back of the stage and away from the crowd. He pushes through a black door with a glowing exit sign above it, and I blink, stepping into the blinding sunlight.

"Let's get you home. I'm sure you want to get cleaned up before we celebrate your success," he says, pulling me along the cement path.

I raise my brows. "You have a funny idea of success."

"You didn't get sent back to jail, did you?"

"I guess. Some of the hunters seemed to think jail would've been the better option."

"Those hunters will never be as brave as you, either."

The hot shower was utter bliss. I've scrubbed away the last remnants of the cement cell and managed to put my stress aside for the night. Laughter echoes through the apartment, and I'm glad to hear the atmosphere lighten up a bit.

I pad into the hallway with wet hair and socked feet, not really dressed for a celebration, but I'm comfortable. I breathe deeply, overwhelming my nostrils with the mixtures of scents wafting through the air. It smells like the fragrance section of a department store, a mixture of warm spices, floral bouquets, and the ever-present zest of lemons.

I step into the living room and smile. Everyone I care about is waiting for me, and my heart flutters with excitement and love. Evan greets me with a kiss before handing me over to Jacie for a long, suffocating hug. I've only met this stunning hunter once, but she left a great impression on me, and I'm happy she's here. One by one, I give out hugs like I've been in prison for ages, relishing my freedom to enjoy the company of my friends—my family.

"You were amazing today," Evan says, wrapping his arm around my waist. He kisses my forehead lovingly, and we take a seat together on the empty loveseat.

"I really had a hard time keeping a straight face when you were preaching about the alliance," Jacie says, plopping between us. "You were a total suck up. For a moment, I thought you were human."

My cheeks redden. "I *am* human—sort of. And it got me out of there pretty quickly, didn't it?"

Jacie rolls her eyes. "I suppose."

"Can we just forget any of that happened?" Alana asks, bringing in a plate of sandwiches. "Cami has a lot to worry about in the next seven days. She doesn't need any more stress on her plate."

"Ew. Me too," Cadence says. "My dad pulled some strings and got me a position on the same shift as Cami. Friends don't let friends do body cleanup alone."

"Body cleanup?" My stomach rolls with nausea. I was assigned for demonic battle cleanup, not body cleanup. "Demons dissipate come sunrise."

"Yeah, I know. Humans don't," Cadence says. She scrunches her nose in disgust. "Remember when Drake killed the woman who sold her soul to Malicevile? Imagine that, but a million times more revolting. But hey, there might not even be anything to clean up this week." She's referring to the woman who tried to kidnap me for Malicevile back in Desertville.

I pull up my legs, wrapping my arms around them. My stomach's woozy, and I take deep breaths to calm down. My eyes lock with Dylan's across the room, and he frowns. Being a hunter in training would be easier if the job wasn't so vile and messy.

"If it makes you feel any better," David yells from the kitchen. "You get used to it. When you're my age, you'll have a stomach of steel." *Thanks, David. You always know the right thing to say to cheer me up.*

I don't think I want to get used to seeing dead bodies or

blood and gore for that matter. I need to be sympathetic to react to the horrors demons cause. If I don't, I'll lose the part of me I cherish most—my humanity.

I grip my legs, stopping the trembling in my hands. Dylan gets up and moves to stand in front of me. He sits on the arm of the couch and gently rubs circles on my back. The room goes silent, and I concentrate on Dylan's soothing touch.

Jacie pushes to her feet, allowing Evan to scoot closer. He tilts my chin to look at me. I stare into his clear, sea blue eyes. His piercing stare helps ease the pain in my chest, and Dylan's angelic touch heals it altogether.

"Oh, jeez. I'm going to be doing all the cleaning up, aren't I?" Cadence asks.

I can't help but laugh. She would do something like that for me. "That's why you're my best friend. You're willing to take one for the team."

Cadence smiles. "You would do the same for me."

I know she's referring to the secret we share. I was the one publicly punished, but Cadence has taken on the same punishment. I'm really grateful to have her as a friend.

I fake a yawn, remembering the reason we went to the research center in the first place. I glance toward the hallway, and Cadence catches my drift.

"If you all don't mind, I'm going to head to bed," I say, pushing from the couch. "I'll see you tomorrow, Jacie. Thanks for your support."

I give Evan a kiss on the cheek. "My room," I whisper. I

stand up and hug the others before heading back to my room to wait for Cadence and Evan. I'm finally going to learn more about Malicevile. I just hope I'm ready for the answers.

A DIFFERENT TIME

I OPEN THE curtains and slide my window open for Cadence. I want to tell Alana about the file, but I want to see what's in it first. She may have already read it a thousand times and just refuses to enlighten me.

It takes all of five minutes for Evan to make his way into my room. He shuts the door behind him, locking it. It's not that Alana would ever barge in, but if she did, I'd rather her think I'm doing something I shouldn't be with Evan instead of her catching us with a stolen file.

"Couldn't wait to get some alone time with me?" Evan muses, climbing behind me on the bed.

"Couldn't even wait five minutes before trying to seduce Cami," Cadence says, poking her head in the window. "Typical boy. Oh, and Angel Boy followed me. Sorry, I couldn't get rid of him in the two seconds it took me to walk around. I can knock him out if you want."

"No, it's fine. Both of you get in here before someone sees you," I say, waving my arms.

Cadence steps through with Dylan on her heels. She jumps onto the bed, and by instinct, I levitate while Evan bounces into the wall. Dylan pulls the chair away from my desk and situates it next to my bed.

"It would've been easier to just follow you to your room," Dylan says.

"You would've never been allowed," Cadence says. "You were lucky to have been permitted to join us in the first place. I don't know what you've done to Alana, but boy, I can see the muscles in her neck twitch whenever you're mentioned."

I cover my smile with my hand. I don't know why Dylan's complaining. He's come in through my window more than he's used the door. I won't be the first to mention that, though. I've hurt his ego enough to last him a lifetime.

"It's complicated," I mutter. "Alana doesn't like when nephilim flash their wings at innocent *human* girls. I'm sure glad you did though. Where would I be if you didn't decide to change my fate?" I pat Dylan's knee and smile.

"Me too," Cadence says. "No other way would you have landed in Desertville after dark."

After a moment of silence, Cadence unzips her leather jacket and pulls a poorly treated file from under her arm. She sets it in my lap, but I don't move to open it. It could contain life-altering information, and I'm content with how everything is now.

I take a deep breath and flip the folder open to the first page. I'm surprised when a photograph of Malicevile stares at me with his intense green eyes. He's dressed like a businessman in a white suit with a dark shirt and tie. His dark hair is gelled back, and he looks exactly how I remember him—an ageless man who could be in his late twenties.

Malicevile's basic information is typed under his picture, and none of it shocks me. He doesn't have a date of birth, but an estimated time of discovery which is believed to be sometime around the turn of the twentieth century.

I flip through the first couple of pages, briefly glancing at the written documentation of his earlier demon attacks. It's nothing new that my father is evil or a demon. If the file doesn't say anything else about Malicevile, then I have to believe that the alliance isn't as thorough as I previously was led to believe.

I sigh. "There isn't much in here that I already don't know." I turn a couple of pages and pause. A small photograph of a girl, a few years younger than me, with bright green eyes and curly brown hair is stapled to the front of an envelope that has been precariously shoved into the file.

Dylan's hand flies out and snatches the folder away from me, tucking it under his arm. "You should stop, love. This doesn't concern you."

"Give it back. This has everything to do with me!" I reach to grab the file back, but he stands, moving out of my reach.

Tears threaten to fall from my eyes. I can't believe Dylan is being such a jerk. He has no right to stop me from learning more about my father. He doesn't even have the right to be here. He can protect me all he wants from the world, but he can't protect me from this. Not now. Not ever.

Dylan shakes his head and turns toward the window. I don't give him the chance to make it halfway across my room. I fly off of my bed and collide into his back. We fall on the floor, and I twist on top of him, forcing his hands above his head, causing him to drop the file. Papers scatter everywhere, and Evan is on his feet in a matter of seconds collecting them and putting them back together.

Cadence watches silently from the bed, unmoving. I breathe heavily, staring into Dylan's chocolate-brown eyes. He doesn't attempt to move. He just stares back with concern lining his brows. My heart breaks because it has come to this. The obsession with my demon half is becoming all-consuming, making me turn on those I care about.

"You know what's in that file," I say.

Dylan nods. I resist the urge to scream at him, to slap him. I'm so angry; the fringes of my vision darken, turning blood red. He's known all along and hasn't said a word about it. The lingering doubt over my decision of choosing Evan melts away completely. Evan would never hide anything this huge from me, even to save me pain and regret. He understands me better than Dylan ever will. Dylan may care about my soul, but he doesn't care about me. I know that now and feel stupid for believing otherwise.

"Cami..." Evan puts his hands on my shoulders. He can tell that I'm losing control.

I release Dylan's hands, grabbing onto the sun stone dangling from my neck instead. Its warmth is comforting, and the room becomes clear again. The shadows vanish, and I become more of myself.

"Who is she?" I ask, my voice no more than a whisper. She looks like a younger version of me, but I know she's not me.

Dylan reaches for my hands, taking them into his. "I never wanted you to find out like this." He grips my hands tighter. "You have to realize this is a different time with different people. You're much stronger and braver. You have people who care about you—who would die for you. You are part demon but your humanity is your dominate part. You live and breathe for the goodness in the world. No matter how hard the demonic part of you thrives, you are still you. You have to realize that nothing, and I mean nothing, will ever change that."

His words terrify me. My core trembles with fear and confusion. I don't understand what he's getting at, or what any of this means. I hate that I can't read between the lines and just know what his cryptic words mean.

"Who is she?" I repeat. I'm tired of him avoiding the topic. Dylan insists on being complicated when it could be so simple.

"She is, well, she was Malicevile's daughter." Dylan frowns like the words leave a bitter taste in his mouth.

And then it sinks in.

Malicevile had another daughter.

I have—I had a sister.

But, what happened to her?

I stumble, falling over Dylan's legs to get off him. My cheek hits the carpet. For the first time in a month, I know what it feels like to hit the ground again. I can't seem to remember how to levitate, how to breathe even. My lungs burn as I gasp breath after breath without sucking in any oxygen. The air is heavy against my clammy skin. I'm stuck in what feels like a vast, deep ocean. I know it's only my imagination, but I'm so scared. I see Evan's arms around me, and Cadence holding my hands. Dylan's glorious wings expand out to wrap around me, but I only see them. I feel nothing. Absolutely nothing.

"Cami? Cami? Can you hear me?" I watch Evan's delicious lips move, understanding what he's saying, but he sounds so far away, like there is another world between us.

"Step back!" Dylan's voice breaks through the barrier, loud and clear. It's like a sweet melody to my ears. "I need to stop it. Her soul is fissuring. I need to heal her before it shatters."

Brilliant, ethereal light explodes from where Dylan was standing. I squint, covering my eyes from the blinding light shining from him. His wings appear as silhouettes against the magnificent light, swooping and encasing me in pure, raw strength, love, and warmth.

The burning pain in my lungs and heart subsides, and I'm able to take a shallow breath. My erratic heartbeat finds its rhythm and beats smoothly.

Dylan scoops me into his arms, and it's like I've emerged from icy water. My head settles on my feather pillow, the light fluffiness hugs against me almost like Dylan's wings.

I roll my tongue in my mouth, searching for the words that have become lost to me. "I need to see the picture again."

Cadence's hands shake as she flips the file open and scours it for the photograph of my dead sister. She pulls it from the envelope and sets it in my hands. I study it, devouring every detail. I can see the similarities between us. Her almond-shaped green eyes mirror my own, and her bottom lip puckers out like mine, though her nose must resemble her mother's because it's not like our demonic father's. Her ears slightly point like mine, an almost elf-like quality I hide under my hair. The more I stare at the photograph, the more of me I see. It's undeniable that she's my sister, and we share the same father.

"Her name was Melanie Wright," Dylan says, rubbing his fingertip across the edge of the picture. "She was a very power-ful demi-demon, not unlike you."

Melanie. My sister was named Melanie. *I wish we could have met. You could've taught me so much,* I think to myself. *Is that why Malicevile tricked my mother? Did he want to replace you? Is it why he wants to protect me now? What were you like? Am I like you?*

"She's beautiful," I whisper. I rub my finger over my face,

imagining what it would be like if she were still alive. We could spend all night talking. We could share our deepest secrets. We could even complain about the difficulty involved in having Malicevile haunting us.

My chest aches with the loss of discovering I have a sister but will never have the chance to meet her. It isn't fair that she was taken away from me the moment I found out about her. It hurts. I never thought I could miss someone I never knew so much. It could be the idea of knowing I have a sister who I'll never get to share my life with that I regret the most.

"She looks like you," Evan says softly. "It's hard to get over the resemblance."

I wipe the oncoming tears from my eyes before they have a chance to stain my cheeks. A billion questions float in my head, and I don't even know where to begin. Was she a hunter? Was she good or evil? Did she know about Malicevile? Did she attend this same academy?

I try to ignore the most obvious question, but if I don't ask it, it'll continue to nag at me. "How did she die?" I ask, holding my breath.

Dylan doesn't respond. He stares at his hands like he is trying to come up with a believable lie. I shut my eyes as my heart sinks into my stomach. It could only mean one thing. Malicevile killed her. He murdered her like he murdered my parents and probably millions of other people. He probably wanted her to join him, and when she refused, he killed her. *Like he's going to kill me when he realizes I'll never join him—that*

I'll always choose the alliance over him.

"You don't have to answer. I know it was Malicevile," I say. "Who else would kill her?"

Dylan glances at the floor instead of agreeing.

"You mean he didn't?" I ask. I couldn't imagine her simply passing away from natural causes. Demi-demons rarely get sick. "Did she die in battle against another demon?"

"No," Dylan answers.

My stomach flips in anxiety. "Just tell me. I need to know. Who killed my sister if it wasn't Malicevile or another demon?"

Dylan sits on the edge of the bed, bringing his eyes back to mine. "The alliance."

And for once, I know he's telling the truth.

ABOVE GOOD AND EVIL

"GET OUT!" I yell. "Get him out! I don't want him here."

I refuse to look at Dylan. If I do, I might do something I'll later regret. I thought he was my friend. Friends don't keep secrets like this. The alliance is responsible for my sister's death. They could be responsible for mine. A person should know that kind of thing, right? It's a slap in the face. I don't even know who I can trust anymore.

"Cami, please listen," Dylan pleads.

"No. Get out!"

I turn on my side and curl into the fetal position. I want to be alone. I have a lot to think about, and I don't need anyone else's opinions or thoughts influencing me. Malicevile was right to be concerned about my wellbeing. It hurts knowing the truth.

I listen to Dylan shuffle to the window and hesitate. Even though I can't see him, I can feel the sadness pouring off him. I don't know what upsets him most—the fact that I'm angry at him or that he regrets not telling me the truth sooner. Either way, it's not my problem. I have more dire things to worry about, like whether or not I'll survive to graduation.

A cool hand touches my arm, and I glimpse the sparkle of Cadence's purple nail polish. "I'm going to walk home with him," she says. "Don't forget to pick me up on the way to cleanup duty."

I nod my head. I peek through my lashes, watching as Evan closes the window behind them. He meanders to the bed and slumps onto the mattress. I curl up against him, listening to his strong heartbeat.

I expect Alana to knock on the door at any moment. She's deaf if she didn't hear the commotion going on in here. She might choose to ignore it though, since I'm sure she's aware Evan is in here with me.

"This sucks." I fidget, playing with the buttons on Evan's shirt. "I'm so confused. I don't know what to do anymore."

"You have to keep going forward. The past is done and over with. You can't change that. All you can do is learn from it." Evan sounds like Alana. I bet he got his insight from her.

"It's hard. I'm tired of the secrets. Why is it so difficult for people to be honest? I thought demons were the ones who lied. I never thought my father would be the one who was telling the truth this entire time. It's scary."

"Don't let him fool you. He may be right about this, but he's still a demon. They only tell the truth if it benefits them. He wants nothing more than for you to start fearing the ones you've relied on. It guarantees to leave you with no other option than to go to him."

"I'd rather be murdered by the alliance than go to him." Melanie probably said the same thing and look how she ended up. Could I really give up so easily? Would I choose death over life if it meant my soul would remain safe? At this moment, I don't know. I don't want to know. I never want to be in that situation. It would be giving in to the lesser of two evils.

"You're not like her. I'd never let you be put in that situation." It's like Evan can read my mind. He always knows exactly what to say to make me feel better.

I lift my chin and kiss him. His lips are warm and inviting, and I can't resist. He pulls me closer, kissing me harder. His hands trail up my back, tangling in my hair. We breathe in unison, our heartbeats mingling, pounding, creating a rhythmic symphony.

"I love you," he whispers. "No matter what."

"Even if I turn evil?"

"Yes, even then, because I know you would overcome it. You're above good and evil—you're real. Unlike anyone around here, you understand the gray areas. You know that it could never be one or the other. You know how to balance it."

"And you know exactly what to say to make me feel better." I kiss him again.

I brush my hand through his hair and look into his crystalline blue eyes. "Do you mind if I look through the file some more. It'll be easier with just you and me." Whatever else the file contains, it can't be any more heart wrenching than what I've already discovered.

"Are you sure about that? I mean—are you sure you want to know more?"

"Positive. I've never been more sure about anything."

Evan sighs, reaching for Malicevile's file sitting on my night table. He sets it in my lap, and I carefully pull the envelope sticking out from the center, which had Melanie's photo attached to it. The seal's never been broken and my curiosity gets the best of me. I shove my finger under the corner and pull it through, opening it. I tug the folded letter from it and run my finger across the old, fragile paper.

I unfold it and study the tight, curly script. It's not my father's handwriting—I'd remember his penmanship. It's addressed to no one, but signed Melanie. I could gaze at her name forever, like I could finally get to know her.

Evan takes my hand, and I begin to read silently to myself.

Terrible, terrible things have been happening lately. The tension around the academy is thick enough to slice with my dagger. I keep telling myself it'll get better after graduation, and that I won't have to work so hard to keep communication with my father secret. Call me crazy for caring about a demon so much. But, what can I say? The man raised me until I was eight when the alliance intervened and kidnapped me like they do with many half-humans.

Even after nine years, they still believe I'm going to turn evil and kill them all. Not many believe that I'm not out for blood. They have this misconception about demi-demons, believing that our souls can be influenced by our demonic parent, which is ridiculous. It doesn't work like that. Being half-human allows me to choose which side I want to fight for, and I've chosen the alliance. Though, for them, it'll never be enough. I could kill my kin, and still it will never be enough—not until my father is dead.

If I didn't know the alliance, I'd think they were insane for wanting a daughter to murder her father, but I understand. Dad could use a good dose of goodness, and I've argued many times with him over his mistreatment of werewolves and humans, but he's never hurt me or tried to persuade me to be like him. He says that he'll let me make my own decision, and if I want to be a hunter, I can, because that means less competition for him. I just think he's grown soft from being on earth for so long. I believe humanity is rubbing off on him like it does angels, but I'd never tell him that to his face or he'd go and try to prove it isn't. If only the alliance saw what I see in him. They'd realize that the lines between good and evil are blurred. What is good to one person may not be good to another. Whose right is it to decide, anyways?

The growing fear of my father within the alliance led me to visit the storyteller today. It was my first time ever meeting her, but it felt like I've known her for years. It was like she knew me, too.

She was sweet and full of life, not exactly what I was expecting from a woman who knows too much. I also met her son. He was handsome, charming, and a great hunter—a total shoo-in for alliance leader in a couple of years. He has great ideas and plans for the future. Could you imagine creatures of the Veiled Realm becoming eligible for an alliance leader position? A change in motto? That good comes first? Fair trials, better protection for werewolves, witches coming out of hiding, blood drinkers not being ashamed of who they are, the reconstruction of the entire alliance? Aston gives me the hope that his mother, Vivian, couldn't. The only thing she could promise me was that my soul would be safe. That I wouldn't fall into the darkness.

I don't understand why her prediction scares me to death. I should be happy that I won't lose my soul. But that wasn't the only thing she told me. She told me to run, to leave everyone I know and care about behind. She told me it was the only way to survive. She saw death coming for me. Not a peaceful death or a worthy death caused in battle, but an unjustified death surrounded by fear, hate, and jealousy...not exactly the way I planned to go. I'm a hunter, a predator—it's in my blood to fight, not to run and hide like a scared little animal. I refuse to believe that the only way to survive is to run. I can't. I. Just. Can't.

I've decided to write this down and keep it in my pocket so the world could know that I was brave, that I'm my own person. I'm choosing to stay because I can't let my fear of death prevent me from doing what I think is right. I'm a hunter first, a human second, and a demon last. I may care for my father, but I'm not him—I'm me. I'll always be Melanie Wright, the demon hunter with a de-

mon father, and no one—not the alliance, not the demons—could ever change that.

I'm squeezing the letter so hard that it crinkles under my fingers. It's difficult to believe that my sister cared so much about Malicevile that it eventually killed her. Her death must've changed him. I don't see that caring person she spoke about. He's manipulative, mean, and has never given me the choice to decide which side of the game I'll be on. Her trust in him could've been the reason for her death.

I scour the file in search of more about Melanie. I'm hoping to find out what happened after the letter. Did she change her mind about working for the alliance? Was that the reason they killed her? I have to find out more.

"We should call Vivian tomorrow," Evan says. He pulls the letter from my hands and folds it neatly, stuffing it back into the envelope. "She could fill in the blanks."

I sigh. "She would've told me about Melanie if she wanted me to know."

"It doesn't hurt to try," Evan says. "She could be waiting for you to ask her. Maybe it wasn't time to tell you before. Would you have stayed here if you knew the alliance had killed your sister?"

"No, probably not."

"Making it easy for Malicevile to attack you again," Evan says. "Vivian isn't like the rest of the alliance. She believes in protecting everyone, not just humans. It was probably her way to protect you."

"Was it this hard for you when your mom was alive?" Evan never talks about his demonic mother, and I wonder if it's just my luck that I have a demon father interested in me.

"It was different. I never knew her as anything but a demon. She didn't have a relationship with my family. I happened to be born a demi-demon by chance. This is going to sound really weird, but my demonic mother was an egg donor trying to spread her seed throughout humanity in hopes of building her own little army. She was smart, but her plan didn't go quite as planned. The alliance put a stop to that quickly. Unfortunately, it wasn't soon enough for my human mom because she was pregnant with me at the time. The alliance kept an eye on my family, but they couldn't save them, just me. I've only ever seen my demonic mother once, the day I helped David cut out her evil-infested heart, and then we celebrated. Knowing that something so evil could have given life to me was the hardest thing to believe, but good in a way, because I killed her for it."

"That means there's hope after all," I say. Melanie couldn't hurt Malicevile, but that doesn't mean I can't. I don't have a problem with stabbing him in the heart. I'll do what I have to do to live a normal life. That's where we're different. Melanie saw herself as a hunter, then human, and lastly a demon. I don't consider myself a hunter or a demon. I'm a human tainted with demon blood. It is part of me, but it will never *be* me. All I have to do is convince everyone else of that.

"There's always been hope, Cami. I'm glad you finally see

that," Evan says, kissing my forehead. "Now, put that file down. I think you've read enough for one night. I wasn't kidding earlier about wanting to be alone with you."

BREAKING POINT

"YOU CAN'T BE mad at me forever," Dylan says.

Vibrant yellow roses blossom from deep green stems. They remind me of Dylan—beautiful until you get pricked by their thorns. The garden is as lovely as ever, but it doesn't make up for the secrets he's kept from me.

"Give me a reason I shouldn't be. I trusted you. I cared about you. I let you into my soul and look how you've repaid me. You've been lying to me this entire time. What were you afraid of? It's not like I have anywhere to go."

Dylan's shoulders slump. "I wanted to save you from the pain. You experienced too much of it already."

I clench my jaw for a moment. "The pain makes me stronger."

"You have a breaking point. People can only take so much before it eats away at them and weakens them."

"I know that!" I ball my hands. "I feel my breaking point every time I get mad. It's like I'm going to suddenly explode and destroy everything in my path. I don't like it, but I can deal. I didn't hurt you last night, did I? I wanted to, but I didn't."

"That's what bothers me. You shouldn't have to struggle to stay in control, love. The littlest thing could set you off. The good thing is that you realize it. Your sister didn't. She snapped and hurt a lot of people. The alliance didn't have a choice."

"You're lying again. The alliance could've chosen not to kill her, but for some reason murder is the easiest option when things get hard."

"You don't understand. It's not easy being Malicevile's daughter."

Dark clouds swirl above us, blocking the golden sun. The beautiful day ruined by my dark emotions. "Just stop it! I don't want to hear anymore. Leave me alone, Dylan. You're ruining my dream!"

<hr />

I startle awake. Evan sleeps next to me, and I rest my head on his chest, listening to his heartbeat. I close my eyes for a moment longer, savoring the few minutes I have before I need to get up.

The digital clock on my night table reads three forty-five. I scramble from the bed, tripping over the forgotten chair that was pulled away from my desk. I levitate moments before I hit the ground in a clatter, releasing a whoosh of breath because my ability has returned.

I stumble across my room and bang into my closet door. Yanking it open, I run my fingers over the hangers for a hoodie. I strip off my pajama bottoms and wriggle into a pair of jeans from my dresser and then pull my hoodie over my night tee before shoving my socked feet into my boots.

As I reach for the door handle, Evan jolts up. "What's wrong?" he asks, sleep muffling his words.

"Go back to sleep. I'm heading out for cleanup," I whisper.

Before I can argue, Evan throws on his T-shirt and ties his boots. He wraps his bandaged arm around my waist, guiding me to the front door. Alana drinks a large cup of coffee near the door, dangling a small backpack from her wrist.

"You may need this," Alana says, hugging me and Evan together. "Don't leave Cadence's side and watch each other's backs. It's still dark enough for demons to be prowling."

"Will do," I mumble, squeezing her tighter than necessary.

The campus is eerily quiet this early in the morning. It's too early for field hunters to be coming home or for other members of the community to be moving about. Small solar lights shine along the cement walkway, covering the greenery in a subtle glow. The stars sparkle like brilliant diamonds scattered across midnight blue chiffon fabric. The mysterious allure of the night enhances the beauty and charm of the redbrick buildings and sprawling lawns.

Cadence sits on the top step of her apartment building. She's casually dressed in a black tracksuit with black sneakers. Her purple hair is pulled into a high ponytail with her bangs swept across her forehead. Her neutral makeup enhances her honey eyes, and she looks beautiful as always.

Evan holds me from behind without saying a word.

"Someone woke up late." She swirls her finger at my thrown together outfit.

"Not everyone can wake up looking like sunshine, and I didn't think it was necessary to dress up to clean up guts," I mumble.

"It's always necessary." Cadence smiles, stands up, and throws a black backpack over her shoulder. "Let's get going. We're going to have to hurry. We have two minutes before we're officially late."

I kiss Evan goodbye before Cadence drags me away. We walk in silence to the main gate, where a square building sits next to the wall. A tall, muscular woman waves us over, and I stay close to Cadence's side.

"I was surprised to see your name added to my crew this morning, Hunter Dubois. You don't strike me as the cleanup type," the woman says. Her sandy blond hair is twisted into two neat braids on both sides of her head. Her hazel eyes shine in the orangey glow cast from the light above the door to the building. She's wearing an academy uniform with a couple of sheathed daggers dangling from her metal studded belt.

"No one knows my type, and this isn't my first cleanup. I needed a break from my new mundane life living on campus." Cadence shifts her bag off her shoulder and drops it next to her. "Also, since my soon-to-be partner got stuck with this gig, I figured I'd help her out."

The woman turns to me and smiles. "You must be Camilla Anders. I'm Natalia Alvarez, your guide. I've heard a lot of interesting things about you. Welcome to the most disgusting job you can get in the alliance."

"Call me Cami," I say, offering my hand. "Only my father calls me Camilla."

I stand awkwardly, waiting for instructions. I feel like I should be doing something besides standing around. Cadence leans against the building, tapping her foot. I shove my hands into the front pockets of my hoodie, hiding their tremble. I haven't been away from the campus since I arrived, and I'm unsure what to expect. I'm worried that Malicevile will be waiting outside the gate. I'm worried I'll be cleaning up a bloody massacre. I'm worried about a lot of things, especially since Alana isn't the one leading the way, and I have to blindly trust that Natalia knows what she's doing.

A flash of headlights illuminates the metal gate, and it whines as it opens. A black truck drives through, stopping in front of us. Four hunters exit the vehicle, tossing the keys to Natalia without saying a word.

"Time to get this party started," Natalia says. "Help me lift those crates into the back, and we're set to go."

The crates weigh a ton, and I need extra strength from my ability to get them situated in the bed of the truck. If I didn't know any better, I'd think that they carried a dead body or two. My fingers take on a mind of their own, caressing the rough wood. I stick my index finger under the lid and ease it open. I gape in shock. The crate is empty with the exception of plastic lining.

"Why the heck is this thing so heavy if it's empty?" I ask.

"Beneath the wood is a fine metal mesh lining. Dead humans aren't the only thing we ever pick up. Some creatures require something sturdier than wood," Natalia says without elaborating.

I wonder if that means we get to pick up living creatures, and which ones need metal to keep them from escaping. I sigh, unable to come up with anything.

Cadence nudges me with her elbow. "The metal helps neutralize magic found in elves, fairies, pixies, genies, and the list goes on and on."

Keeping track of all the different Veiled Realm creatures makes my head dizzy just thinking about it. Life was much simpler a month ago when the only ones I knew about were demons. Sure, they are the most wicked, evil creatures out there, but I preferred knowing it couldn't get worse than that. But now...I don't know. The idea's terrifying—what exactly do those creatures do or eat, how do they live? Are they simply trying to survive in the human world? Do they fight against the bad guys? Or assist them? They sure aren't lining up to join the Hunter's Alliance—we're made up of a bunch of humans and half-humans, and who's going to admit if they fall outside of the human, demon, angel, or werewolf category? It'd probably be their death sentence because *Humans Come First*, and I suppose half-humans second, but creatures without human genes are seen as the bottom of the barrel. The truth is, there isn't a place for them, even Annabelle really, and it breaks my heart thinking about it.

"I'm not capturing some innocent creature so the alliance can execute it." I drop the lid, and it slams shut harder than I expected.

"And if it tries to kill you?" Cadence asks softly.

"Let it try. I honestly believe that creatures kill because they have to do it to survive, not because they're evil. Think about it, Cadence. What would you do if three knife wielding people cornered you? You would fight for your life and think about what you had done later." I lean closely to her ear. "The alliance's dogmatic ways and lack of understanding would drive anyone to kill."

"Okay, okay, I get it. If we come across some live creature, we'll make sure it gets away. But, and I'm serious about this, if it attacks, I'm attacking back. I'm not going to get myself killed like some antelope refusing to run from a lion in hopes of it not being hungry."

"I'd never let you get killed. You're not the only badass one around here," I say, giving Cadence a hug.

Cadence rolls her eyes, sighing. She bends down and grabs both our backpacks off the ground, handing mine to me. I unzip it, curious about what's inside. Alana has packed a pair of latex gloves, goggles, a nose plug, a bright yellow hand towel, a flask of holy water, and a plastic bottle of hand sanitizer. Wedged at the very bottom are a bottle of water and two chocolate donuts. *I better eat these on the ride over.*

"Anything good?" Cadence asks.

I shrug, handing her the bag. Cadence looks through it and pulls out the plastic bag with the donuts, untying it and handing one to me. We eat the donuts while watching Natalia throw a couple of duffle bags behind the seat.

"We'll leave in five. Go ahead and get in," Natalia says.

I slide across the bench seat, uncomfortable about being stuck in the middle, but Cadence doesn't give me a choice. She feels the same way I do, but since she's an official hunter and I'm not, she wins the window seat.

A rectangular printer is neatly tucked into the dashboard where a stereo should be. It's small and inconspicuous, with a slot the size of a compact disk to print from. Above it is a fold-down navigation system with computer capabilities. A newsfeed flashes across the bottom of a local map defining the city outside of the academy walls.

Natalia opens the door and gets behind the wheel. She presses a couple of buttons on her steering wheel and brightly colored stars blink on the map. I count five, two blue, one yellow, one green, and one red.

"They're color-coded by level of priority. As you've probably guessed, the red is first." Natalia turns the key in the ignition, and the truck roars to life. Diesel fumes pour through the cracked window, and I cover my nose.

"Please, tell me that red doesn't stand for raging, bloody death," I say. I'm not ready to start the morning like this. It should be started in baby steps, like cleaning debris off the street, not mopping up guts and gore. I'm becoming nauseated thinking about it, which isn't good for Cadence or Natalia since I'm sitting snuggly between them. Alana should've packed a paper bag in the backpack.

"We won't know until we get there. Just prepare yourself for anything and everything, and then imagine it being ten times more disturbing."

Natalia eases down on the throttle, and we surge forward, driving through the plush lawn to turn around. The wrought iron gate automatically opens, and we drive through without further delay.

I glance through the back window as the gate whines shut, leaving us on the wrong side of the protective barrier. Natalia slowly drives up the gravel path, and I nervously wring my hands as the trees thin out on both sides.

I breathe shallowly, calming the nerves pinching my back. I can make out the dim glow of streetlamps ahead directing us to the road. I tense when we reach it, expecting to see a demonic army, or at least my father, but it's empty. Maybe this job won't be so bad after all. *Yeah, right.*

DEMON BROKEN

THE DISGUSTING SMELL of burning flesh, blood, and moist dirt reaches me before we turn onto a crumbling street with old, rundown houses lacking any signs of life. It's dark and eerie. The streetlights either need bulbs replaced or they've been broken by someone or something afraid of a little extra light. Seeing that the entire street is shadowed in darkness, I guess it's the latter.

Natalia eases off the throttle, slowing the truck down to a crawl. I cover my nose with the sleeve of my hoodie. The closer we get to the bright red star on the map, the fouler the stench. I scan the street and sidewalks for any signs of life...or death. The neighborhood is overrun with weeds and trash, but there's no demon sludge, or what I fear the most, human bodies.

Natalia stops the truck in the middle of the road and then shuts off the engine. According to the map, we're parked exactly where we're supposed to be. The fumes overwhelm me, and I can smell the reek of death nearby. It smells vaguely familiar, and I'm terrified to see what comes with that stench.

I cough into my sleeve while yanking my backpack open. Digging around, I feel the rubber cord of the nose plug catch on the nail of my middle finger. I pull it out and immediately put it on. I grab the goggles next, adjusting the rubber band over my head until it sits snugly behind my ears.

Cadence slaps my hand as I reach for the latex gloves. "You haven't even seen anything yet, and you're acting like we're about to step into a house contaminated with the plague."

"By the way the air reeks from here, I'm sure it'll be pretty damn similar. I think I'm going to need a gas mask to get out of the truck."

"I thought you were demi-demon, not werewolf," Natalia says.

"The dog-men and I share a lovely ability, except I don't shift. I can levitate a couple of feet though, which can be handy. My boots will at least stay clean."

"That's lame. Who wants the power of scent?"

"Not me, that's for sure. I'm hoping to one day meet a demon whose power is the inability to smell, so I can borrow it. Deflection and absorption can be handy when they have something I want to borrow."

"I guess that makes up for the rest," Natalia says. "Now, if only you could see through the walls and tell me which house it is and what to expect."

My cheeks redden. I can't see through the walls, but like a tracking animal, I can sniff it out. It's embarrassing being able to detect something like a werewolf, and I really don't want to admit to it. I refuse to be used like hound dog for the rest of the week.

I open the nose plug and breathe deeply, trying hard to keep my stomach from heaving. I know exactly which house the stench is coming from. I stare intensely and notice a detail that Natalia and Cadence missed. All the doors on the surrounding houses are closed except for the one with the demonic aftermath inside.

I point at the foreboding yellow house. "It's the house with the open door."

"All right then, let's get moving. We're running out of night," Natalia says.

The stench of gore intensifies as we reach the broken path leading to the dilapidated house. The yellow stucco exterior cracks from years of not being cared for. A rusted metal awning covering the porch is bent out of shape and looks like it will collapse if it's bumped the wrong way. The door wasn't left open like I thought; it has been forced open. The frame is splintered and there's a foot-sized hole in the center.

Electricity sizzles from my fingertips. I'm terrified to discover what lies inside. I'm not afraid of being attacked by a demon because hunters have already been through the house. It's what they've left behind for me to clean up that has panic squeezing my heart.

Cadence's dagger shines in the light of Natalia's miniature flashlight. She squares her shoulders, preparing for anything. She taps the door with the toe of her boot, and it creaks all the way open.

I cough as a pungent cloud of stinking air whooshes around me. I'm going to suffocate if Natalia doesn't have a bottle of air freshener in her supply bag. By the frown on Natalia's face, she must be able to smell it, too, and she's not wearing a nose plug. She's probably used to stinky situations by now.

"Cami, I want you to do the walk through while Cadence and I grab the supplies," Natalia says.

My stomach lurches. "You've got to be joking. Why me?"

"Because..." Natalia pauses. I bet not many hunters question her authority, especially a student.

It's not that I want to cause problems or sound like a brat, but I need to know that she's not sending me first because to the alliance and many hunters, I'm expendable because of my demonic heritage.

She sighs. "Because you're the one with electricity sparking from your fingers," she says. "It doesn't require close contact like a dagger does."

I sigh in relief. Natalia recognizes the benefit of having a demi-demon on her side. I'm not exactly excited about having to enter alone, but at least I know Natalia trusts me enough to put her wellbeing in my hands.

"Okay, but if I throw up, one of you gets to clean it."

Cadence rolls her eyes. "Not it."

I strengthen the electricity in my fingers until it's bright enough to light the entryway. I step over the threshold and onto the dirty brown carpet. The house is empty of furniture, making it easier to look around.

The living room is off to the right of the front door, and I peek in to see it covered in dirt and leaves. I stick my head into the kitchen, the bathroom, and a small bedroom, still finding nothing out of the ordinary. I continue down the hallway, my heart racing, when I spot a long, dark stain running down the center of the hallway, glistening in the light of my power.

Something has been dragged behind the last closed door. Black burn marks discolor the walls, and it seems the battle started here. I levitate an inch off the ground, refusing to touch anything, even with my boots.

Gliding forward, I gather my bearings, steeling myself for what I'm about to discover. I gag as rancid air blows from under the door. I stop moving and hover inches away, glaring at the door like I have X-ray vision and can see the gory remains left over from the demonic showdown.

I reach out and gingerly touch the gold-painted door knob, feeling the cool metal through my gloved hand. It takes every ounce of my will to turn the knob. It groans as I push the door open.

My eyes widen. "Ugh! Oh, my God."

Perspiration dampens my forehead, and I brush the sticky bangs out of my eyes. I grab onto the doorframe, steadying myself, the shock of the scene shaking me to my soul. My knees weaken, threatening to buckle, and I concentrate on not passing out.

I avoid staring at the mounds of flesh on the carpet. Instead, I focus on the blood splattered walls. It reminds me of a horror film movie set with a mixture of handprints and paw prints painted in sticky crimson. Except this is real.

The bloody walls weren't designed and predetermined. They're the remnants of a fight to the death. Proof of the sick and twisted ways of both hunters and demons—with innocent humans trapped in the middle.

When I see a pile of discolored, melted flesh and bones resting near a shattered window, gorge rises in my throat. The room reeks of burnt sugar and rot, the scent of a deceased demon.

I swallow hard, glancing at the broken, dead figure slumped in the corner. A tangled mass of curly black hair covers the lifeless eyes of a demon-bound woman. Her jeans are dirty, the tough material shredded at her oddly bent knees. A pool of fresh blood seeps from a gaping wound across her neck. She died from a slash to the throat, the weapon that killed her, unknown to me.

It could've been the demon, yet it could've easily been done by a hunter's dagger. Either way, I'm saddened that this poor woman had to die. She's another nameless lost soul taken before finding her redemption, if she even wanted to find it.

I turn away from the woman to the last body crumpled on the floor. I step into the room for a closer look.

"What the—?" I whisper. The creature looks like a hairless werewolf stuck in the midst of transformation between human and animal. It has the skin of a human covering its grotesque doglike body. The naked werewolf's back is covered in black slime and its muzzle looks to have been dipped in blood. My skin crawls when I notice its open eyes gazing lifelessly at me. Disturbingly human, they're hypnotic green and oval-shaped, and I expect them to blink.

I hold my hands out to brighten the room a bit and notice something strange. Small tendrils of steam swirl from the werewolf's skin like a cool rainstorm on hot asphalt. The creature is obviously not an ordinary werewolf, and the memory of a night I spent battling demons in Desertville flashes through my mind. *It's a demon-broken werewolf, a hellhound.* I didn't recognize it right away because the wolf wasn't engulfed in the flames I'm used to seeing. And the eyes—they're not round, fiery coals. The werewolf hasn't been demon-broken very long, just long enough to get itself destroyed.

I've seen enough to say that any threat that was here is now gone. The hunters took care of everything just as I expected they would. We're here to cleanup, not to destroy demons.

"Cami?" Natalia calls from down the hall.

I step backward out of the room and glide weightlessly

through the hallway and back to the living room to see my companions hovering in the doorway.

"It's nasty, but nothing tried to kill me. I think we're good to get started," I say, waving them in.

I don't bother to help with the duffle bags slung over their shoulders because I was forced to face the disturbing scene alone. I'm more confident knowing that I survived without passing out or vomiting, so I might do all right after all.

I silently lead them to the last bedroom and freeze when I glance in. The blood and gore is still the same as it was just minutes ago, but something's different.

I thrust my arm out, blocking Cadence from going ahead of me. "No, no, no. Where is it? It was dead. I know it."

"What was?" Natalia asks, concern shaking her voice.

"The hellhound! It was there a sec—"

A scream rips from my throat as the naked Hellhound leaps toward the doorway, half engulfed in demonic flames. My legs refuse to move, and my eyes widen as it leaps toward us in its fiery glory, with me as the only thing blocking its path.

WOLFIE

THE BREATH WHOOSHES out of me as two hundred pounds of pure muscle slams into my chest, knocking me into the wall. Sharp pain bursts in my ribs, and I cry out. It happens so fast, I don't have the chance to shock the beast or slow down the course of our collision.

The hellhound growls with its glistening, flaming jowls inches from my face. I flinch, staring into its human eyes that seem to be shadowed in pure panic. The icy fingers of fear brush my heart, but I can't hurt a poor creature that might still have a chance at redemption.

I reach out with a trembling hand. Before my fingers have

the chance to pet its greasy, fiery coat, the hellhound scampers back and dashes between a shocked Cadence and Natalia.

I scramble to my feet, using the wall as leverage, and race after the flaming werewolf. The cold air of the unheated house whips at the bare skin of my chest peeking through the burned fabric.

Cadence yells out, but I don't stop. I need to find the hellhound before it's destroyed by another hunter or worse, another demon that can finish breaking it.

I rush into the dark street, easily spotting the zooming ball of fire on four legs. "Stop! I won't hurt you!" I scream.

My boots hit the ground hard as I push to run faster. I can't concentrate enough to levitate, and it's making it difficult to pursue the hellhound quietly. It disappears from sight as it skids around the side of the last house on the right, but its pungent, burning scent is thick in the air, leaving an easy trail to follow.

I slow down before reaching the end of the street. I don't want the Hellhound to resort to attacking me. Like most animals, if frightened enough and unable to run, it will fight for its life, even if I intend it no harm.

I sniff the air, peering around the dark street. My cheeks heat in embarrassment because I have to rely on the humiliating ability I really wish I hadn't acquired from Malicevile. I don't care if I can scent out demons and creatures—it's a stupid ability that is debilitating more often than it's helpful.

The dry grass crackles under my boots as I tiptoe across the abandoned lot. I spot the hellhound, bowed with its muzzle touching the dirt, panting heavily. Its skin is slick with black slime instead of fire. A gaping hole oozes crimson blood on its side under its ribcage, a wound that could be fatal if not properly cared for. The broken werewolf doesn't have a chance of surviving trapped in canine form. The quick escape has worn down its life force.

I cross my arms over my chest. "Please, stop running. Let me help you."

The hellhound growls a deep sound that vibrates in its throat, warning me. It opens its bloody mouth and lets out a guttural whine that almost sounds like "let me die."

I shiver. "Not happening."

I brave another step closer to the beast with enough electricity stored in the palms of my hands to knock it out but not kill it.

It growls again, and I pause. "Knock it off. We're running out of time. The sun will come up soon and trap you until tomorrow night."

I steel myself and close the distance between me and the hellhound. It doesn't look strong enough to put up a fight to incapacitate me. It doesn't look like it can do much at all, except threaten with meaningless growls.

I glance around for signs of Cadence and Natalia before I kneel on the hard-packed ground. It would look really bad if I was seen aiding a creature deemed evil, and they wouldn't understand. This hellhound hasn't submitted completely to the dead demon pulverized back at the house. Now that the demon is gone, there's a chance that the broken werewolf could be saved. My reasoning is farfetched, and I've never heard it discussed before, but it makes sense to me. For me to find out, the hellhound must be alive, and at this point, the likelihood is slim to none.

I lift up my sweatshirt, yanking my pajama top tight. With my free hand, I singe the material right below my bra and rip it away. *This should do.*

"I'm going to wrap your wound. If you even think about biting me, I'll zap you." I press my gloved fingers against the side of the hellhound's muzzle, firmly pushing it away from me. I drape the frayed fabric over its slimy back. Instead of leaning over its back, leaving my side exposed, I move around to its other side before cautiously reaching under and pulling the other end of the fabric through. I tie the loose ends to prevent shifting.

I pet the top of the Hellhounds head. "We've got to get moving before we're spotted."

I coax the injured beast to its feet. We need to get out of this clearing and to shelter before sunup. If I'm spotted by an unfamiliar hunter or creature, they'll automatically assume I'm pure demon and will attempt to take me out. I've had enough action for these last couple of months to last me a lifetime. Once this morning is over, I just want to lay low for a while.

I guide the hellhound along the rotting back fences of the shabby houses until I spot the metal roof of a shed. I tap along the fence until I discover a weak spot. Pressing my back against the fence, I use the heel of my boot to kick two of the boards free. The space is narrow, but I manage to squeeze through behind the broken wolf.

We enter a backyard overrun with weeds. I levitate just above them as the hellhound slinks through them in the direction of a tiny, weatherworn garden shed just big enough to hold a lawnmower and a couple of tools.

"You can hide here until dawn. I'll be back for you at dusk," I say. It sounds ridiculous having a conversation with a demonic animal, but I know a human is trapped somewhere under its slimy, flammable skin.

The beast releases a low growl, nudging its muzzle through the crack in the rusted metal doors of the shed. The doors squeak as I pull them open wide enough for the hellhound to enter. It maneuvers through the space and slinks into the far corner, taking refuge in the dark shadows. I quietly close the doors, relieved that the broken wolf will be safe long enough to heal.

"Bye, Wolfie," I whisper, glancing up at the purpling sky. The sun will rise in a couple of minutes, which means the majority of the human world will be waking up to start their days.

I glide through the backyard, taking a shortcut through the gate on the side of the shabby, brown stucco house. It leads to the street, where I see Natalia's truck with its engine still running a block away.

I creep down the sidewalk inconspicuously and lurk for a

moment on the front porch, thinking about how I'm going to explain myself. What I've done, chasing after a hellhound, was not one of the best ideas, and I hope I'm not thrown back in jail for not following orders.

I knock loudly on the open door before stepping inside the house where the stench of death assaults my nose. It's best not to startle two lethal hunters. "Hello? I'm back."

Natalia strides from the bedroom covered in blood, a fitting look for someone hiding the evidence of a demonic crime scene. Cadence is close behind her without a speck of dirt on her. Only Cadence could scrub down a bloody room without getting a drop of blood on her outfit.

Natalia lifts a delicate eyebrow. "Stupid move, Cami. You're lucky Cadence has spent the last hour convincing me that you knew what you were doing when you went after that hellhound. We're not supposed to hunt unless we're in danger, and that monster just wanted to get the hell out of here."

"They expect us to ignore and let something that dangerous run free?" I ask, exasperated. It surprises me that the clean-up crew has to follow such a ridiculous rule, yet I'm relieved that she believed that I wanted to kill it.

"In this case, yes. You're an untrained hunter and as human hunters, Cadence and I could get seriously injured facing a creature with fiery skin."

"I've faced a pack of hellhounds before with Alana," I argue.

"Did you fight?"

"I didn't know I was demi-demon at the time, so no."

"Did Alana?"

"Well, no," I say, frowning. I can sense I'm losing the argument I started.

Natalia puts a hand on her hip. "Exactly my point. So next time, let it go. And if you're worried about someone getting hurt, we can report the incident to someone in the field," she says.

"I'll remember that." I brush a loose strand of hair behind my ear. "At least we don't have to worry about that this morning. I killed it."

I usually feel terribly guilty for lying, but not so much this time, and I don't know if that's a good thing. *It's for the best. The alliance would never allow a hellhound, even if it isn't completely broken, to live.*

"I knew you would put it out of its misery," Cadence says, finally speaking up.

Not yet, but I will. I fake a smile, hating that I'm leading Cadence on. I'll tell her later, when the time is right. We had an agreement not to kill unless attacked, and the hellhound didn't. She'll understand...I hope.

"It was the right thing to do. I felt bad for the poor broken werewolf. It didn't deserve to live like that." I shift from foot to foot, anxious to hurry up and get out of here.

Natalia pulls a towel from a hook on her belt, wiping her forehead. "You got that right," she says. "As your reward, you get to help me carry out a body."

I swallow hard. I've been so concerned about the hellhound that I almost forgot about the disgusting job I've been assigned to.

I twirl my finger in the air, rolling my eyes. "It's like I've won the lotto," I mutter.

I follow Natalia back into the bedroom, holding my breath as the scent of dead demon and human overwhelms me. I suck up my squeamishness and hope the rest of the morning is uneventful.

REDEMPTION

CLASSES FLY BY uneventfully to my relief. My brain is muddled with thoughts of Malicevile, Melanie, and the hellhound. I have a lunch date with Cadence and Evan at Cadence's apartment, and I'm dying to tell her about the letter left behind by my sister.

The last week has blurred together in a series of ridiculously scary events, and I want to be able to sort things out so I can move on and get my life back to normal—if that's even possible.

"Cami? Earth to Cami," Hunter Garcia says.

I glance up and realize I'm sitting alone in the room, and

my classmates have already been dismissed for the day.

"You've been distracted the last hour. Is everything all right?" she asks.

I don't know why, but I shake my head. "No—yes..." I pause, sighing. "It's nothing. I should go." I stand up and turn on my heels to leave.

Hunter Garcia grabs my wrist. "Wait. You can talk to me. Everything you say remains confidential."

I slump my shoulders. I want to trust her, but she works for the alliance, and my faith in them has been shaken. "It's just—I saw something really disturbing last night, and I can't get the image out of my head."

Her eyes line with concern. "Clean up duty is tough. I've been there. You have to remember those lost souls couldn't be saved. They're better off now."

I nod, keeping my expression blank. "I suppose you're right." I bite my lip as a burning question pops in my mind. Being the instructor of all things related to the Veiled Realm, she might be able to help me. "But what if that wasn't the case? What if death wasn't the only way to save a lost soul?"

"I'm not sure how to answer your question, but my theories are that if a person willingly deals with demons and loses their soul in the bargaining process, they don't stand a chance of ever regaining possession."

"And if they don't willingly do it? Like broken werewolves?"

"Once a werewolf transforms into a hellhound, they're demon-bound. You can't fix or change that. It's not possible because they're no longer human."

My heart falls. "And if they're not completely broken?"

"That's unheard of. Demons are always successful in breaking a werewolf."

That's strange. I've seen two werewolves this year alone that haven't been completely broken, including one of Malicevile's, and he's the most powerful demon I know. It gives me the hope I need to save the hellhound, knowing the alliance knows nothing about it. But how do I save a soul? I can't...but maybe Dylan could.

Hunter Garcia pats my arm. "Don't worry so much. You're not a werewolf."

"Okay," I say, before making my exit to meet Cadence and Evan. "I guess you're right."

<hr>

The campus buzzes with life. Students mosey around enjoying the clear, sunny sky. I pass the dorms and head to the singles apartment building. I'm not sure whether it's good or bad luck, but I see the back of Dylan's curly black hair through the double doors.

I quicken my pace, jogging the short flight of stairs into the building. "Dylan," I call. I don't want to miss my opportunity to talk to him now, instead of having to seek him out later.

He turns, his eyes sparkling in amusement as I rush toward him. "I'm assuming you're in a better mood than last night," he says, brushing his black locks behind his ear.

I sigh, taking in a deep breath of his comforting, fresh scent. "Not really, but I need your help." I'm not one to beg, but I'll grovel if he turns me down because of his hurt feelings.

"Oh," he says curtly, shoving his hands into his jacket pockets. He glances at the floor before bringing his eyes to mine. "If this has anything to do with your wild plans to find out more about your sister, then the answer is no. I won't be an accomplice when you get yourself hurt or worse."

My chest tightens. It's like a slap in the face that he refuses to tell me everything he knows about Melanie, when it's my right to know that information. I cross my arms, holding back my anger. I can't let his protective thinking bother me so much.

I resist the urge to walk away and swallow my pride. "It has nothing to do with her, and I don't know who else to go to. No one else will understand." *Except Evan, or maybe a werewolf, but neither one can help me.*

He scrunches his brows, lining his face with concern. "Okay, I'll help you."

I smile widely, my heart soaring with relief. "Thank you, thank you, thank you," I say. I stand on my tiptoes and brush my lips against his smooth cheek. "Meet me in the far northeast corner of the wall at sunset. I'll explain everything later," I whisper, giving him a warm hug.

Before he has a chance to respond, I turn and run to the elevator, stepping in as soon as the doors ding open. Dylan tilts his head in confusion, and I press my index finger to my lips making the silence symbol, informing him that our rendezvous later is our little secret.

I fling open the door without knocking. Cadence's apartment smells delicious, like fluffy garlic bread mingled with Evan's seductive scent of amber and patchouli. Evan sits on the couch with his feet propped on the coffee table. Cadence waves from the kitchen, and I shut the door behind me.

"I don't know how you both survived school here. If I hear one more 'demons are evil' lecture, my head is going to explode," I say, kicking my shoes off at the door. I pad across the living room and plop down on the couch next to Evan.

"That's because you're with the new recruits—the ones who've only met the tainted ones. They had me trained and out of here by the time we first met and skipped most of that stuff," he says as he greets me with a gentle kiss before draping his arm across my shoulders. "Maybe Cadence's time here was different."

"It's because they've run out of new material," Cadence adds with a laugh, coming into the room and setting a steaming bowl on her small dining room table.

I push from the couch and follow her into the kitchen to fill up three glasses of water. I hold two in my hands and one in the crook of my elbow and carry them back the table.

Evan joins us at the table as Cadence dishes spaghetti onto three blue ceramic plates. He grabs a piece of bread from the small basket and takes a huge bite.

"I'm starving," he says at my raised eyebrow.

Cadence laughs, smacking him on the shoulder. "You must

have worked up your appetite lying in your pajamas all day while Cami and I were sweating blood doing cleanup duty."

"No, I spent my morning waiting in line at the infirmary to have my hands and arms checked out before getting my bandages removed. You gotta love quick healing," he says, showing off his scabbed palms.

"Thanks for making me lose my appetite," Cadence comments.

I grab Evan's hand and inspect the shiny, healing skin on his palms. They've healed faster than I expected because of the intensity of power that was flowing through me that night. It wasn't the average amount I use when practice fighting with him, that merely shocks him if he lets it hit him.

Cadence scoops a forkful of noodles into her mouth despite her comment. I twirl my fork, simply moving my food around. I'm too nervous to eat.

"I have something important to tell you," I say, setting my fork on the plate with a clank. "My sister knew your grams and father. She mentioned them in a letter I found in Malicevile's file."

Cadence's eyes widen. "I wouldn't expect my dad to tell me, but Grams? She never said a word."

"She warned her of her death. And your dad, well, I don't know. Melanie seemed fond of him."

"That's so weird. You could've been my aunt if they'd hooked up." Cadence grins, and I laugh. Why am I not surprised that her first thought would be that we're related. Of course, that's not possible since Cadence is human.

"Focus," Evan says. "That's beside the point. You know your father would've never been elected an alliance leader if he had."

"A girl can dream," Cadence mutters. "What should we do with this information? I can't blackmail my dad. He's the only one on our side right now."

"I don't want to do anything. I just need to know what Melanie did to get a death sentence. I need to know the alliance isn't out to get me."

"We can call Grams, see if she can persuade the alliance to let us visit her," Cadence says.

"Why can't we ask her on the phone?" Evan asks.

"Grams thinks the lines here are bugged. And, maybe I miss her."

My stomach churns in fear. My last visit to Desertville almost got me killed on several occasions. I'm not sure I could handle another trip. I don't even know if Alana would let me go. She still has final say on what I can do until I turn eighteen.

"I miss her, too," I say, putting my hand on Cadence's. "I just don't know if that's the best idea. The pack there and I aren't on the best of terms."

"I wouldn't worry about that now that you've accumulated your abilities. We could be in and out within a day if we leave at sunrise," Cadence says. She pushes away from the table and picks up her phone off the kitchen counter. "I'll see if we can head out there this weekend."

I open my mouth to argue but then shut it. There's no point. Her mind is already set on taking a road trip from campus.

Cadence puts the phone on speaker and dials. The phone doesn't even ring before Grams' voice sounds out. "Hello, dear. I've been expecting your phone call."

"Figures." Cadence smiles at me. "Do you know why I'm calling?"

The line is silent for a moment. "You know I do," Grams finally says. "And I've already made a call to your father. Cami can only leave campus if she agrees to be escorted by that lovely nephilim Dylan."

"Why Dylan?" I ask, aggravated. I don't need a babysitter, especially one who wants nothing to do with helping me find out about Melanie. "He's not even a hunter."

"That's something you're going to have to ask him, Cami. It's not my place to give away the boy's secrets," Grams says. She sure knows how to stay neutral.

"Come on, Vivian. Don't you think I've dealt with enough secrets already?" I ask.

"Which means you should be used to them. You wouldn't want people to be blabbing about your secrets now, would you?"

I cradle my face in my hands. The truth is she's right. I wouldn't want her telling my secrets to anyone. They're dark and disturbing enough to get me killed instantly. I really hope it's not the same for Dylan. He might annoy me and sometimes piss me off, but I'd never want him to deal with carrying around information that could kill him if it ever got out.

"No, definitely not." Cadence and Evan probably assume that Vivian is talking about my sister or even my inner demon. I have a strong, nagging feeling she already knows about the hellhound, which is my own deadly little secret. What's worse is I'm about to drag Dylan into it, too—I don't have a choice.

"Good. Then it's set. I'll see you Saturday." Vivian breathes heavily into the phone, creating static. "Oh, and Cami, please be careful tonight," she adds ominously before hanging up.

Cadence and Evan don't notice the hidden meaning behind Vivian's words to my relief, but I caught it quickly. I know she knows about my plan tonight just from the sound of her voice, but I also know she'd never admit to it. Vivian knows a lot more about the Veiled Realm than she lets on. Her storyteller nickname isn't fitting. She's psychic, but the alliance doesn't want to believe in her predictions. They can't believe in stuff that isn't set in stone or that can change. Dress her in some beads and stick a crystal ball in front of her, and she'd look the part, too.

I glance up and notice the golden sky gleaming through Cadence's window. I'm not as afraid as I thought I'd be. I'm more anxious than anything. What if the hellhound is gone? Or dead? What happens if my plan doesn't work? And, what if I'm caught? Would the alliance see me as a traitor for aiding something they think is demonic?

The questions swirl through my head. It's frustrating that I don't know the answers to any of them. If I did, would I still risk everything for one broken werewolf? Yes. I would. Not because I like werewolves, because I don't, they actually freak me out, but because if there is a tiny chance that their souls could find redemption without death, I'm going to take it.

I get up from my chair. "I need to go speak to Dylan," I say. "I'll see you later."

I kiss Evan on the forehead and blow one to Cadence before heading to the door. They both stare at me with narrowed eyes but don't move to stop me. I click the door closed and lean against it, composing myself, stilling the fear raging in my heart.

I hope this works.

BROKEN ONES

I CUT THROUGH the scattered lemon trees in the orchard, swiftly making my way to the northeast corner of the wall. I glance around for signs of Annabelle but don't risk calling her name for fear that I'll be heard. It's still early enough that people could be nearby, and the last thing I want is to have to explain why I'm out here just before dark. They'd automatically assume I was up to no good with my new, super evil reputation.

I lean against a tree with my back toward the wall, giving me a perfect view of my surroundings. It's quiet and serene, and reminds me of the peaceful dreams Dylan creates for me. A light breeze musses my hair, and I sweep strands behind my ear.

The scent of dewy apples wafts around me, engulfing me in a cloud of sweet air. "You can't sneak up on me. I can smell you coming."

Dylan emerges from behind a lemon tree across from me. His glorious wings flash in and out of visibility in the warm, golden glow of the setting sun. It's simply breathtaking. He hesitates, keeping his distance, like he's unsure whether or not he should be here—or at least, be here with me.

I shove my hands into the pockets of my leather jacket. I'm still angry at Dylan, but that doesn't stop my heart from pounding in overdrive. His brown eyes sweep around him before settling on me. He half smiles, flashing his dimples, nearly melting the ice I've packed around my heart to keep me immune from his irresistible charms.

"I'm really glad you didn't bail on me," I say. "For a minute, I wasn't sure you'd show up."

"I told you I'd help you, love." Dylan strides closer, and his translucent wings caress my cheeks like the soft whisper of a breeze. I close my eyes, enjoying their feathery lightness, and the stress I've been carrying begins to melt away.

He's making it extremely difficult to stay angry at him. "I hope you're true to your word, because I haven't even told you what I need help with."

Dylan frowns. "You know I'd do anything for you, even if it's dangerous."

"How do you know it's going to be dangerous?" I ask.

He steps closer, staring down at me. Shadows cover his shining eyes as the sun sinks lower. "Because you can't seem to stay away from it."

I look away from his hypnotic gaze, using the moment to clear my mind. Staring into the face of an angel, a half-angel, is distracting. It's like the lure a flame has on a moth, except I don't have to worry about getting burned, just being captured by his presence.

"I don't have a choice. I was born into it," I whisper. "I'm not going to run away from it anymore. I can't. It's not who I am. I'm a demi-demon with an insane demon dad, living among human hunters who would execute me the moment I mess up. No matter how hard you, Alana or Cadence, or even Evan try to change that, it can't be done. I'm sorry if you don't like it. I'm the only one who has to be me, so that's what I'm going to be."

It feels like every conversation I have with Dylan lately turns into me defending myself. I know it's not his intention to push my buttons, and I know the last thing he wants to do is upset me, but I can't help picking a fight. It's like my inner demon wants me to despise him while my heart wants to love him. I'm tired of the struggle between my humanity and my demon.

"You don't have to defend yourself. I love you for who you are, good and bad. Don't think you have to change for me or anyone. It wasn't your humanity that I fell in love with. It was your curiosity, your feistiness, your stubbornness, your strong will."

No matter how often Dylan admits his love for me, it never fails to surprise me. "We should go," I say, changing the subject. I need to be clearheaded for the hellhound, not a soppy mess of emotions. "There's not much time before dark, and I promised Wolfie I'd be back for him."

"Wolfie? You want me to take you to a werewolf?" His eyes line in confusion.

I smile innocently, grabbing his hand. "Not exactly, but we do need to go. You can fly, right? Or are those wings of yours just for decoration?"

His eyes widen, and I think I've caught him off guard. My smile widens, knowing I'm not the only one susceptible to surprises.

"Please, tell me you're joking. You want me to fly you off campus ten minutes before dark? Is that what I'm helping you with?" he asks, thrusting his arms out. "You need a ride? There are cars available."

I pout my bottom lip, grabbing his hand. "Yes, and there's more, but we're running out of time. I'll tell you when we get there."

Dylan sighs. "Do you at least have a weapon?"

"I am a weapon," I say. "But if it makes you feel better, you can borrow my dagger." I yank up my pant leg, revealing the blade strapped to my combat boot. I slide it out of its sheath and offer it to him.

He shakes his head. "It'll be safer in your hands. You know

I'm not a hunter. I trust you to protect me, love."

I slide the dagger back into its sheath, nodding my head. "Always."

I wrap my arms around Dylan's neck and he scoops me up, cradling me like a blushing bride. Hornets buzz in my stomach, zinging around in nervousness. I don't know why I'm afraid. It's not like I can fall to my death with my levitation. It's just that I've never had to protect someone else's life.

I close my eyes as the wind whips through my hair. The whooshing sound created by Dylan's flapping wings is soothing, like the lapping of gentle waves on soft sand. I peek through my eyelashes at the brilliant crimson, gold, and violet colors cast by the setting sun, lighting the world with amazing beauty.

The world is far enough below that if anyone were to look up, we'd be mistaken for a large bird. I scope the landscape, imagining the streets we drove down this morning, retracing the directions from my bird's-eye view.

"Follow the main road for about five miles. The house is in an abandoned neighborhood next to a clearing," I say into Dylan's ear.

"I know exactly where that is," he says. "It's a demon hotspot."

I press my cheek into his chest, protecting my watering eyes from the chilly wind. I hope the neighborhood is as empty as it was this morning. Dealing with demons, or the ones who hunt them, is not on my agenda for this evening.

"We better fly around and inspect the area before we land."

"I already planned on it," Dylan says into my hair.

I easily spot the neighborhood; the dead lawns and broken roof tops are a dead giveaway. My stomach drops as Dylan descends for a better view. It looks as empty as it did this morning, eerie and lifeless, like everything has had its soul sucked out of it by demons.

The last sliver of the dazzling sun disappears on the horizon, and twilight grabs hold of everything, dimming the yards, trees, and houses in a faded haze. My heart pangs with sadness over such a beautiful sight masking the evil that lingers, waiting to come out once the sun is gone.

Dylan smoothly lands on the roof of one of the sturdier looking houses. The shingles quiver, some slipping free to clatter to the dead grass in the yard. He carefully sets me on my feet, tightly holding my hand to keep me from sliding on the crumbling shingles.

I peer around the dilapidated backyards. The metal roof of the shed I left Wolfie in is three yards over. I lift my arm and point my finger at it. "Over there," I whisper.

I pull Dylan to the edge of the roof and wrap my arm around his waist. I balance on the edge, levitating to keep my balance.

"We should walk from here. It wouldn't be a good idea to surprise Wolfie," I say.

I release Dylan, stepping over the edge, hovering just off the roof. I offer my hands to him, and I carefully lower him to the grass with me.

He doesn't let go of my fingers, but instead, he grips them tighter. Panic masks his face, and I'm afraid if I let go of him, he'll take flight and leave me behind to find my own way back to the academy. From experience, fear causes people to act on instinct, and his instinct is to run, not stay and fight. I'd know. Mine used to be the same before I realized I wasn't as helpless as I thought I was.

"Now that we're here, tell me what I'm helping you accomplish," Dylan whispers. His palm is clammy against mine, and I resist the urge to pull away and wipe my hand on my jeans.

"Not yet," I say.

"Then how are you going to know if I can really help you?"

"I don't, but I have faith in you." I stare into his chocolate-brown eyes. "You're going to have to trust my judgment."

Dylan nods, his Adam's apple bobbing as he swallows hard. I know I should tell him what I'm getting him into, but I can't risk him automatically turning me down before seeing what he's up against.

I make the first move, dragging him with me as I climb through the knee-high weeds overrunning the yard. I kick in the wooden slats of the fence, creating a narrow opening to slide through. I poke my head out, glancing around for signs of life and death. The air is clean, fragranced only with Dylan's aroma, so I know it's safe to exit.

I shimmy through the fence to the other side and wait for Dylan to follow before heading in the direction of the shed. He nervously looks around before determining I'm not luring him into a trap or a demon-infested forest. The darkening sky quickens my pace, and Dylan jogs to keep up with me so I don't yank his arm from its socket.

When we reach the fence that I busted through this morning, Dylan hesitates. I roll my eyes, entering ahead of him. After a moment's pause, he follows suit, staying a couple feet behind me.

"Wolfie? I'm back. I brought a friend who can help you," I say.

The shed doors are closed just the way I left it before sun-up, and I cross the weed-laden yard. I knock once on the shed and yank the brown, rusted door open, wincing at the awful screeching noise coming from its tight hinges.

My heart skips a beat. "No. No. No. Oh, please, no."

Electricity crackles in my palm, and I use the light emitting from it to illuminate the small shed. To my horror and fear, it's empty. The hellhound is gone without a trace. The smooth ground is paw-print free, and there are no signs of struggle suggesting that Wolfie was taken. *So, where can he possibly be?*

"He's gone!" I exclaim. "I told him to stay here, and he didn't listen. You can't save his soul unless he's here."

"Save whose soul?" Dylan asks from behind me.

"Wolfie's!" I yell.

"Wait a minute. Are you telling me you want me to save a werewolf's soul? That would mean—that would mean it's a—a hellhound." Dylan runs his hand through his dark hair, pushing it away from his forehead. "Are you freaking insane, love? Hell-hounds can't be saved. That's why they're called the Broken Ones."

"Shut up." I can't think with Dylan panicking about the hellhound. "I need to concentrate."

I gulp a deep breath of air, picking up the faint scent of burning skin and nature. I cross my arms, pacing back and forth in front of the shed. *What can I do? The hellhound is gone. I've lost.*

Tears prick my eyelids, threatening to escape, and I wipe my eyes on the sleeve of my jacket. I can't believe I've failed. Sorrow and regret beat at my chest like a hammer. *Why didn't I just risk taking him closer to the academy?* I could've kept a better eye on him.

"Cami..."

"I said be quiet," I snap. "I'm trying to think of where he could have gone."

"But, Cami," Dylan says louder, forcing me to look in his direction.

"What? What is it?"

"On the roof."

I swiftly turn on my heels toward the house. Nothing appears to be out of the ordinary, and I glance back at Dylan. "You're seeing things."

Dylan's eyes widen, and I turn back to the roof in time to see two hundred pounds of flaming Hellhound soaring directly toward me.

FEEL HUMAN AGAIN

I GASP AS the air rushes from my lungs. The fiery hellhound knocks me to the ground before I have a chance to defend myself. Its steaming jowls drip warm saliva on my face, and I wince at the guttural growl erupting from its throat.

It bares its sharp, glistening teeth, and I struggle to gain enough leverage to knock it off me. It's impossible to move with its front paws placed squarely on my shoulders.

I hear Dylan moving through the brush behind me, and the hellhound ferociously barks, snapping its jaws inches above my face. My fingers tremble, pinpricks of pain tingling in my hands as I lose feeling.

"Stay back, Dylan!" I yell, my throat burning from the pressure sitting on my chest.

Hot breath coats my skin in sweat, and small tendrils of smoke wisp from my clothing as it burns under the heat of the flaming beast. I flinch as it touches its warm nose to mine, and I imagine the excruciating pain I'm about to feel when it decides to snack on my face.

My vision hazes in red, the creature blurry and unfocused at such a close distance. "Please, don't eat me," I say, my voice barely audible over the sound of the flames licking the hellhound's skin.

It opens its black mouth, glistening with veins the color of molten lava, and I scream. I thrash and kick my legs, determined to fight my way free before I'm mauled by its deadly sharp teeth.

I turn my head, squeezing my eyes shut, waiting for the unbearable pain to consume me. Its deep, throaty growl is deafening. I can't hear anything, not even the frantic beating of my heart.

I startle at the warm, slimy sensation sliding across my cheek. Squinting, I see the hellhound's wide black tongue slipping from its mouth to lick my face again.

"Wolfie," I whisper. "Can't breathe."

The hellhound shifts its weight off me, and I sit up, wiping my face off on my sleeve. The broken wolf sits back on its haunches and stares intensely at me.

"You scared the crap out of me!" My voice is shrill from the realization that I'm not going to die.

I scramble to my feet, dusting off my hands on my jeans. I turn to see Dylan, whiter than a ghost, clinging to a piece of wood pulled from the fence. I laugh, partly to calm my frazzled nerves and partly because he looks ridiculous with his makeshift weapon that wouldn't even daze a fly. He wasn't kidding when he said he wasn't a hunter.

"You can put down your weapon, Dylan. Wolfie won't hurt you."

Dylan reluctantly tosses the wood to the dead grass, only inches out of his reach in case he has to grab it again. He rubs his hand across his face, wiping away his blatant fear.

"You've trained a hellhound," Dylan says, astonished by the idea that not all demon-bound creatures are out for blood. "Impossible."

"That's weird coming from the boy who once told me anything was possible," I say. "Wolfie isn't like most hellhounds, and no, I didn't train him. He's not completely broken. Look at his eyes."

Dylan inches closer, pausing when the hellhound releases a low growl deep in its throat.

"Stop that. You want Dylan to fix you, don't you?" I ask, stroking behind the broken wolf's flaming ears.

The hellhound whines, lowering its head in the only way it can apologize. Dylan steps forward another inch, reaching out his hand, palm up, in a non-threatening way. Wolfie sniffs his fingers and whines again before flopping to the ground.

"I can't attempt to heal him unless he cools off some. I'd be in too much pain to concentrate," Dylan says, his voice low with concern.

I bite my lip, considering the circumstance. I completely forgot that unlike Evan, Dylan isn't immune to fire. Yeah, he heals quickly, but his body would probably try to heal itself first instead of the hellhound. What happens if Wolfie can't snuff out his blazing body? Then what? I'd be all out of options.

"You need to do whatever you did yesterday to put out your flames," I say to the hellhound. "You don't want to burn poor Angel Boy when he's trying to fix you."

It's magical, watching the blazing red flames blow out like candles in the wind. It looks as if the hellhound has stepped into an invisible lake; his fiery skin simply washes away to slimy black.

I breathe a sigh of relief. That was a lot easier than I expected without water. Steam radiates from Wolfie's skin. If I were closer, I'd get a steam facial, but I don't think I could handle the stench. It's one thing to breathe the outer traces of stench, sticking my face into it is a whole other story—I'd be knocked out by the fumes.

I trace my finger down the hellhound's back to check the temperature. It's cooler than before, but I can't tell if it's cool enough for Dylan to touch. Being immune to intense fire dulls my perception of hot and cold, and if I didn't know any better as a child, I'm sure I would've touched a hot stove without learning a lesson because there isn't a consequence for me.

Dylan steps closer, peering over my shoulder like hiding behind the wall at a zoo to study a wild animal. Black slime coats my finger, and I twist around and hold it out to Dylan. "Tell me if this is hot."

He reluctantly runs his finger across mine, and I shiver from his gentle touch. "Feels like warm Vaseline," he says, wiping the slime on his jeans.

"Good." I swipe my finger along his cheekbone, creating a line like football paint. "Then it's time for a miracle. Who knows, you could change history and get a mural painted in your honor for everyone to adore."

"Wouldn't that be nice?" Dylan leans his head to the side, brushing the sludge on his shoulder. He grimaces, pursing his lips together. "You owe me a shirt."

"Add it to my bill for your sheets."

He shakes his head and then kneels next to the placid hellhound. The steam dissipates as he waves his hand over Wolfie's back without touching him. Dylan closes his eyes in deep concentration, and I truly think he's summoning a miracle. His forehead beads with sweat, the mixture of the heat and his healing ability taking its toll on him. His translucent wings softly glow in the darkness, casting shadows across the yard.

I hold my breath, staying as still as possible, even though I'd rather be pacing back and forth like a worried mother waiting for news from a doctor.

"I can feel it," Dylan murmurs without opening his eyes. "His soul is faint, but it's there, dangling by a thread."

I let out my breath. My heart beats rapidly, overcome with the anxiety tightening my chest. I drop to my knees, cupping the broken wolf's head in my hands. Its human eyes shine with tears, and I smile my encouragement, praying this works. *It has to work. Oh, please, let this work.*

I wish there were something I could do to help. I'd give anything to save this poor, wounded soul. It breaks my heart to see someone trapped in Purgatory, not demon but not human either. It's how I feel about my life, but seeing this werewolf, this half-human transformed into a creature he can't escape, is ten times worse. His freewill was stolen, leaving him without an option between good and evil. Evil had won...until now. If Dylan can heal a soul, bring it back from evil, then I know that I can fight against my inner demon—I can win freedom for my shadow-coated soul.

Dylan's brilliant, ethereal wings stretch out, wrapping us in their pure, shining light. He presses his hands on the hellhound's ribcage, and I watch in fascination as small tufts of fur sprout through the thick sludge coating its skin.

The hellhound whines, nuzzling its nose in my hands. It rolls onto its stomach and struggles against the pressure of Dylan's hands as he shifts them to its back, forcing the wolf to remain down.

The hellhound jerks its head out of my hands as rolling muscle spasms shudder through its limbs. A loud guttural sound startles me, and I fall backwards into the weeds as heart-wrenching convulsions consume the broken wolf.

Dylan releases the hellhound, scrambling back on all fours, and slumps against my shoulder. His breathing is heavy and strained, and I wrap my arm around him before he can fall over.

"I've done all I can." His hoarse voice is low, barely audible over the loud scream of the broken wolf.

My gorge rises watching the hellhound flop like a fish out of water. Tufts of fur break through its skin and disappear as it fights to regain control over its soul. Bones crack louder than thunder, and its limbs snap and reform, transforming from human to wolf and back again. It's excruciating to watch, but I can't take my eyes away. My hope dwindles as the struggle between human and hellhound wears Wolfie into submission. I don't know if he can survive this—if he even wants to survive.

"Stay strong. You can do this," I coax.

The broken wolf howls, its back arching and its legs bending in awkward positions as though the strings of a puppet are being yanked by a careless puppeteer.

It feels like hours have gone by, and the poor hellhound is still trapped in a soul shattering transformation. *What if it doesn't stop? Could I put it out of its misery?* My heart pounds in fear. This is too much to handle.

I push away from Dylan and leap to my feet, sliding the dagger from my boot. I can't let the wolf go through this pain any longer. It isn't right. *At least its soul is safe...*

Moving slowly through the weeds, I position myself a foot away from the struggling broken wolf. I squeeze my eyes shut, bringing the dagger over my head, preparing for the death blow.

It's better this way. It's better this way. It's better this way, I chant to myself.

"Cami!"

I thrust the dagger downward, but I'm knocked off my feet inches before I stab my mark. I skid across the ground, and my dagger flies from my fingers, clanking against the metal door of the shed.

I gasp, shrugging Dylan off me. "What were you thinking?"

Dylan's slimy hand slaps over my mouth, shutting me up. "Look," he whispers.

My mouth drops open in surprise. Where the hellhound struggled with humanity lays a naked, slime-coated body. Its back is facing us, and I notice the slight rise and fall of its midsection as it breathes. Not a single hair protrudes from its skin—its head is as bare as a newborn baby's head.

I scramble to my feet and jog the short distance to the once broken werewolf. I gently push it on its back and glance down in surprise. *Wolfie's female!*

I strip off my jacket, covering the woman's shivering body. Her eyes remain closed in exhaustion, her expression serene, no longer consumed by pain. I caress her smooth cheek, noticing how her high cheekbones dip into her slightly pointed chin. Her full lips puff in and out as she breathes through her mouth. Her hairless brow bone crinkles above her twitching eyelids as she struggles with waking up. Her flushed, caramel-colored skin is clammy like she's fighting off a fever, but she's alive. *Dylan did it—he really did it!*

"It's over," I whisper. "Your soul is safe."

The woman moans, opening her eyes. She jerks away from me, tears pouring down her black, slimy cheeks. Glancing around in fear, her eyes are round as she looks from me to Dylan. She pulls her knees up to her chest, hugging my jacket like a baby blanket. Her chest heaves, and she breaks down crying, sputtering and choking through her tears.

I bite my lip, unsure of what to say. What exactly do you say to a person who has been through Hell and back to comfort them? I don't want to scare her, and I can't say something cheesy like "I feel your pain," because I've never been through something like that. It's unimaginable to even try to relate to her. Sure, I've been kidnapped, beaten, imprisoned, and almost killed a dozen times, but I've never transformed into a fiery dog and fought my way back before. I don't know what it feels like to be her.

"Do you know your name?" Dylan asks, kneeling next to the blubbering girl.

She nods her head, gasping through her tears. "Lola," she manages to say.

"Good," Dylan says softly. "I'm Dylan, and this is Cami. Do you remember what happened?"

She nods again, wiping her trembling hands over her face, smearing the remnants of her transformation. "I-I-I was broken, b-but you saved me," she stutters. "It was horrible!" She sucks in a breath and wails, smacking her delicate hands against the hard packed dirt.

I reach out and pat her shoulder. She grabs my hand, squeezing it in her fingers, surprising me with her strength. "It's over now. You're safe. I won't let anything hurt you again."

She pulls me to her, hugging me, sobbing into my shoulder. "You really saved me," she repeats, burying her face in my shoulder.

I rub soothing circles on her back. "I promised I would."

"I know—I just—I thought you meant you were going to kill me. I've never been so happy to think I was going to die."

I bite my lip, guilt clenching my heart. *I almost did kill her.* "It would've only been a last resort," I admit. "If Dylan couldn't heal your soul, I would have killed you. But, let's not think about it. You're alive and free and human."

I hug Lola a moment longer before pulling away. Now that the worst is over, I don't know what to do. I never fully thought about what to do if Dylan was successful. The reasonable thing to do would be to bring her back with us to the academy, but then what? The alliance would probably turn her into a science experiment, and there wouldn't be anything I could do to help her, because I'd be arrested again on ridiculous charges for helping a demonic creature get its humanity back. And Dylan...I don't know what would happen to him.

"Is there somewhere we can take you? To your pack, maybe?" Dylan asks, reading my mind.

Lola shakes her head. "They've faced the same fate as me," she says, sniffling.

My chest clenches. It doesn't seem like it, but Lola was the lucky one. "We can't take her back to the academy. Who knows what would happen then."

"There's a safe house not far from here. We can take her there," Dylan says. "The only problem is that I can't carry both of you. I can take you back to the academy first and then come back for her."

I scrunch my face, contemplating the idea. "No," I say, raising my chin to gaze at Dylan. "I'm not leaving her alone. It's dangerous for her to be out here in this state after dark. She could easily be overtaken by a demon again."

"What about you? I can't leave you here either." Dylan rubs his hand over his face, smoothing out his torn expression.

"Then what choice do we have? We can't sit around and do nothing. I can take care of myself. I'm a freaking demi-demon who can fry an entire town, levitate out of reach, and can't be easily surprised. I can *smell* danger coming."

Dylan sighs. "You're right."

"I'll be fine. The academy's not that far away. If I start jogging now, I can make it back before anyone suspects I'm missing."

I reach out my hand, helping Dylan to his feet. He embraces me, kissing my forehead. "If anything happens to you, I'll hunt you down, love. I'll find you, and then I'll lock you up for safe keeping for talking me into this mess."

"Deal," I say, stepping back. "And when I make it back, you have to buy your own shirt, and a new jacket for me," I add, teasingly.

Dylan scoops Lola into his arms, cradling her like a small, fragile child against his chest. She locks her arms around his neck, burying her face against his shoulder. He bends his knees and prepares to take flight, his brilliant wings flashing through the darkness.

"Be safe," he says as he jumps into the air. The wind from his wings whips through my hair, engulfing me in his rainy, crisp apple scent.

I stand with my feet apart, staring up into the glittering night sky, watching as my angel disappears into a small pinprick of light, blending with the stars.

I sigh, my heart soaring in relief that Lola will be able to live a normal life again, safely tucked away from the demons out to break her. This precious moment has finally made me realize what I need to do with my life. I don't want to be a hunter, or some desk clerk filing away information about demons. I want to find lost and broken souls; saving them could be my way of making up for my demonic heritage and demon taint. It would make me feel human again.

DEADLY DECISION

I RUN SOUNDLESSLY down the cracked sidewalk, levitating inches off the ground to keep a fast pace. To humans, I'd look like a girl merely out for a night jog, gutsy and confident, running through the eerily quiet neighborhoods. I breathe deeply, in and out, sniffing my surroundings for signs of demons and creatures. The air is nearly odorless, and I occasionally catch the hint of people cooking dinner, nothing out of the ordinary for a neighborhood around dinner time.

I push my feet to run harder when I see the main road that leads to the academy two blocks away. From there, it'll be a straight jog to safety.

A dark truck turns the corner, heading in my direction. I dive into the nearest yard and take shelter behind a hardy rose-bush. The headlights illuminate the street but aren't bright enough to reach me in my hiding spot. I wait until the truck disappears around another corner before heading back to the sidewalk.

"That was close," I mutter.

The streetlamps shine brighter, illuminating the dark street as I reach the main road. It's wide, surrounded with trees instead of houses, and the lack of sidewalk doesn't look good for my cover of a nightly jogger.

I maneuver around the large the trees, weaving in and out and between to stay off the road. It's darker on this side of the tree line because of thick, leafy branches that block the dull orange glow of the streetlamps.

A branch snaps, causing me to skid to a halt. The noise came from somewhere up ahead since I'm not making any noise at all. *It's just an animal.*

Another branch cracks, and I duck behind a tree. I sniff the air, unable to pick up the scent of demon or animal. I peer through the shadows, watching as a dark silhouette steps out from behind a tree. *Oh, crap!*

The figure is bulky with broad shoulders. He clumsily steps over the shrubs and weeds, cursing when he trips on a fallen branch. For a minute, the man looks bald, but it's only a navy blue baseball cap covering up his stick straight, shoulder length hair.

Goose bumps prickle on my bare arms, and I rub them away with dirty hands. Fear brushes my mind, and I quickly dismiss it. The man isn't a demon or hunter, just a human out for a late night walk.

I stand from my crouch, straighten my shoulders, and walk into view. I don't want to startle the guy and have him come after me in self-defense.

Crossing over the ground, I lower an inch to appear to be walking on the ground instead of blatantly levitating. It takes my eyes a moment to adjust to the bright light of the streetlamp I'm under. I wipe my eyes, casting away my shadowed vision.

I take a step back when the man emerges from the trees in front of me. I squelch the urge to gather electricity in my palms for protection. The last thing I was expecting was to come across some human man on my jog back to campus.

Instead of confronting him, I cross the road to the other side of the street. *You've got to be kidding me!* The man follows suit and crosses ahead of me blocking my path. *Who does he think he is?*

I place my hands on my hips. "Can I help you?"

The man grins widely, and I shiver. "A pretty girl like you shouldn't be walking around these parts at night."

Just the words I wanted to hear... I shift from foot to foot. Every instinct in my body tenses, begging me to show this man my nastier side. The only thing holding me back is the possibility of punishment from the alliance.

Stay calm. "How kind of you to consider my wellbeing," I

say sarcastically.

The man takes a step forward.

I bend, keeping my sight locked on the man, and reach for the dagger in my boot, except it's not there. I didn't remember to pick it up after Dylan knocked me to the ground. *Crap. Crap. Crap.*

I raise my palm in a stop motion. "Stay back."

My blood boils when he doesn't listen. He takes another step forward. His eyes crinkle in excitement, but I don't let him intimidate me into moving. His boxy face is shadowed with a day's worth of stubble, and his greasy hair sticks to the sides of his cheeks. He's in desperate need of a shower. His thin, cracked lips peel back into a jagged smile, and I grimace at his yellowing, decaying teeth. *Someone not only needs a shower but a tooth brush.*

He's wearing a gray and black flannel shirt over a white ribbed tank top tucked into filthy boot cut jeans held on by a leather belt adorned with an ungodly large, oval-shaped metal buckle with the name Buck etched on the surface.

"I *said,* stay back." I fist my hands, bringing them level with my chin in what I hope is a threatening enough pose.

Buck chuckles, raising his hands in surrender. "Take it easy. I'm just messin' with ya."

Great. A guy who gets thrills off scaring people. I lower my hands an inch, narrowing my eyes. "Then let me—"

The man pulls out a pocket knife and points it at me. "Empty your pockets, pretty girl."

"Do I look like I have something for you to steal?"

"Let's find out." Striding forward, he reaches out for me but only has time to grab one of my wrists before I thrust the heel of my palm at his face, striking him squarely in the nose.

He wails but doesn't release me. Instead, he swings the pocket knife up and nicks my cheek, the sting of the cut blurring my eyes with tears.

I don't let the pain overwhelm me. I could easily zap the guy and knock him out, but that's my last resort. I shove my free hand against his chest, using my levitation to put enough force behind me to push him back.

"What the—" The man's eyes widen as I continue to push against his chest, my feet hovering a foot from the ground. I pull my hand away from his chest, and he startles when I don't fall. I slam my fist into his stomach, and he groans, tumbling over and hitting the dirt with a thud.

Scrambling to his feet, he rushes at me, spitting in rage. The last thing he expected was to get knocked on his ass by me, and I just pissed him off. I side step, but not far enough from him because a second later, his arm hooks out, catching my neck. His chest presses firmly to my back, and I struggle to breathe against the pressure cutting off my air supply.

Digging my fingers into his arms while stomping my boots hard, I hope to crush one of his feet. "You don't want to do this. I'm warning you."

The man breathes his gross, alcohol-laced breath in my ear. "Whatcha gonna do about it?" he asks, muttering. "Didn't your daddy ever tell ya to do what you're told?"

My nose begins to burn, and I can't respond. Fear grips my stomach as the intoxicating scent of cinnamon and clove tickles my nostrils. I struggle harder, desperately, the man holding me hostage is no longer a threat.

"Many times. But I didn't mean she should take orders from a pest like you. Now let go of the girl before you regret it." Malicevile steps out from behind a tree, his startling eyes flashing green in the streetlights. He saunters closer, a devious smile playing on his lips. His dark hair is neatly slicked back, styled with the sticky gel he seems to favor. He looks ethereal yet dangerous, like a slinking black panther stalking some poor, helpless prey.

"You don't scare me, pretty boy." Buck releases a weird noise from his throat, like a growl and half yell while he digs his chin into the nape of my neck.

The nickname is fitting for Malicevile, who is decked in a lavish midnight blue suit with a black tie neatly knotted around his white collared shirt. He looks like he's just come from a business meeting, which is highly possible when it comes to dealing with souls.

"Such fearless words coming from a man shaking in his boots." Malicevile leers in our direction, mischief dancing in his eyes.

"What're ya? Her boyfriend or somethin'?" His words are disgusting but make sense. It's easy for a human to mistake Malicevile for my boyfriend because of his ageless, youthful appearance.

"That's gross," I say through clenched teeth, my throat aching under his painful hold. "He's my father."

Buck steps backwards, yanking me with him. Now he's only holding me to shield himself from Malicevile. I levitate to keep my feet from skidding but don't try to escape. I'd rather spend the day with Buck-O than a couple of minutes with Malicevile. I can take Buck down in a second—unfortunately it isn't the same for Daddy Demon.

"I'll give you a thousand dollars if you can get us out of here alive," I add, shifting to look at Buck.

"That breaks my heart, daughter," Malicevile drawls. "You resort to bribing this repulsive man to help you when I'm not the one who has you trapped in a headlock."

"He can't steal my soul," I say. "Hell, he can't really hurt me either."

Malicevile smiles wickedly. "Then what are you doing? Going for an evening stroll?"

"I was heading home from—" I pause, reconsidering my words. "I'm just on my way home." *Why are you even talking to him? You should be running.*

Buck loosens his grip and drops his hands to his sides. I rub my neck, staying between him and my father. The man might be the scum of the earth and not worthy of my protection, but I'm not going to let Malicevile get his greedy hands on him. I'd prefer it if the police handled the situation.

Electricity erupts in the palms of my hands, and I hold

them out in warning. "Now if you don't mind. We'll be on our way."

"Oh, but I do mind, Camilla. You are free to go, but this gentleman stays with me. He hurt you."

I rub the cut on my cheek against my sleeve, shifting uncomfortably, not knowing what to do. I can leave this man to his fate, or I can stay and risk my soul. It shouldn't be such a hard decision. I can almost hear Alana screaming, "Run!"

My legs refuse to move. Thoughts of Lola and Dylan play through my mind. I need to stay—I have to save this man's soul before he becomes tainted. He's bad already—I can just imagine what my father will do to him. The world will be worse off dealing with a soulless psycho. I can't let the fear of my father prevent me from doing what's right for the rest of humanity.

"No. I'm not leaving."

Malicevile produces a ball of energy in his hand, and the man whimpers behind me. As my demonic father strides a foot closer, I scamper back, pushing Buck with me. Five feet of distance between me and Malicevile is too close for my comfort.

"Don't be difficult, Camilla. This man doesn't deserve your chivalry. I can taste the evil coursing through him. He'd be perfect for my collection."

I swallow hard. "People can change."

"And you trust this man will suddenly change his ways? It's impossible. He'll be out tomorrow night hunting for some unlucky person to attack just like he tried to attack you. Can you live with the knowledge you helped a criminal escape?"

His words strike a nerve. He's right. How can I trust that Buck won't continue with his evil ways? Letting Malicevile have his soul would only escalate his way of life. That's what demons do. They use their evil influence to corrupt souls, turning humans into monsters.

"Yes, actually, I can." Against my better judgment, I turn my back on my father and stare into Buck's frightened eyes that are focused on the power in Malicevile's hands.

"Buck?" He doesn't move or look up at me, his fear of my demon father overpowering. "Buck! Look at me." I grab his chin, forcing him to focus. "Do you want to live?"

"Y-y-yes," he stammers.

"Okay, then listen to me very carefully. You will be a model citizen from this day forward. You'll work hard to make a living, and you'll never, and I mean *never,* scare, hurt, stalk, rob, or do anything bad to anyone ever again. If you so much as look at anyone in a way you shouldn't, I *will* hunt you down, cut you to pieces, and fry you up to feed to hungry demons. Is that a deal?"

My stomach churns. I sound like a true demon negotiating, but I need to make sure he won't make me regret letting him go.

Buck furiously nods his head. "I swear."

Malicevile applauds, and I glance back at him. "Do you really think that's going to stop me from taking him?"

"No," I say slowly. "But I know what will."

Malicevile raises his eyebrows curiously, a small smile playing on his lips. "And what would that be?"

My mouth dries, the words sticking to the back of my throat. I run my hand over my hair, brushing it out of my eyes, wishing there was another way out of this mess, but there's not. I'm out of options. I can't fight Malicevile for the safety of the man's soul—it would only lead to his death and me having to live with the guilt that I didn't try hard enough. And it's not like I can just call up the alliance and ask for help. I doubt they'd come running to the rescue anyways. So that leaves me with one deadly decision I'm sure to regret.

"I want to make a deal," I quietly say, wrapping my arms around my chest for comfort. "And I know you won't be able to resist."

RECKLESS

MALICEVILE STROKES HIS smooth, jutting chin with his manicured hand. "You have my full attention." His voice is as silky as milk chocolate, and I shake my head, clearing my thoughts. I have to be careful what I say next.

I shift back and forth on my heels. I need to stop opening my mouth before I think things through. My impulsiveness is going to get me killed. Not worrying about my soul every day has turned me reckless—the academy has lowered my guard.

What would Alana say to this? What would Evan? The Hunter's Alliance will surely twist this awful situation, blaming me and accusing me for dealing with demons. I just hope they'll understand I'm doing this to save a life, a soul, one of the very human souls they fight on a daily basis to save. The soul of a man who'd probably destroy many if he were tainted.

I mull over my next words, considering all the ways Malicevile could twist them to benefit him. I need to make a solid deal that doesn't have any loopholes.

"I will trade you twenty-four consecutive hours of my time to visit, talking only, with one phone call that I can make at the time I choose to actually talk to a person of my choice. Answering machines don't count. It has to be at your home somewhere within walking distance of the Hunter's Academy, where I currently live, with free meals of my choice, a room of my own, and your protection and guarantee that I will be released without any harm to my body, mind, and soul caused by you or anyone—" I pause, taking a breath. I swear Malicevile looks bored. I don't let that affect the rest that I need to say, though. "For the freedom of this man's—Buck's—soul, mind, and body, with the guarantee that you will not seek him out, bother him, hurt him, or ever try to make a deal with him alive or dead."

"Done," Malicevile says, shocking me.

"Really?" I ask. He didn't even try to bargain with me. He agreed too quickly, made it so easy. I question whether or not this deal was really successful or will benefit me.

"Yes, really. It's too late to question your judgment, Camilla. If you breach our deal, your soul is mine."

My heart skips a beat. *This is so not good!* I forgot about the consequences that would happen if I don't complete my side of the bargain. "Then I get all your power if you don't complete your side," I add hastily.

Malicevile laughs, his shoulders shaking, before he composes himself. "You couldn't handle it. You can barely manage what I've given you."

I huff, placing my hands on my hips. If I thought he had a soul, I'd ask for that, but I doubt he does. "Is it a deal?"

"Whatever you want, daughter." Malicevile shifts his eyes behind me, staring at Buck, shivering with fear. "Your presence is no longer required, you may leave now. Just don't forget what my daughter has told you. I'll make sure she's good on her word to kill you if you fall into your old habits."

Buck spins on his heels and runs faster than I thought possible for a human. He races down the middle of street before turning down another street, disappearing from sight.

I stand awkwardly, wringing my hands together, wondering what happens next. What if Malicevile lives in some run-down shack infested with man-eating spiders? I don't know if I could last twenty-four hours. At least by this time tomorrow, I'll be home and safe in my own bed.

Malicevile pulls out a cell phone from his breast pocket, shocking me with his savvy use of modern technology. He's called me before, but it's just plain weird seeing him actually use it. He taps the screen a few times before holding the sleek, black phone to his ear. He winks at me, but not in a creepy way. It was definitely a dad wink—one that says it's all good. I don't know whether I should barf or start crying my eyes out. This entire situation is not what I expected. It's so *normal.*

"Hello, Rebecca, please send a driver and have my daughter's room ready for her arrival."

A woman squeals through the phone, and Malicevile ends the call without listening. Rebecca sure seems excited about my visit. This is all so strange. I can't seem to shake the foreboding feeling settling in the pit of my stomach. That's what I get for agreeing to visit a demon's lair.

"I already have a room at your house? It better not be pink," I say, awkwardly trying to make conversation. I can't let him fool me into believing he actually cares about me.

"Yes, you have a room at all my estates. I've been ready for your arrival since you were born."

I want to bring up the fact that they probably weren't my rooms to begin with, that they were Melanie's, but now doesn't seem like a good time to push any of his buttons. I don't want to spend the rest of my time discussing the travesties created by the alliance, because even if I'm not fond of them, I do want to go back. That's where my life is, where everyone I love is. *Oh, God. Evan's going to freak when he finds out…maybe I should call someone who won't try storming in to rescue me, forcing me to breach my contract. That leaves me with David.*

I open my mouth to make a sarcastic comment instead but pause when bright headlights shine on us. A black Lincoln Town Car stops in the middle of the street, and a uniformed chauffer jumps out and opens the door.

"Good evening, Sir. Mademoiselle," the driver says.

Malicevile sweeps his arm out, giving me permission to get in first, and I hesitate. "I'd rather sit up front," I say, reaching for the door handle.

Malicevile's hot fingers lock around my wrist. "Don't be ridiculous. Get in."

My heart pounds against my ribcage as I slide across the black leather seat. The windows are darkly tinted, and I can't see anything through the glass. I push the button to roll down the window, but the child safety is on, and it doesn't even make a noise. I'm trapped, and I can't even see where I'm going. The deal was that his house is walking distance from the academy, but you can walk anywhere. *Crap. Crap. Crap. What have I gotten myself into?*

The driver shuts the door, and my eyes water because of Malicevile's potent spicy scent. It's thick enough to cut with a butter knife and strong enough to linger in my pores for weeks. I carefully click my seatbelt into place, jerking slightly when the driver accelerates, taking me to complete my bargain.

***

I've been slowly counting the mileage meter as it changes, and we've driven ten miles—not unbearable, but not exactly a distance I want to be running. When I thought taking a bus was a miserable way of transportation, it's a walk in the park compared to this. Malicevile hasn't said a single word to me since we've left, and I kind of like it that way, but it has me on edge. It's like he's quietly planning my visit, and I don't like the thought of that.

My shoulder bumps the door when the driver turns off the road. We stop in front of a black metal gate with the same emblem as the letter he sent me, welded into it. The driver enters a code on the keypad, and the gate creaks open. A ten foot privacy wall surrounds the property, almost the same as the academy, but I highly doubt this one is blessed—more likely cursed.

Flashes of light illuminate the trees, zigzagging and moving alongside the vehicle, allowing me glimpses of the surroundings through the dark tinted windows.

The driver parks in front of a large plantation-styled house lit by spotlights. I don't wait for the driver to open my door. I step out of the car onto the granite driveway. Spinning in a circle, I take in the fountain and the beautiful, moonlit landscape.

I gape at Malicevile's house. It's huge with white pillars as thick as I am that reach the high, slanted roof. The wraparound porch is big enough to comfortably fit a house full of guests and is decorated with a porch swing and brightly patterned outdoor furniture. Potted trees are carefully placed along the railing, adding privacy, even though it's not needed.

I rub my hand over my face, wiping away my surprised expression, feeling Malicevile studying me. "Not quite the gates of Hell I was expecting," I say.

Malicevile chuckles, and his warm hand grabs my arm, causing me to flinch. "I hope you're not disappointed."

I shrug free from his grip and stroll a few feet forward. I hesitate at the bottom of the white steps leading to the porch, pure terror batting in my chest. *Just get it over with already.*

The stairs squeak as I nervously ascend to the porch. A low growl erupts behind me, and I spin in time to see a hellhound leap at me. I duck, narrowly escaping a full force collision and gather sizzling power in my palm. The hellhound skids to a stop, flipping around to face me. Its jowls glisten with steamy froth, snapping and biting at the air, threatening me. I muster the courage to stand strong, refusing to be intimidated, and glare into its glowing coal-like eyes.

"Get out of my way before I zap you," I say, lowering my voice.

The hellhound barks and snaps, refusing to budge. *Show him who's boss. You can't save this one. It's already too far gone.*

"I said *move!*" I yell, throwing a ball of blue energy. It smacks into the hellhound's broad chest, and the broken were-wolf convulses at the shock. It realizes that it's no match against my power and flops on its side, revealing its stomach. I push my guilt aside and step onto the porch. "I'm sorry I had to do that, but you know you would've tried to eat me," I say, patting the hellhound's belly.

Malicevile climbs the stairs with a wide, dazzling smile. I'm sure he's enjoying every bit of my discomfort, seeing that he hasn't done a single thing to welcome me or keep his guard dogs away.

The door swoops open the moment Malicevile steps foot on the porch, and a tall, model-thin woman in her early thirties stands in the doorway, greeting us with a smile. *What has she done to get herself into this mess?*

"Welcome back, Mr. Hellshire," the woman says, beaming a perfect, straight smile. "And Ms. Hellshire, it's a pleasant surprise for you to finally come home. I wasn't expecting you to arrive until after graduation. Mr. Hellshire says that you love your school so much, you never want to come and visit."

The woman hugs me against her, and I stand with my arms at my side. *What the hell is going on?*

"Rebecca, please. Don't overwhelm the poor girl. She's only been here for a minute."

I'm speechless. When did Malicevile get a last name? And who is this woman and where is she getting her information from? She smells normal, like most humans smell, which surprises me because she has to be tainted to be living under this roof, yet she doesn't smell like Malicevile at all.

I open my mouth to correct her, but Malicevile puts his arm around my shoulders, surprising me. I jerk my arm, but he's intent on keeping me at his side.

"Sorry, Mr. Hellshire. I'm just so excited to have her here." Rebecca moves from the doorway, stepping aside to let us in. "Are you hungry, Ms. Hellshire? The kitchen staff will make you whatever you want."

"Of course Camilla is hungry. She's had a long trip," Malicevile says, answering for me. *Long trip? It only took like twenty minutes to get here. What am I missing?*

Rebecca turns quickly, gliding down a narrow hallway. Without her distraction, I notice the stylishly decorated room.

The black, hardwood floors gleam under a crystal chandelier with gold candelabras that sparkle with flame-shaped light bulbs. A circular table is covered in a satiny turquoise tablecloth with a unique flower design embroidered along the hem that brushes the floor. A shiny, white ceramic vase, blooming with white roses, sits in the center. The cream-colored walls are accented with white crown molding, and turquoise and white abstract paintings are cleverly placed above rosewood furniture pushed against the walls on both sides.

A buffet table with golden knobs sits against the wall, and the matching rosewood chair, its seat covered in fabric that matches the tablecloth, is pushed up next to it. A glass-fronted display case holds different kinds of crystal glasses, from delicate flutes to thick goblets. The grand foyer alone is absolutely amazing.

I shake my head, bringing my attention back to Malicevile. "Why does she think I've been at a boarding school, and when the hell did you get a last name? And why doesn't she reek of your scent?"

Malicevile presses his lips together. "No one has ever told me I *reek*. I'm highly offended." He narrows his eyes. "If you must know, Rebecca is simply hired help, a mere human, so it would be in your best interest to play along. As for your other question, normal people can't get around anywhere in this world without a last name." *Normal? He thinks he's normal?*

Oh. My. God. It shouldn't surprise me that Malicevile lives a double life, as a human to the public eye and a demon to everyone else. But why? Why would he take the time and effort to hire and pay humans when he can simply barter for their souls and have free help? It doesn't make sense.

I frown. "I don't understand. Why not trick her into selling you her soul?"

Malicevile smirks. "Because sometimes you need someone who wouldn't try to destroy you the moment the opportunity arrives."

I guess not every human has the same moral standards as the alliance. Malicevile probably pays his staff well enough that they're able to overlook a couple critical, scary flaws. Self-centeredness is part of being human—if it doesn't affect them, then why should they care, right? *And the alliance claims that humans are the innocent ones.*

"This is freaking weird," I say. "One day you're a complete monster, and now you're trying to be fatherly. You should've worked on your approach."

He shrugs, nearly killing my horrible idea of him. Seriously, a shrug? "I'll admit, I have a temper, and you've never made things easy. But I've also changed. I've seen my mistakes and understand how you think, Camilla."

"You don't have a clue—"

He raises his hand up, cutting me off. "Is there anything else I need to clarify for you? Or do you think you can manage to just enjoy our lovely visit together?"

More like being a prisoner in an expensive hotel. "Actually, yes, there is one more thing." I hope my next words aren't a big mistake, but I'm tired of the small talk and need to use this time to get the answers I seek to things the alliance wants to keep hidden from me. "When were you going to tell me I had a sister?"

Malicevile stares at me with his vibrant green eyes peering deep into my soul. Anger, sadness, hate, and disgust mar his features before he has a chance to compose himself. I've caught him off guard, and it feels like he's about to shift from father to demon on me any second.

I cross my arms protectively over my chest and step backwards to put distance between us. I should've waited until I was free to leave to ask him about Melanie, but I couldn't stop the question from coming out of my mouth.

"Never," Malicevile says, a glint of firelight in his gaze. "I didn't want you to know."

THE RIGHT SIDE

AFTER SERVING OUR late dinner, Malicevile ordered the staff away for the rest of the night. He stands by the large picture window, staring off into the darkness. I sit with my legs pulled to my chest on a deep blue chaise lounge chair. The large flat screen television plays some comedy sitcom without sound. Malicevile hasn't said one word since I asked him about Melanie, and maybe the rest of my stay will be just as peaceful.

"For being so persistent on hunting me down to bring me to your home, you're sure quiet now that I'm actually here. Do you regret making the deal?" I ask, breaking the silence.

Malicevile sighs, turning from the window to face me.

"No," he says, rubbing his smooth chin with his hand. "It's just been a very long time since someone has surprised me like you have. It's quite annoying."

Join the club, Daddy Demon. I roll my eyes, unwilling to fall for his demonic charms. He might be kind to me now, but it doesn't make up for the years of torture he's put me through with the excuse that he has a temper. I should be civilized for the sake of my soul, but I'm tired of playing the good daughter. There's no one here to listen in on our conversation now.

"You wouldn't have been surprised if you'd told me about my poor sister, who you brainwashed and left to the fate of the alliance," I say. I wince, expecting Malicevile to strike out at me, but he doesn't.

"She wasn't brainwashed just like you're not. She was well aware of what I was and who the alliance was. She made the mistake of choosing the alliance, which got her killed. They accused and found her guilty of the murder of a nephilim when it was I who killed him. Fortunately, I was able to acquire her soul before they got to her." Dylan crosses my mind, and I can't help the fear gripping me. Would history repeat itself?

"You have her soul?" My heart pounds furiously in my chest.

"Why wouldn't I have her soul? She's my daughter...like you."

I swallow hard. This is wrong. Very, very wrong. Why can't Malicevile collect coins or something? But souls? What could you possibly do with a soul? It's not like she has a body anymore. *Why doesn't the alliance teach us about these things? I could really use the knowledge...*

"Because it's *wrong*. What do you gain from holding her soul hostage? Don't you want her to rest in peace? Some father you are." I can imagine Melanie's soul accumulating dust on a shelf somewhere in this house among all the other souls he has acquired over the centuries. Why does he need hers when he probably has so many others?

"You ask too many questions," Malicevile says.

"And it's your job to answer them, *Dad*." I swing my legs onto the floor and stand. *Don't be stupid. Sit back down.* I force my legs to work, shuffling closer to Malicevile. His cinnamon and clove scent overpowers me, the sweet spiciness coating my tongue. "Convince me to choose the right side. Don't let me make the same mistakes as my sister. I'm not going to end up as a keepsake on your shelf."

What am I saying? Malicevile isn't on the right side. But I don't know if the alliance is either. If the good guys are just as evil as the bad guys, what side am I supposed to be on? *The side that lets you live...*

I ball my hands into fists, levitating higher the closer I get to Malicevile. I hover inches away from his face, heat and anger rising into my cheeks, my inner demon begging to come out and play.

"You have my eyes when you're angry," Malicevile says quietly.

"Shut up."

"You have my desire for greater things."

"I said *shut up!*"

"You have my thirst for death and destruction. I can see it on your face. You want to cause pain and anguish. You want the people who've hurt you, lied to you, mistreated you, even stolen your heart to pay. You want the same things I want, Camilla. You crave power—control. You need it. It helps you survive."

Crimson red coats my vision as deadly rage seeps into my mind. The threads of my sanity are drawn tight, threatening to snap, causing the backlash of allowing my demonic blood to take control. Hot, liquid power zings through my veins, burning and devouring the small tendrils of humanity that cling to my soul.

Drinking in Malicevile's hypnotizing scent, my breath becomes ragged, heavy. His scent trickles over my skin, and every pore on my body absorbs it like a drug, tantalizing the beast within me.

My fingers tingle with traces of electricity, crackling and popping, ready to be at my service. I dig my nails into the palms of my hands, but the pain of my nails cutting into my flesh does little to distract me.

Calm down. Control yourself. He could easily snuff you out like a fragile flame in a tornado. This is what he wants.

"I'm nothing like you," I whisper, the hoarse sound burning my throat. "You're evil."

It takes every last ounce of my willpower not to lash out

and attack him. I want to dig my fingers into his emerald eyes and show him that I'm not like him. I'll never be like him. *Don't resort to violence. He will kill you.* The thought nags me, pushing against my brain.

If he harms you, it's a breach of your contract. You'll get his powers. I could get out of here early...

"You're a lying, manipulative, abusive, destructive—you're the embodiment of Hell." I stab my finger at his chest, sparking enough energy to sizzle the fabric of his designer shirt.

"That's enough, Camilla. You're just working yourself up." He grabs my wrist, swiftly and gently removing my finger from his chest.

Tears sting my eyes, clouding my vision in red-tinged haze. My rage is slowly sputtering out, turning into heartache. The sun stone tied around my neck radiates with heat, battling the dark shadow of my personal demon.

My toes touch the ground, and my knees buckle under the sudden weight. I slide to the shiny wood floor, closing in on myself. I cradle my knees to my chest, tears slipping free, marring my cheeks with wet, salty streaks. He's better at bargaining than I thought. No matter what I say, he won't hurt me—it's frustrating.

"Please," I beg. "Just tell me why you hold onto Melanie." I've given up hope in shortening my stay. I can't unleash my demon...not to save my soul. Not for him. Not ever.

I glance through my salty tears at Malicevile, his grotesquely angelic face smooth, calm, and collected. He reaches out his hand and pulls me to my feet. I teeter on my heels, using my levitation for balance.

"I can't let her go to the wrong side," he says. "I can't let her make a bad decision twice."

I sniffle, wiping my sleeve across my eyes. "You can't make that decision for her." My voice is hoarse, barely audible over the pounding in my ears.

"Yes. I. Can. As her father, I have a right to her soul. I have a right to your soul as well. Do not be mistaken, Camilla. You can pretend to be human all you want and live with those pesky hunters, and even fight with them. But when it comes down to the side you'll choose. It *will* be mine. I'll see to it that you have no other option."

Like a grenade hitting the ground, I explode. Electricity shoots from my fingers, slicing through the air like sharp daggers, right into Malicevile's chest. The tight chains binding my soul loosen as I release every ounce of power. My hair floats around me, trapped in the static field created by the energy.

Malicevile raises his hand at me, and I smile, preparing to be slapped. He pulls his arm back, narrowing his eyes and swings with full force at my face. I squeeze my eyes shut expecting a flash of pain that doesn't come. I peek through my eyelashes at his palm a mere inch away.

My body grows lighter and lighter as his unwanted power flows freely from me and back into him. I laugh hysterically at his discomfort, his appalled expression priceless. He can't do anything to stop me.

"Camilla, no!" he bellows. "You need that!"

My chest heaves in agony as the last drop of power is forced out of me. I'm cold and shaken, dizzy from the sudden jolt of power and then the sudden emptiness I feel now that it's gone.

"I don't need anything that belongs to you," I whisper.

Dark shadows fringe my vision, and all I want to do is sleep. *Wait for the sun!* I stumble back, pressing my back to the wall for support. I'm exhausted and drained, weighed down by everything that has happened tonight. I just want it all to end.

Malicevile rushes toward me, and the last thing I see are his vibrant green eyes piercing into my soul.

"Cami! Cami, love, where are you?" Dylan's voice laces with sheer panic. His wings open to the heavens, and his skin glows the most glorious of golds—his pure, ethereal light shining through.

I never thought I'd be this exhausted in my dreams, but I am, and it takes all my energy to pull my muddled thoughts together.

"I'm fine," I say instead of answering his question.

"You're lying. Your soul...it's—you have to tell me where you are."

His chocolate-brown eyes line with worry, and I wish I could see what he sees. What's wrong with my soul? What has Malicevile done to me? "I can't."

"But, love!" he says, exasperated. "You've damaged your

soul! You're weak."

Damaged. Forcing all of Malicevile's power out of me has damaged my soul. "I need rest. That's all."

"No, you need me. I can heal you."

"It'll have to wait. I can't go home," I say softly. "At least not for a couple more hours."

"What is so important that you can't come home now? The alliance is riled up, thinking you've run away to avoid finishing your sentence. You have everyone freaked out. Alana is searching for you, thinking the worst has happened."

My heart hammers in my chest. "Make them stop. No one can find me." If anyone finds me, I'll lose my soul for sure. It's best they stay out of it for my sake.

"Cami, you're shaking." Dylan grabs my hands, pulling me close. "Why are you so scared?"

Tears burst from my eyes, and I sob into his shoulder. I cough and hiccup, ineffectively trying to pull myself together. "I made a deal with a demon." I'm not even sure I've said the words out loud.

"You did what? Cami, how could you? After everything I've done to keep you safe."

Guilt consumes me, and I cry harder. "He was going to claim Buck's soul. The man would've destroyed the world."

"Calm down. It's okay." Dylan rubs soothing circles on my back, and I cling to him like a life raft on an unrelenting sea.

I suck in slow, shallow breaths, pushing my fear and regret to the back of my mind. Dylan guides me to a stone bench, pressing his knee to mine when he sits down next to me. He cups my face in his hands, kissing the streaming tears from my cheeks. His comforting presence calms my nerves, and I feel like there's hope for this disturbing situation after all.

As he kisses my cheek, I can't help but think about Evan and Alana scouring the night for me, worried sick. Why couldn't Evan be the one with the dream walking ability? I could at least talk to him and let him know I'm okay.

"Now please, tell me exactly what happened after I left you," Dylan says.

"Everything was fine until some creep attacked me. I didn't want to use my abilities on him because he was human, so I left myself vulnerable when Malicevile showed up as a knight in black armor." I sigh before continuing. "He was going to take the man's soul, but instead I traded twenty-four hours of my time with him for the man's soul, and he accepted. If I leave, it'd be breaking our contract, and he'd get my soul by default."

"Are you sure you're not a nephilim?" Dylan asks, brushing the moist hair from my eyes. "You bargained with a demon to save a man who tried to hurt you. The alliance should be ashamed for ever punishing you."

"So, you're not mad?" I ask.

"I'm furious. But you did what you thought was right, and I can't blame you for that. It still doesn't explain what happened to your soul, though."

"I kind of gave Malicevile all of his power back. Evan's going to be disappointed when he realizes that our practices aren't going to be as entertaining."

"I'm relieved," Dylan whispers. "Malicevile's evil has done nothing but harm you."

I nod my head, wishing I could truly believe him. How am I going to protect myself from the alliance now if they turn on me? I can't levitate forever. I've grown to rely on Malicevile's power to keep me safe. But Dylan's right. It wasn't good for me.

The world begins to shake, and I know my peaceful dream is about to end. "I don't want to wake up!" I cry. "Dylan, don't let me go back."

His fingers slip from mine as everything begins to spin out of control. "I can't! Something's blocking me. Tell me where you are so I can come get you when your contract expires."

I open my mouth to speak when Dylan is yanked away from me, pulled out of existence.

I scream, the loud, shrill sound of my voice echoing around me as my dream world is torn apart.

THE COLLECTION

MALICEVILE HOVERS OVER me, and I scream, surprised and afraid of waking up to him. I twist and turn on the strange bed in this strange room. He smiles wickedly, pressing his index finger to his lips, telling me to be quiet. I slap my hand over my mouth, suppressing the shrieking sound before he resorts to covering my mouth to shut it up for me.

The ivory curtains are pulled open on the window, revealing the dark night. I grasp the soft, matching comforter between my fingers, yanking it up to my chin. A weird, girlie lamp, shaped like a butterfly, glows dully through its orange shade on a glass-topped night table, matching the lace throw blanket draped across the end of the bed. A mahogany vanity table with elegantly shaped perfume bottles neatly arranged against the mirror is pushed against the wine red walls.

I shift to my side, glimpsing the intricately painted orange flower design on the head board of the bed that matches the feminine theme without seeming childish.

Malicevile steps back, taking a seat in an upholstered chair. He's strangely mundane in a simple pair of jeans and a button-down shirt, pressing his bare feet into the light brown rug over the off-white carpet.

"Is it almost morning already? What am I going to do all day?" I ask, yawning into my hand. Since he agreed to twenty-four consecutive hours, it means that I'll have half the time to myself.

Malicevile runs his hand through his freshly showered brown hair, disheveling it. "It seems I've made a terrible bargain with you, Camilla. Out of the twenty-four hours allotted to me for visiting, you've spent most of them knocked out because of how fast you released all that power I had given you. You make better deals than I thought. No question that you're my daughter."

I shake the confusion from my mind. If I've slept through the day then my bargain is complete, and I'm free to go. How I managed to pull this off, I'll never know.

"You didn't have to let me sleep," I say, pushing the blankets away. I stare in horror at the black cotton night gown I'm wearing. The fabric hits just below my knees, dark red lace peeking out from the hem. Definitely not the pajama pants and tank tops I'm used to wearing. *Who the heck dressed me?* My face warms, and I yank the comforter with me when I get out of bed. My bare feet sink into the soft carpet, and I glance around for my clothes.

"And interrupt the peace and quiet I got to enjoy with you asleep? I do hope you grow out of your tirades soon so we can have a civilized conversation. There is so much catching up we need to do. I thought you might be willing to stay." Over my dead body will I stay a moment longer.

I'm not sure if I should be insulted that a demon called me uncivilized or that he prefers me asleep because I annoy him. "We can have a civilized conversation when you get a soul."

Malicevile smiles, and I swear he rolls his eyes. "I have thousands of souls, Camilla." He interlocks his fingers and places them in his lap.

I can't resist rolling my eyes back at him. "Those don't count. Now, if you'd excuse me, I'll be heading home."

I stroll to the door, giving up hope on getting my clothes back. I'll just levitate home without shoes. Malicevile jumps from his chair and strides across the room, bracing his hand against the door, preventing me from opening it.

"Please, stay. I have so much more to offer you," he says, gazing intensely at me. "It isn't safe for you to go back to the academy."

"I can deal with the consequences. Can I please make my phone call now?"

"At least let me refill your power," Malicevile says. "You never know when you'll need it."

"I'll pass. I'm sure I can manage to live fine without it, just like I did before you gave it to me the first time."

"Very well. But don't think I won't intervene in your life if I feel it necessary."

I narrow my eyes. "I'd like to see you try."

Malicevile slams his hand on the doorframe, making me jump. "Don't underestimate me."

I keep my head high. "I could say the same thing."

With a sigh, Malicevile removes his hand from the door and guides me down a narrow hallway leading into his study. When I step in, I'm taken aback by the dazzling sight of glittering crystal cylinder-shaped vials the size of a finger tucked within the built-in shelves. A large, sturdy desk sits center stage on a leopard skin rug. A red stitched, black office chair faces the door, allowing Malicevile a complete view of the room while sitting in it. A black iron chandelier hangs from the ceiling, its light sparkling off the wall-to-wall built-ins. There isn't a window in this room; it must have been covered, leaving the door as the only exit.

I don't bother asking where the telephone is. A black, multi-lined phone sits next to the obsessively huge monitor on his desk. I push past him, taking a seat behind the desk.

"A little privacy?" I say.

"No." Malicevile crosses his arms and leans in the doorway.

I roll my eyes and pick up the receiver, dialing Information, before quickly hanging up when I realize that I can't ask for the Hunter's Academy. They'd think I was crazy.

I wasn't planning on calling Evan, but I'd rather talk to him instead of Alana, and I never memorized David's number. I dial the nine digits, and count three rings before his deep voice sounds in my ears.

"Hunter Whiteshaw," he says.

"It's me," I whisper, closing my eyes, listening to him inhale deeply. "I need a ride home."

There's a long pause and tears build up in my eyes, afraid he's hung up on me. "Evan? Did you hear me? I said I need a ride home."

"It's so good to hear your voice," he says, and I can picture the relief spreading across his face. "Where are you?"

I cover the phone with the palm of my hand, glancing up at Malicevile. "Where am I exactly?"

"Do you really think I'm going to give you my address so you can tell your hunter boyfriend where I live?"

I sigh, bringing the receiver back to my mouth. "Do you by chance know where Malicevile lives?"

"Don't joke with me like that," Evan says.

"I'm serious. I'm at Malicevile's, and he won't tell me the address. It's about thirteen miles west of the school. If I start walking, I'm sure Dylan can spot me from the sky."

"Okay, I'll find you soon," he says.

"Please hurry," I say.

The line goes dead, and I carelessly drop the phone back

into the cradle. Thank God Dylan can fly or else I'd be stuck wandering around for hours. I move from the desk, drawn towards Malicevile's glass collection.

"You have an odd taste in collectibles." I run my fingertips along one of the cylinder vials before noticing it's engraved with a name. *Bethany Townsend.*

I look over my shoulder at Malicevile, a wicked smirk playing on his lips. "You shouldn't touch what doesn't belong to you," he says.

My heart sinks into my stomach as I put the pieces together. It's not the crystal trinkets that he collects. It's what's inside of them that makes them so precious. *Souls.* The idea of Melanie's soul gathering dust on a shelf somewhere wasn't farfetched after all. She's probably among the thousands of souls Malicevile has trapped here.

Now that I'm aware of what they are, I swear I can hear tormented whispers floating through the air. Their voices are faint, like the sound still projecting from a muted television when you press your ear to the speaker. My insides wrench in pain—the pain I know they're feeling not being able to move on.

"Cami."

I lift my eyes to Malicevile's, and he raises a curious eyebrow. "What?" I say annoyed.

Malicevile shrugs, and I turn back to the wall.

"Cami."

My ears begin to ring at the sound of my name. *That's not*

Malicevile. I close my eyes, forcing myself to listen carefully. I want to pinpoint where it's coming from.

"Where are you?" I whisper so low I can't even hear my own voice.

"Cami." The voice is coming from somewhere near the door.

I glide along the shelves, rubbing my index finger on the slick wood. *Chastity Smith, Daniel Long, Mark Hale, Amy Fitzpatrick.* I read the names as I go, waiting to spot someone familiar.

"Melanie, are you here?" I ask silently, my heart pounding furiously in my chest.

The names go on forever, running together like a list of children on Santa's naughty list. *This is worse. Way worse.* Instead of getting a lump of coal, these names belong to tainted souls who have dealt with Malicevile and lost.

I pause, reading and rereading the only name I recognize. My stomach churns, and I press my hand to my mouth to keep from vomiting. My breath quickens the rise and fall of my chest, obvious under the thin material of my nightgown. I turn my shoulder, angling away from Malicevile, pretending to be studying the bottom shelf.

Elizabeth Anders. A scream burns in my throat, hot and dry, and a sharp pain twists in my heart, breaking it to pieces. The last name I'd expected to see on Malicevile's shelf was my mom's. All these years I believed she was in a better place, simply gone from this world by my demon's hands. But, that isn't the case. Her soul blends in with the rest of the souls, placed neatly in alphabetical order by last name. *She was a good person, the best mother I could have hoped for, and her only fault, wanting to have a baby, damned her soul to eternity in Malicevile's hands.*

I move forward before Malicevile notices me lingering, but I can't help sneaking glances at the glittering cylinder with my mom's name engraved on it.

I swallow hard, cold fear sloshing in my stomach. I'm not going to leave tonight without my mom's soul, even if Malicevile tries to kill me. I can't. She needs me. *But how?*

Every idea that pops into my mind has way too many possibilities of me ending up trapped here as a soul on the shelf. I can't make a deal with Malicevile again, and I'd surely be caught if I tried to sneak back here to steal it later.

So that leaves me with one option.

I straighten my shoulders, glance over at Malicevile, and punch the section of cylinders next to my mother's name, shattering them to pieces. I grab my mother's soul in my free hand and drag my arm across the shelf, knocking every soul within arm's reach off the shelf to break into pieces on the floor.

I clutch my mom's soul to my chest, praying for the strength to survive as Malicevile rushes toward me in all his terrifying, demonic glory.

SAVING GRACE

MY BLOODY FIST connects with his nose, pressing the crystal shards deeper into my knuckles. He screams in rage, blindly grabbing at the strap of my nightgown, ripping it from my arm. I duck, maneuvering out of his reach, stepping on sharp glass in the process.

Hot pain washes through my bare feet, but I don't stop. It pushes me to run harder until I can concentrate long enough to levitate.

He hesitates for a few precious seconds, concerned over his precious souls, giving me a small advantage. I crash down the hall, knocking anything and everything I pass onto the floor to slow him down.

"Get back here, Camilla!" Malicevile yells.

I push my body to move faster, faster than I've ever had to run before, because if I don't make it out of this maze of a house now, Malicevile won't take pity on me because I'm his daughter. *Almost there.*

As I reach the foyer, Rebecca pops in from another hallway blocking my path. Her lips press together, and her hands rest on her hips. "What in Heaven is going on here?"

"Hell, not Heaven!" I scream, knocking into her. She stumbles backwards, and I leap over her effortlessly. "He's going to kill me!"

"Why do you th—"

Vibrant, purple electricity smacks into the front door, splintering the wood. Warmth tingles on my back, the smell of burning fabric perfuming the air, as the electricity singes the flimsy material of my nightgown. *Crap!*

My body absorbs the energy, and I launch an energy ball behind me, sending the gorgeous, satin covered table on its side, blocking Malicevile's way, slowing him down.

I skip the small flight of stairs, running through the air three feet off the ground. Gliding across the dimly lit property, I swerve around the lush trees and vegetation instead of staying on the path.

The smell of burning flesh reaches me in time to move out of the way of a flaming hellhound that jumps out from behind a tree. The broken wolf snaps and growls, ripping the hem of my night dress before setting it on fire. I launch higher into the air, kicking the hellhound in the head, sending it clattering into a nearby tree.

Various growls echo around me, and I can hear Malicevile bellowing behind me. It feels like all of Hell is breathing its hot breath down my back, demanding me to stop and give up, to wave the white flag and beg my daddy demon for forgiveness.

Shut up and run!

The soothing voice interrupts my thoughts, and I clutch onto my mom's soul tighter. The deeper I run into the property, the harder it is to see. *What if I'm running in the wrong direction? What if it goes on for miles?*

My blood boils, fighting the chill of the wind against my sweaty skin. My feet and hands sting from the embedded glass, and it's hard to stay focused. I brush my hair out of my eyes with my shoulder, shaking my head in the process to help me think clearly.

I jerk my head to both sides, searching for hidden hellhounds or my father, without seeing anything. Suddenly, I collide with a solid stone wall; air whooshes out of my lungs and my cheek bursts with pain. My knees buckle, and I collapse to the hard packed dirt, the shock of the collision knocking me off my feet.

I claw my bloody fingers into the ground for leverage and slowly push to my feet. My entire body screams in pain and shadows cloud my vision, blurring the night momentarily. The trees moan and crack as the hellhounds draw near, sniffing out my blood.

My heart races, smacking my ribcage against the flimsy fabric of my night gown, and I close my eyes to concentrate. *Come on, come on, come on! Work stupid ability, work!*

I jump into the air only to fall hard on the balls of my feet. I wince in agony, adding to the pain of the glass. I'm too stunned to levitate, and I can't make it over the wall without it.

I tuck my mom's soul under my arm, digging my fingers into the slightly indented, cemented spaces holding the stones together. One of my nails cracks as it grinds against the stone while I force myself to climb. My foot slips, and I fall to the dirt, landing on my back.

Now's not the time to stop working, stupid abilities! You're supposed to keep me alive!

A hellhound zooms from the coverage of the trees and lands heavily on my chest. I jam my knees into its stomach, pushing it high enough to kick it off with my bare feet. Without my boots, it doesn't launch as far as I'd like it to from this awkward angle but just far enough to where I can roll to my side and jump back to my feet.

I don't wait for the hellhound to lunge at me. Instead, I charge with one arm spread away from my side and collide into the broken wolf, the weight of my body knocking it into the wall. Fire slime coats my cheek in rancid goo, and I choke and spit as the smell intrudes my nostrils. I punch the hellhound on the side of its muzzle, smashing its skull into the wall, and it drops to the ground with a thump.

"I didn't want to have to do that," I say, a bitter taste coating my tongue.

I drag myself onto the lifeless pile of burning flesh, my feet slipping and sliding on its slick back. I clench my mom's soul in my fingers while reaching up. *Still not tall enough.*

My stomach churns, nauseated, when I jump, bouncing on the hellhound like a kid on a trampoline. My hands latch on to the top of the wall awkwardly with my mom's soul digging in between my index and middle finger.

I swing my leg, but I can't get it high enough to pull myself up and over. I dangle helplessly like a piñata waiting to be torn to shreds by the fiery hellhounds closing in around me.

"Camilla, you can stop running. I won't hurt you. I just want you to stop fighting." I glimpse the flash of crackling electricity through the trees, and I bite my lip to keep from screaming out in frustration.

Cami, calm down. Panicking will only get you killed.

I inhale a deep, stinking breath of the rotten air, slowly releasing it. The pain in my fingers subsides immensely as my feet touch the invisible barrier of my ability. My heartbeat slows as I rise higher and higher to my escape. I toss my leg over and straddle the thick wall, taking one last look at Malicevile's beautiful, nightmare-inducing property. It's ironic that such an evil creature could have such luxurious taste.

I'm yanked from my thoughts when molten pain tears through my leg, almost dragging me back to the ground. I scream, watching in horror as fiery, razor-sharp teeth bite into my calf, shredding my leg open in an excruciating, bloody mess.

I flip, the hellhound's teeth dislodge from my leg, and I fall to the other side of the wall, catching myself an inch from the ground. Tears pour down my cheeks, my sobs echoing through the night. The intense pain consumes my every thought.

My body lands on the ground a moment later, my ability to levitate gone with all my concentration focused on not passing out. I stumble to my feet, dragging my gored leg behind me. The crystal cylinder containing my mother's soul wills me to keep moving, to get away. Because if I don't, Malicevile will rip my mom away from me all over again. I can't lose her.

The dim glow of a streetlamp guides me through the wild terrain, and I spot the road close ahead. Every step is like walking on hot coals, but I push my feet to keep moving.

I reach the paved road and head east, not stopping to look behind me. If Malicevile really wanted to catch up, he would've already, but I think he only wanted to make me suffer.

It's eerily quiet, like someone pushed the pause button on the world, and I'm the only one left running about. Dawn is still hours away, so most humans are tucked safely away in their beds. Most people have a sense for evil, and this whole area screams to stay away.

I squint, blinded by bright headlights illuminating the road. I wave my arms, praying that the driver is a Good Samaritan willing to help me. It's hard to tell for sure when it's only the bad or brave who ignore their sense of evil.

The car honks without slowing down, and I jump out of

the way seconds before it almost runs over me.

I stumble on the dip between the road and the vegetation and land hard into a pair of strong arms. I scream, flipping and struggling to get free, the will to live stronger than anything.

"I found her," a familiar voice says.

Glancing up through my wet eyelashes I can see the brilliance of Dylan's translucent, glowing wings. He snaps his cell phone shut, lifts me into his arms, and cradles me against his taut chest.

I cry, my shoulders shaking, relieved to be in the arms of my angel. I clutch my mom's soul to my chest like a baby blanket. *You're safe, Mom. You're with me now.*

Cold wind whips through my hair as Dylan, my saving grace, takes flight away from the hellhole where I nearly died escaping. I bury my face against him, dirtying his white shirt with hellhound slime, blood, dirt, and tears—the night's events summed up in stains that I'll never be able to wash away from my mind.

"Hold on, Cami," Dylan says. "We're almost there."

I cling to him for dear life and do exactly what he says. I hold on.

CHANCE FOR SALVATION

I SQUEEZE MY eyes shut; the sudden wind whips at my face making my tears ice cold. Shards of glass poke from my bleeding hands, but I can only stare at them until we land. I refuse to loosen my grip on my mom's soul because I don't know what would happen to her if the cylinder breaks. Would she get lost in this world unable to move on? I hope not, or else I'm going to feel guilty for the rest of my life because of the souls I tried to set free.

"Brace yourself," Dylan says.

My stomach flies into my chest at the sudden drop in elevation, our descent quicker than I expected. I shiver in my flimsy night gown, my toes numbing, alleviating the pain of the glass stuck in the bottom of my feet.

A black truck speeds down the shadowed road we're flying above. The faster we fall, the more I panic. Our landing will put us directly in its path, and I don't think I could handle any more pain.

"Dylan, slow down! You're going to get us killed!" I scream, burying my face into his chest.

The truck's engine roars as the driver shifts gears, picking up speed. *Oh, God, help us!*

The world shakes as Dylan's boots hit the top of the truck's roof, and he shuffles quickly to the bed, jumping into it. He doesn't let go of me as he crosses his legs and drops into a sitting position with his head resting against the rear window.

"You should have a little more faith in me," Dylan says. He shrugs from his jacket, draping it across my filthy lap to help stop the chill vibrating through my bones.

My teeth chatter uncontrollably. "I-I-I'm s-sorry. A lot of p-p-people want me d-dead tonight," I stammer.

"I can see that."

Dylan lifts my leg in his hand, and I scream in pain. My calf oozes sticky blood, and jagged, flayed skin hangs from the open wounds. Bile rises in my throat, and I slap my hand over my mouth to keep the situation from getting worse.

Dylan pulls the jacket from my lap and wraps it over my bleeding leg to staunch the blood flow. "Evan said you were fine. You are *not* fine." His low voice tickles my ear.

"I *was* fine. I just forgot that once my contract expired, I was free game," I say, groaning at the throbbing pain reverberating through my body.

Dylan presses his hand on my calf, and I scream again. "That hurts!" I complain. "Heal me already, would you?"

His brows furrow. "I wish I could, love. Souls are my specialty, not this." He nods his head at my injured leg.

I shift uncomfortably, my arm pressing into Dylan's sturdy chest, rising up and down with each of his shallow breaths. His skin is warm through his cotton T-shirt, and I lean my cheek on his shoulder, inhaling his apple, rain-shower scent. It almost makes the pain bearable, being cradled in his arms, but my mind wanders to Evan, and I wish it were him holding me instead.

The houses blur by, and I can't keep my eyes focused on where this truck is taking us. I stare down at the crystal cylinder, peering through its thick case to try to make out my mom's soul. There isn't enough light to glimpse her, so I take comfort rubbing my skinned finger across her name.

"Dylan?" I say weakly.

"Yeah?"

"What happens to your soul after you die?"

I can feel his heavy stare boring into the cracks and fissures of my soul, and I can't help but wonder if he's trying to read me.

Dylan sighs, gently rubbing his hand up and down my bare arm. "You're not going to die, love. I wouldn't worry about that just yet."

"I'm not talking about me. I'm talking about souls in general. Malicevile didn't attack me simply because my contract had expired. He attacked me because I did something that I thought was a great idea at the time. So, please answer my question."

"Cami." I glance up into his chocolate-brown eyes, narrowed with concern. He only calls me by my name when he thinks I've done something completely insane—which of course, I have. "You didn't try to release his hellhounds did you? You know Lola's situation was different. A precious rarity."

I shake my head, tangled dark hair falling into my eyes. "I'm not stupid. I can tell the difference between something that has the chance for salvation and something that doesn't."

"Then what could you have possibly done to upset him so much that you ended up like this?" he asks, exasperated.

I look at the crystal cylinder in my hand, and Dylan follows my eyes. "I, um—I may have purposely knocked over an entire shelf of souls so I could have this one."

Dylan sucks in a breath and reaches out his hand to touch it. I slap his hand and quickly regret it as the glass bites deeper into my skin.

"Oh, no, love. What possessed you to steal a soul from a demon?"

Tears creep into my eyes, and I blink them back before Dylan notices. "I couldn't just leave her," I say, my voice trembling at the thought of not having my mom's soul with me now. "She's my mom. And if my dad's soul was among his collection, I would've taken that, too. But my dad wasn't the one who made the deal. She was. So please, tell me what will happen to the souls I set free? I have to know."

"I could get in a lot of trouble for telling you this," Dylan says.

"Screw the alliance!" I slap a hand over my mouth, shocked at my reaction.

"You don't understand. You're not looking at the bigger picture. The alliance doesn't rule Heaven and Hell—they don't even rule earth. They're merely a group of humans who attempt to control things that are uncontrollable to give their lives meaning, and until you pick your side, I can't tell you anything."

Malicevile's words spin through my mind. *I won't let her pick the wrong side again.* Melanie chose good over evil, interfering with Malicevile's sick plans of demonic conquest. I don't know what he has to gain by holding her soul hostage, but I know it isn't good.

"I'm on your side," I say quietly. "I always have been."

Dylan smiles sadly, gently rubbing my arm. "I wish it were that simple, but you don't make that decision. Your soul does, and I see yours is on the fence teetering both ways."

My inner demon. The demonic blood running through my veins taints my soul enough to leave me straddling the line of good and evil, and there doesn't seem to be anything I can do about it. I don't even think a blood transfusion could save my soul from playing on Team Evil. The possibility of me being demon bound—evil bound—doesn't seem right. How could I be born with a fifty percent chance of automatically falling for evil? It doesn't seem fair.

"Why hasn't anyone told me this sooner? You know, when I still thought I was human?" I'm not asking Dylan for an answer, but I can't help wonder out loud.

Dylan shrugs. "It wasn't my place."

I smile sadly. "I know. Alana would've kicked your ass anyways if you'd tried. And don't change the subject. I need to know the answer."

Dylan pulls me against him with the hand that's cradling my back. "All I'm going to say is that if there isn't a guide to direct the souls where they should be, Malicevile can recollect them."

My stomach heaves, sick over the information. I didn't do anything for those souls but simply left a mess for Malicevile to clean up.

"No." I moan into Dylan's shirt, heavy guilt lacing around my heart. "I should've grabbed more."

"You didn't know, love." Dylan kisses the top of my head. "And you did well. You saved three souls this week. That's more than most people can save in a lifetime."

I clutch my mom's soul like a life preserver amid a stormy sea. I just hope it's enough to save my own soul in the end.

My muscles ache, and I'm in more pain than I was before I fell asleep in Dylan's arms. Evan parks the truck at a gas station with bright, fluorescent lights illuminating the pumps. I've lost track of time, confusion clouding my mind, because we should've been back at the academy by now. I know I've slept more than thirty minutes.

Dylan lifts me in his arms, carefully jumping from the tailgate and onto the cement ground. I wince at the sudden movement and manage to open my eyes a sliver.

Evan and Alana talk quietly, standing in front of the hood of the truck. Cadence messes with the nozzle of the gas pump. I'm elated to see them here but nervous because they aren't waiting for me back at the academy. I thought Evan was the only one in the truck.

"I was able to stop the bleeding, but we need to get her medical attention sooner rather than later. She was badly bitten by a hellhound," Dylan says, placing me into Evan's arms.

I bury my face into his shoulder, breathing in his warm amber and patchouli scent. His lips gently touch my forehead, and I wrap my arms around him, squeezing him as hard as I can manage.

"I'm going to destroy that bastard," Evan says, his deep voice vibrating in his throat.

He opens the door of the truck and maneuvers into it without letting me go. Dylan slides in on the other side, my dirty, bare feet resting limply in his lap. I cringe, noticing how disgusting they look, and I can't help the embarrassment warming my cheeks.

Alana and Cadence sit in the front, with Alana behind the wheel as usual because of her control issues. She glances over her shoulder, sadness rimming her eyes, before starting the truck and pulling back on the road.

The silence is deafening, like my friends are mourning the loss of my life even though I'm still hanging on. I've felt death on my doorstep before and this is nothing compared to the feeling of my life coming really close to being snuffed out, but I'm hurt and cold and afraid for what happens next. I'd be seriously surprised if Malicevile hasn't burned his white flag yet.

"Stop acting like you're at a funeral," I mumble, shifting in Evan's lap to find a more comfortable position.

"This isn't a time to joke," Dylan says softly. "We were close to arranging yours."

I sigh. "Did you ever think that maybe I need some comedy after what I've been through? I feel like crap, look like crap, and I'm pretty sure I smell like crap. It's over, and I'm safe, so can we all just move on?" The words come out harsher than I expect. I don't mean to be catty. I just want to forget this ever happened.

"We can move on after you give us an explanation," Alana says, her white knuckles gripping the steering wheel.

I swallow as a million lies swirl through my mind. "It's not a big deal. I just happened to be in the wrong place at the wrong time." I sound like a cliché, but the truth is harder to deliver.

"Go ahead, Cami. Tell them," Dylan says, patting the top of my filthy foot.

I inhale a long, lung-expanding breath. "Remember when I said I killed that hellhound?" Cadence turns, looking at me from over her seat. "Well, I didn't."

Cadence purses her lips. "But—"

I raise my sore palm to interrupt her. "I couldn't. She wasn't completely broken, so I thought, well, I hoped I could save her soul with a little help."

The muscles in Evan's arms tense, and he releases his breath, blowing into my hair. "Dylan, you—"

"Stop! It wasn't his fault." My shrill voice echoes through the cab of the truck. "He didn't know what I was getting him into. But, it worked. He saved Lola from eternal damnation. He helped her transform back into a werewolf."

"Oh. My. God," Cadence says. "This is huge! Imagine what we could do for the werewolf community."

"You're getting off topic. That doesn't explain how you ended up bargaining with Malicevile," Alana says calmly. "But it is amazing news." A small smile plays on her lips, and I can see glowing pride in her steely gray eyes.

"It's my fault," Dylan says, speaking up for me.

I wish he hadn't though. Evan's face lines with rage, and I notice fire blazing behind his eyes. Turning my head, I look him dead in the eye, pleading with him to stay calm and to not get upset.

"After Lola turned human again, I realized I couldn't fly

with them both, so I left Cami to walk back to the academy by herself."

"You stupid angel! This is your fault." Evan motions to me lying placidly across their laps.

"Calm down, Evan." Alana taps her fingers on the steering wheel. "I'm sure Cami didn't give him a choice, just like she didn't give us a choice when the church was burning. Be mad at Cami, not Dylan."

Thanks a lot, Alana. What a way to stand up for me. I know she's right, that Evan—all of them—have a right to be mad at me but blatantly stating it out loud makes me feel worse than I already do.

"I can't," Evan whispers, kissing my hair.

"If you guys keep interrupting me, I'm not going to finish," I say. "Anyway, to make a long story short, I saved a man's soul by offering Malicevile twenty-four hours of my time, but then once it was over, I couldn't just walk out peacefully. I shattered the cases he keeps his souls in to save this one." I hold up the crystal cylinder for everyone to see. "I went through Hell because this soul deserves better. It's my mom's," I whisper. I don't regret the hurt, fear, and pain I've been through because it was worth it. I'd do it again if I had to.

"Oh, Cami. God, I'm so sorry," Alana says. "I didn't know."

"No one did. But it's over now. She's safe." I lean into Evan. He rubs his fingers over the crystal cylinder in amazement. Dylan watches with a frown furrowing his brows.

"So, can we please go back to the academy? I just want to sleep in my own bed tonight." My heart thunders when no one responds to my request. "What aren't you guys telling me?" I ask.

"Until David can prove your innocence, the alliance has found you guilty for breaching their punishment. If you go back, you'll head straight for jail."

DON'T LET GO

IT'S LIKE THE world is closing in on me, washing away every-thing I've worked so hard to get. The safety and protection from the alliance, honing my abilities, a place to live—and here I find myself on the run from the people I trusted to be on my side. The people I thought were good.

It's like the Hunter's Alliance is picking on me, judging me as if I'm a demon myself. My sister's life is shadowing mine, where it feels like everything she did wrong is coming back to haunt me, even though I have only just found out about her existence.

"They're going to think I'm guilty, and that I purposely

disobeyed them." I gaze out the window, watching the scenery blur by. "What about your dad, Cadence? Couldn't he do something?"

Cadence peeks over the headrest. "Um, about that. My dad is walking a thin, dangerous line right now because of his previous insistence of a lighter punishment."

Great. This is just great. Not only does the alliance believe I'm evil, but they're going to start blaming my friends for associating with me. If an alliance leader can get in trouble, my friends will be the next ones in the spotlight.

"Can I please catch a break?" I say it to whoever is on my side who will listen. Dylan's lecture about the bigger picture floats through my mind. How will I know if I have chosen the right side? *I suppose it's the one that Malicevile isn't part of.*

Alana turns down a winding road, and the headlamps illuminate the dry, empty dirt fields. The faint glow emitting from the porch light of a house in the distance welcomes our arrival. There's an old, beaten up minivan that looks like it hasn't been driven in a while parked on a gravel driveway. It's coated in a layer of dust thick enough to make the color look brown, which reminds me of Desertville, the small town where Cadence's grams lives.

The house looks like it belongs in a neighborhood of tract homes. Its structure is identical to those in new communities sprouting everywhere in California, with its stucco walls that come in the standard peach, gray, yellow, and brown colors. The garage door is shut, probably hiding the junk people tend to accumulate and store in there instead of cars, and the second story windows are dark. I don't know if the owners are expecting our arrival, or if we're going to drop in.

"Who lives here?" I ask, curious to discover who I'm going to meet.

"Someone you already know," Dylan says cryptically. He gets out of the truck, shutting the door behind him and jogs to the door alone.

A girl steps out, her brown hair tumbling over her shoulders, and hugs Dylan a little too tightly. I watch their silent conversation, with Dylan furiously waving and pointing at the truck. The girl subtly nods.

Alana shuts off the engine, gets out, and comes around to open the door for Evan. He hands me to her, and she graciously accepts my weight like the strong hunter she is. Cadence slides from the truck, hovering next to my head, then lightly kisses my forehead before I'm handed back to Evan.

My teeth chatter from the sudden change in temperature, from the heated truck to the cool night, and I press closer to Evan. He strolls so smoothly to the door, my body doesn't rock or sway in his arms.

I immediately recognize the girl as Dylan's nephilim friend who brought me something to eat when I was in jail. Katie frowns, assessing my bloody, beaten body, wrinkling her smooth complexion. Her dark black eyes roam from my face to my toes, stopping on my mom's soul clutched in my hands. Her plump lips are stained a deep red color, while the rest of her face is made up with subtle, natural browns that accentuate her natural nephilim beauty. She's wearing a simple, deep brown shift dress with golden ballerina flats, which she taps lightly against the cement patio.

"I'll do the best I can to fix you up, but you have to leave by morning," Katie says, speaking solely to me. She cautiously peers around before motioning us to follow her inside.

For the way Katie presents herself, her living room is surprisingly drab. There's an old, blue couch positioned against a white wall and a scuffed up coffee table in front of it. A threadbare tan rug covers the stained sky blue carpet, and a soot blackened fireplace across from the couch doesn't look like it's had a warm fire blazing in it in years.

Alana and Cadence disappear with Katie down a hallway, and Evan sits on the couch with me still snuggling against him. My arms lock tightly around his neck, and I'll refuse to let go even if he asks me to.

Dylan shifts his feet, standing in the middle of the room, before moving to perch on the arm of the couch. His white T-shirt is stained with dirt and blood, and his eyes look tired, but he manages to smile at me.

I nuzzle against Evan, breathing in his warm scent. "I thought the alliance took care of its employees," I say, breaking the solemn silence.

"It does," Evan says in my ear.

"Katie technically doesn't work for the alliance," Dylan says, interrupting. "She visits when her presence is needed but tries not to get involved. What she does though, is provide refuge to creatures in need of a place to stay when the alliance won't offer them one. You could call her a non-human activist of sorts."

My heart warms, knowing that there are people in the world who fight for rights the alliance has taken away. "Why didn't we come here instead of the academy in the first place?" I ask. "I would've been better off, don't you think?"

"No. The alliance provides demonic protection with the help of religious affiliates, and even though Katie is seen in grace with God to the alliance, she could never ask for that kind of help. They wouldn't give it to her because the alliance thinks we're abominations. You know they only ask for our help and let most of us live peacefully because they don't have a choice. A purely human organization would easily be destroyed, so they've traded holy protection for the use of our powers and strength but only to those who are half human to maintain a good reputation for whoever they think they're fighting for," Evan answers.

His voice deepens as he continues. "This has been happening for so long that creatures have forgotten there are other options and choices they can make. Alana made the decision for you because she thought it was best. That's until the alliance started paying close attention to you. Even if David were able to bring you back into their good graces, we're not going back. He's only trying to stop them from hunting you down."

I close my eyes, suppressing the anxiety filling my chest. If

I hadn't made the deal with Malicevile, I would've never found out about any of this. *When will the secrets stop?*

I'm too exhausted to be angry, and my demonic abilities have shut down, leaving me feeling empty and useless yet preciously human.

"Cami, say something," Evan whispers.

"What am I supposed to say? That I'm fine? I'm sick and tired of finding out things when I'm too weak to make my own decisions. Do you know what it's like to feel like you don't know anything? That your options have been limited? I've always thought there were two sides—good and evil. You don't know what it feels like to be hunted by the good and bad guys. I have nowhere to go, no place to fit in, and apparently I can't even make my own choice of which side I want to play for because my *soul* has the authority to make that decision, and right now it wants nothing more than for all this to go away. Maybe I'm better off being on my own team."

I thought I was too tired to be angry, but I guess I was wrong. Tears burn my eyes, and my heart pounds in my ears. It takes everything in me not to scream. How did my life turn into such a mess? I'd take being on the run with Alana any day rather than sitting here, figuring out what happens next for me.

"Cami, calm down," Dylan says softly.

"I don't want to calm down!" I yell. "Stop telling me to calm down. It's not like I have any dangerous powers anymore."

"Cami—"

"Dylan, leave. Now," Evan snaps.

Dylan raises his hands in defense but doesn't argue. I watch through narrowed eyes as he disappears down the hallway.

Hurt, fear, anger—all these negative emotions roll through me, causing my body to tremble. Evan holds me, petting my tangled hair while kissing the tears dripping down my face.

"Don't cry. Please, don't cry," Evan whispers. "We're going to get through this."

I inhale deeply. "How do you know?"

"Because I have faith," he murmurs.

"In who?" I ask, my fragile nerves beginning to settle.

"In you—in us. We're getting out of here tomorrow, and we won't look back. We'll live by our own rules on our own terms. You have me, Alana, Cadence, David, and even Dylan if you want him around at your side. We'll figure this out."

"What about Malicevile and the alliance?"

Evan's words should comfort me, but the lingering fear of my enemies makes it hard to believe it'll be easy. Malicevile will be after me come nightfall, and I'm sure the Hunter's Alliance already has an army awaiting orders. The people around me— the people I love most in this world—will get hurt. They could get killed or worse.

"We'll be ready for them when the time comes."

Evan kisses my cheek, then my lips. I respond, shivering, the pain subsiding the longer and deeper he kisses me. His hand draws circles on my back. His other tangles in my hair, pulling me closer. I wish this moment wouldn't end. My love and de- sire for him outweighs every negative thing in my life. It feels like with him, nothing bad could happen—he won't let it happen.

His warm breath tickles my collarbone as he nuzzles my neck, kissing along my jaw line. I lean my head back, enjoying the tingling sensation rolling through me. Each kiss is like the lick of a flame, searing its touch into my memory.

Someone clears their voice. "Looks like you're feeling better." Katie stands in the entrance of the hallway holding a first aid kit with Dylan gazing with sad eyes over her shoulder.

I suppress the pang of guilt and nod. "A little," I whisper, bowing my head in embarrassment.

Katie rolls her eyes before strolling into the room. Dylan takes a step to follow, then hesitates, turns around, and disappears again. Katie glances at his fleeting shadow from over her shoulder. She shifts her gaze back toward me and frowns.

She sets the first aid kit on the coffee table. "Without his help, this might take a while."

"I can help," Evan says, easing me forward to get off the couch.

She waves her hand, stopping him from moving. "No. I need you to hold her down."

My stomach twists. The only reason why Evan would have to hold me is if her healing techniques will hurt me. *Please, don't let there be holy water involved.*

My breath comes in shallow puffs as my hands grow clammy. I know the hellhound bite was bad, but how bad? I haven't tried to walk since Dylan swooped from the sky, just like the guardian angel he is. I don't know if I could walk if my life depended on it.

"It'll be easier if you cradle her again," Katie says.

Evan shifts my weight to his lap without a word.

She touches her cool fingers to my cheek. "Now, Cami, I suggest you close your eyes. This is going to be nasty."

I squeeze my eyes shut for a second but peek through my lashes when cool air stings my leg. My gorge rises at the sight of the damage to my leg from the hellhound bite. The skin around the gaping wound swells and turns a deeper purple by the minute. The wound itself doesn't even look like my leg; it looks like a bloody steak, skinless and raw, with several deep slashes where the hellhound's teeth penetrated and dragged when I fell over the wall.

I bite my lip, the fear of pain slicing through me deeper than the wounds on my leg. Katie lifts my leg and places a dark towel underneath it before pulling a long pair of tweezers from the first aid kit.

"How in the world did you end up with both of the hellhound's fangs embedded in your bone?" Katie asks, shock lacing her words.

I gag at the revelation. "We played tug of war."

"I'm glad you won, but this is going to hurt like Hell. Extracting teeth is never easy, and unfortunately I don't have painkillers."

I dig my fingernails into the palms of my hands. "Just get it over with. Talking about it is making it worse."

She holds up a long pair of tweezers. "Got it. I'm ready when you are."

"Do it."

"Take a deep breath on the count of three. One. Two. Three."

As I try to inhale a gulp of air, pain erupts in my leg like nothing I've felt before. I scream a long, high-pitched wail and thrash against Evan. I'd rather live with the hellhound teeth in my leg than go through this. I'm sure I'll die from the pain.

My stomach lurches, and my eyes widen as fiery pain explodes from my leg again. Evan squeezes me against him, my arms flailing, grabbing for anything I can hold onto. My throat aches, burning from my screams, and the world darkens as I gasp for air. I begin to panic and kick furiously, my leg jerking and twitching with uncontrollable spasms.

"It's almost over." Evan sounds far away, his voice muffled from my screams.

Shadows cast across the room; everything darkens around me. My eyes twitch, and I lose focus. It feels like I'm separating from my body. I can't handle the pain, the suffering. I don't want to fight this anymore. I need to let it all go.

My ears pop, and suddenly the pain stops completely. I watch as Evan cradles my lifeless body, whispering into my hair. The room blurs, covered in an eerie, filmy haze. I'm levitating a foot off the ground, startled and uneasy looking down at myself.

"Dylan, get in here! I'm losing her!" Katie screams.

"What's happening?" Evan shouts, tears shining in his eyes.

"Her soul is too weak to handle the pain. It's ripped itself free."

I gape down at what I know is not my body. It looks like I'm covered in shadows with small pinpricks of light glowing through deep cracks in my translucent skin. I don't feel any different besides the absence of pain. It's like I'm using my levitation to defy gravity, except for the fact that my body is shuddering and convulsing five feet away.

Dylan rushes into the room with Cadence and Alana behind him. He stops short, and I'm caught by surprise when he looks directly at me and not my body. He reaches out his hand to me, but I don't move.

"You have to go back, love," he whispers. "You're going to die if you don't."

"I don't know how," I say, but I don't hear the words. It's like I'm speaking telepathically.

I glance at Evan rocking my body, his face buried in my hair. Black mascara is smeared down Cadence's cheeks and she wraps her arm around Alana's shoulders. Alana's mouth moves without sound, and I think she might be yelling.

The light from Dylan's wings brings my eyes back to his. They look different, painted in gold and solid. They expand from his back, brushing the ceiling, before they swoop forward and wrap around me.

"Take my hand and don't let go."

Dylan's wings encourage me to glide forward, pushing me closer to him. He offers his hand to me, and I slowly reach out

to take it. The moment our fingers meet, the world melts away.
I'm left hovering in a white void with no one around except my
guardian angel.

FLAME OF HOPE

"WHAT'S HAPPENING TO me?"

Dylan grips my hands in his fingers, his deep, chocolate-brown eyes peering into my very soul.

"Please, forgive me, love." He brings my hands to his lips and kisses them. "I was reckless and unthinking, and I let my emotions get the best of me. I let you down."

Fear slithers up my spine. "Am I dead?" I glance around the white space. It's not what I thought either Heaven or Hell would look like. There's not a silver-lined cloud or fiery pit in sight. Just the bright, stark white atmosphere. *Purgatory. I'm trapped in Purgatory just like in life.*

Dylan sighs. "No, but you were pretty damn close because of me."

I frown, tilting my head to the side to determine if he's joking. Why does he think it's his fault for me being here? "You didn't do anything wrong. I almost died because of Maliceville."

Dylan shakes his head, and his curly black hair falls in his eyes. "I should've healed your soul the moment I saw you. I knew it was weak. I saw the damage. But I didn't do a damn thing about it."

"It's not your job to constantly have to fix the damage I do to my own soul," I say.

"Then what else am I supposed to do?" Dylan cups my face, his serious expression making me lean closer.

It takes everything in me to look away. "I don't know. Get a hobby or something."

He glances down, cheeks flushing, and then laughs. His musical voice lightens the morbid mood. "I have a hobby."

I find the will to smile at him. "And what's that?" I ask.

"You."

<hr>

Evan's shallow breathing tickles my ear, and I twist to face him, my leg tender as the bandages rub against the couch. My skin's clean, and my hair is braided down my back. I'm wearing an unfamiliar baggy T-shirt and pajama shorts and seem to be the only one awake at this early, dark hour.

I kiss Evan softly, my lips lingering on his until his eyes flutter open. He smiles, his eyes shining with relief as he kisses me again. My fingers touch his scratchy cheeks and I pull him closer. I don't want to let him go after last night. The realization hits me hard. *I almost died.*

"I love you," I whisper through eager kisses.

"God, it's so good to hear you say that." He gently bites my lip, then kisses me deeper. "I love you more than life itself, Cami. I've never been so terrified in my life of anything until I thought I lost you," he whispers against my lips.

I run my fingers through his silky, dark blond hair. "I could never leave you. I'd haunt you if I had to."

I wrap my leg over his, pressing closely against him. His heart beats hard, thudding through his thin T-shirt as I slide my arms under his, touching my chest to his. He inhales sharply, excited by our closeness, and runs his hands under my shirt, rubbing his warm fingers along my lower back, sending chills through me.

He carefully rolls on top of me, his legs inside of mine. I kiss him harder, desperately, enjoying the heat of his skin on mine. My hands trail under his shirt, and I trace light circles on his taut back, memorizing every curve with my fingertips.

The phone rings, startling me, and Evan rolls to his feet. I moan, wondering who would be calling Katie so early. Dawn isn't coming for another hour.

The answering machine clicks on, Katie's voice speaking smoothly and happily through the speaker before a loud beep announces for the caller to leave a message.

I hold my breath, hearing an all too familiar voice. "Hi,

Katie, this is David Whiteshaw."

Evan dashes to the phone, yanking it off the receiver to answer it before David hangs up. He presses it to his ear, and I watch as his flushed cheeks turn chalk white. After mumbling something I can't hear, Evan sets the phone down, bowing his head.

He rubs a hand over his face before looking at me. "You've been found guilty," he whispers. "The alliance received an anonymous phone call relaying that you had made a deal with a demon. There's a warrant out for your arrest."

I'm shocked speechless. I knew I was a fugitive, but I didn't think the alliance would seriously put effort into finding me. It's not like I can conquer the world and kill everyone. I'm not a threat to their precious existence.

And the phone call? My friends wouldn't betray me like that would they? They're here with me now, and David, he's been fighting to save me. But who? Who hates me enough to want to guarantee that I have nowhere to go?

Malicevile...My father's name stabs my heart like a serrated knife, cutting and twisting, ripping it from my chest. I double over, my head resting on my knees, and I dig my fingers into the couch cushion, squeezing it like it's the only thing I can hold on to.

My mouth goes dry, and all of the happiness, excitement, and love from being so close to Evan rushes out of me, leaving behind a bitter residue of loss and defeat.

I knew this could happen. Evan warned me of the consequences, but it doesn't make it easier to deal with. Finding hope is like trying to find a crack of light in a pit of darkness. If only I could find it, I could keep fighting, keep trying to fix things. No matter how hard I look for a small flame of hope, it just isn't there. The darkness is all-consuming. I'm hopeless.

I lean my head to the side, my chin resting on my knees. "It'll be okay. We expected this." My voice falls flat, like the unconvincing words I said out loud were more for my benefit than Evan's.

His crystalline blue eyes darken. "There's one more thing I need to tell you." He shuffles forward, placing his shaking hand on my back. "If a hunter finds you, their order is to kill you if you resist their arrest and anyone who tries to stop them."

I swallow the dread rising up in my throat, torn and outraged that the alliance could do something like this. It's one thing to want me dead, but to murder the people who love me because they want to save me is just as evil as a demon's action. I can't let them get away with this.

"They can't do that." I glare at the floor. "It doesn't make them any different from the monsters they try so hard to destroy. We have to do something. We have to fight."

"We're not strong enough. It'd be suicide," Evan says quietly.

I sigh. "Does it really matter? I'm already dead. At least I can take a few of them with me."

The idea sends dizziness rolling through my head, and I close my eyes until it subsides. It feels like my soul has shifted, leaving me unbalanced and on edge. Would I really kill alliance members so that I could live? *Yes.* The foreign thought doesn't leave a bitter taste in my mouth. Instead, it fills me with relief and the hope I've been looking for. If the alliance chooses who lives and dies, then so can I.

"Cami, please, don't say that. You don't really mean it." Evan's voice cracks with the words.

My inner demon awakens, hungry and excited, and I can't stop the craving for revenge. "I do mean it. If the alliance has their black little hearts set on believing I'm demon bound, then I will be. I won't be bound to Malicevile or any other demon. I'll be bound to me."

Small tendrils of rosy light beam into the window as I watch the sun rise. It warms my cool skin, filling me with the energy I need to make it through another day. The lingering thoughts of death and destruction are banished by the cleansing light, giving me the strength to think clearly.

I'm not going to put my friends at risk because of my thirst for revenge. I don't even know what came over me. The stress of my death sentence was all-consuming, but when it comes down to it, I could never resort to the alliance's ways.

Evan kisses my cheek softly, wrapping his arm around my waist. "So, you'll run away with me?" he asks, tickling my ear with his warm breath.

I lean my head on his shoulder. "Yes," I whisper. "I was just so angry. I said some things I shouldn't have."

"I'm glad, because I don't want to lose you. You mean everything to me."

Alana and Cadence walk into the room, both dressed in the same clothes as yesterday, looking like neither of them got any sleep.

I wave my fingers, smiling. "Are you sure you can handle this, Cadence? You can change your mind."

Cadence narrows her eyes. "Are you trying to get rid of me? You know I made the decision to run with you the day we met. So what if I'm giving up my fabulous apartment for long car rides and sleazy motels? We'll have a whole lot of fun while doing it."

I smile, shrugging my shoulders. "If you say so."

"I'll make sure of it." Cadence winks, strutting to the door in her skinny jeans and halter top, her purple hair bouncing against her back. She opens the front door and turns before going outside. "Five minutes or your ride is leaving without you," she says, shutting the door behind her.

I raise my eyebrows, glancing at Alana who shrugs. "We're taking turns."

Evan pushes to his feet, offering his hand to help me up. My knees wobble, but I manage to find my balance, wincing only a little at the tenderness of my feet. I concentrate on levitating but fail, unable to access my demonic abilities.

Katie rushes into the room with two plastic bags hanging from her wrist. She gives them to Alana before turning to me and hands over a black track suit, socks, and sneakers from under her arm.

"You're all set to go," Katie says, wrapping her arm around me. "Good luck."

Tears spring to my eyes knowing that the entire world isn't against me. That there are people like Katie to help those in need. She truly is an angel—a saving grace.

"Thank you," I whisper.

Evan leads me to the door, and Alana follows as we make our way to the alliance issued truck they somehow obtained. Evan slides into the backseat, and I hesitate, looking around for Dylan.

He appears at the door next to Katie but doesn't move. I wave, motioning him to hurry up, and I see him noticeably slump his shoulders before coming to meet me.

His chocolate eyes, lined with worry, stare deeply into mine, causing my heart to skip a beat. He grabs my hands lightly, pulling them against his chest, his heart beating faster than a dragonfly's wings. He doesn't speak. He just stares at me with his sad, sad eyes.

I bite my lip, my stomach twisting into a thousand knots. "You're not coming with us." I can see the answer in his eyes, and I know it's the truth.

He nods his head without answering.

"But why? I need you." Hot, salty tears rim my eyes. This can't be happening. He's supposed to come with me. I was only kidding when I said it wasn't his job to look out for my soul. I don't want to be without him. He's *my* angel.

"I'm sorry," he manages to say. I step closer, hugging him as tightly as I can. "I just can't."

"I can't do this without you." My heart breaks. "You're my best friend."

"Yes, you can, love," he whispers. "Just remember that whatever your soul has decided, there's still hope."

Dylan breaks away from me, and I know there is nothing I can do to change his mind. I watch helplessly as he strolls back to the house, going inside without one last glance.

Katie raises her hand to me, and I smile weakly, trying to hold myself together.

"Goodbye, Dylan," I whisper. "Goodbye, my angel."

OUT OF TIME

I REST MY head on Evan's arm as we drive down an all too familiar freeway. My heart flips in my chest, the brown, dry landscape whizzing by as Cadence races well over the speed limit.

"We aren't seriously going to Vivian's," I say as Cadence merges off the freeway and onto good old Highway 395.

"We don't have a choice," Alana says, peeking over the headrest. "We need her help." She shifts in her seat, bringing her eyes back to the road ahead of us.

"But I'm not welcome here anymore because of the werewolves," I mutter.

"Don't worry about it. We're only going to stay for a few minutes," Cadence says. "Grams can tell us where to go, and we need to get the weapons I left there."

Cadence has a good point. It would be too risky to stop by any safe house because they're all run by the alliance. It's our only chance of getting off to a good start.

Evan squeezes my hand reassuringly, unfazed by my reaction toward Dylan's goodbye. I breathe in his amber and patchouli scent, letting the warm aroma ease my sorrow. I just wish it didn't have to end like that, but I know it's for the best. Dylan was my guardian angel, but Evan is my heart and soul, and has been nothing but good to me.

"I love you," he says, breathing into my hair. I lift my chin and kiss him sweetly on the lips.

The old, faded yellow, Victorian house comes into view, exactly as I remember it. Cadence turns off the highway and onto the dirt road, parking just before the wrought iron gate. She opens her door, gets out, and pushes the gate open since she doesn't have the remote to it.

She hops back into the truck and slowly drives forward, the tires bumping and shaking on the gravel driveway. She pulls behind the house instead of the front, parking by the back porch. I see Vivian standing in the kitchen doorway.

I rush out of the truck and limp to her, throwing my arms around her frail shoulders. Her honey brown eyes crinkle as she smiles, and her short gray hair is neatly brushed behind her ears.

"It's so good to see you, Cami," she says. "But didn't I tell you not to come without the nephilim?"

I pull away and look Vivian in the eyes. "Dylan, he—" I pause, taking a breath. "He couldn't make it."

Vivian frowns, clutching my hands harder than I thought possible. "This isn't good. If he's not with you, then he's with *them*." She says the "them" like whoever they are, are our worst enemies. My heart sinks when I realize she's talking about the alliance.

"What is that supposed to mean? Will the alliance hurt him?" I couldn't live with myself if the alliance harms Dylan. He's the epitome of good with his angelic status, and I pray that the alliance takes that into consideration since they believe they're the protectors of good.

"No, not physically. But what it does mean is that you're running out of time." Vivian swiftly turns on her heels and walks into the kitchen.

What is that supposed to mean? I'm running out of time? Time for what? I hate when Vivian gives unclear predictions. They always leave me feeling unnerved and out of control.

I rush into the kitchen with Evan, Cadence, and Alana right behind me. Vivian wrings her hands together, staring at the kitchen sink. The memory of her in this exact position when the werewolf pack arrived to drag me to my execution comes to mind.

I can't suppress the irksome feeling of foreboding rolling through me.

"You know where everything is, Cadence. I want you to

grab your things and leave," Vivian says.

"But, Grams, we just got here," Cadence argues.

"And now you must leave. I don't want you bringing the alliance to my door," she says.

I've never seen Vivian act like this toward Cadence, and I can see the hurt and betrayal glowing in Cadence's honey brown eyes. She bows her head and jogs from the kitchen. I rush behind her and catch her before she makes it into her room.

I grab her arm, stopping her. "It's okay, Cadence. We weren't planning on staying long anyways."

Cadence peeks at me through tear-soaked lashes. "I know. It's just—I don't know what has gotten into her. She's supposed to be happy we're here, not throwing us out like we're bringing Lucifer himself to her doorstep."

I release her arm and follow her into her room. She runs her fingers along her bed, probably remembering what it felt like to live here. She heads to her dresser, thrusting the third drawer open, and pulls out a wooden box. Setting it on her dresser, she flings the lid open and grabs a long, sheathed dagger.

"We'll need this," she says, dropping it into a backpack sitting on her desk.

I nod my head, placing the small pile of clothes I had tucked under my arm on the bed. "You don't happen to have alliance repellent do you?" I say jokingly to lighten the mood.

She smiles, shaking her head. "It would be useful now

wouldn't it?"

I pull off the baggy T-shirt and slip into the racer back tank top before putting on the track pants. I step into the sneakers, which are a size too big, before glancing over Cadence's shoulder to look at the photograph of her and her father she's staring at.

"Is it wrong that I'm starting to hate him?" Cadence asks, placing the photo face down. "All my life I've looked up to him. And now, the things he's doing for the alliance makes me sick to my stomach. I miss his hunting days when he actually stood for something, you know."

I pat her shoulder. "Maybe he still does. Like you said earlier, he's walking a fine line. I'm sure he's doing all he can to help me."

"You're probably right," Cadence says, sighing while giving me a hug.

A light tap sounds on the door, and Alana pops her head in and says, "We need to get going. The farther we get, the easier it'll be to find a safe place tonight."

Cadence follows behind Alana, and I hesitate, glancing one last time at Cadence's room. I shut the door quietly and shuffle down the hall back to the living room. Cadence and Alana stand at the door to the kitchen and don't move to enter.

Muffled voices sound out from within, and I slowly back up, fear seizing my heart. Alana looks over her shoulder at me, her brows knitted together, and mouths, "Run."

I don't question her. I just do it.

I race back to Cadence's bedroom, my jaw clenching when I hear Alana and Cadence join the argument in the kitchen. I swing open the bedroom door and lock it behind me. I don't know who's in the kitchen, but I know whoever it is can't be good. I bet it's the werewolves back to finish what they started, but I'm not going to risk finding out.

I carefully pull back her curtains an inch to make sure no one is standing on the other side. I slide the window open, pop off the screen, and step out onto the balcony. Alana told me to run, but she didn't say where, so I climb down the ladder that Cadence kept for an easy escape, and press against the wall as I glide toward the front of the house. I reach the corner, my heart beating wildly in my chest.

A strong hand grabs my arm and I scream, but the sound is quickly muffled when another hand slaps over my mouth. My heart jumps from my shirt, sheer panic racing through my veins. I use my free hand, punching blindly without making contact. *Oh, God, help me!*

"Cami, it's me," Evan says. "Come on. We have to hurry."

He scoops me into his arms and breaks into a jog, jumping and moving quickly through the desert brush. Evan's heart pounds, the comforting feeling easing the fear of having to leave Alana and Cadence behind. *They'll be okay...*

The fence surrounding the property is no more than twenty feet away, but I don't know how far we can keep running without a vehicle.

"We have to hide," I whisper, afraid my voice will echo

through the silent day.

Evan ducks behind one of the large boulders scattered throughout Vivian's property. He leans against it, his chest heaving, and sets me on my feet.

"I can't believe the werewolf pack had the nerve to come here," I say, angry that I didn't even have a moment to catch my breath.

"I wouldn't be running from a mangy pack," Evan says. "Two hunters have arrived."

I gasp, covering my mouth with my hand. I grip the surface of the sun-heated rock to steady my wobbly knees. If the hunters find me, I'm going to die. I can't go back to the academy. I just can't.

"She's not here!" My breathing quickens hearing Alana's scream. I crouch low, my palms touching the grainy dirt. I crane my neck, peering from behind the rock to an unfamiliar hunter gripping her short blond hair, pressing a dagger to her exposed neck.

"You're lying." The man's voice comes out like a growl. "I should kill you right now for aiding a demon. You're a disgrace to all humankind."

I squeeze my eyes shut, unable to watch Alana struggle in the hunter's arms. I can't bear the thought of her giving her life up to save me.

Evan jerks out his hand, grabbing onto my tank top. He furiously shakes his head, holding up his index finger to his lips.

"Kill me and you're no better than a demon." Alana spits,

wriggling in the hunter's arms. He's just out of her reach, and she can't do anything to break free without injuring herself on the dagger.

I look past Alana and see Cadence crying on Vivian's shoulder while another hunter threatens them with his dagger. My stomach lurches, and I think I'm going to be sick. Even though the hunters don't know I'm here, they'd probably kill my friends to get to me.

"Cami Anders! You better show yourself, or I'm going to kill your guardian!" the hunter yells.

Evan's eyes plead with me to stay put, but I can't watch as Alana is threatened, when she hasn't done anything wrong except for save my life a million times over.

I break away from Evan and thrust myself from behind the boulder. "Wait! I give up. Please, just don't hurt her," I beg. "I'll go with you."

The man doesn't loosen his hold on Alana. I step forward, my hands raised in surrender, keeping my eyes locked on Alana's. She begs me not to do this with her eyes, but I'm not going to listen to her this time. I'm not going to let my friends die for me. It's not worth it.

"You stupid girl. You should've have run. I didn't want to have to do this." The hunter jerks his arm, the blade sliding across Alana's neck before he shoves her face first to the ground.

"No!" I scream.

I rush forward to get her, but someone collides into my side, knocking me to the ground. We roll across the rough gravel, legs and arms flailing, until I'm trapped beneath another hunter's weight.

I scream, my voice sounding like a wounded baby animal, reaching my arm out for Alana as she struggles on the ground. The hunter shoves my head to the side, dirt and gravel sticking to my skin. My chest heaves, the world closing around me.

A sharp pain explodes in my cheek and my jaw cracks. My vision blurs, and the last thing I see is blood drip from Alana's fingers before absorbing into the dirt.

HELL-BOUND

"ALANA!" I SCREAM.

Dylan wraps his glorious wings around me. I sob, sparkling tears reflecting in the bright, shining sun. My knees buckle, and I slide to the redbrick ground, gripping my arms around his legs. My shoulders shake, each sob tearing my throat to shreds.

"Cami, what happened?" Dylan tilts my chin up, but he's blurry in my vision. I'm blinded by his luminous light shining through my tears.

"S-send me b-back," I cry.

"I can't, love," Dylan says, petting my hair.

"You have to! Alana's dying!" A long, high-pitched wail

rips from me, but I can't pull it back.

Dylan drops to his knees, embracing me. His warm, ethereal glow penetrates through the darkness shadowing my soul. I can't move. I can't breathe. All I can think about is the world I left behind. Cadence crying in Vivian's arms, Evan begging me not to go, and Alana, my protector, my best friend, the woman who saved my life, dripping blood on the dirt.

I curl up, cradling my knees with my arms as Dylan covers me with his wings, his love, and his soul, trying to push away and protect me from the heartache penetrating me so deeply, I don't know if I can recover from this mess.

"Cami, please calm down. Your soul is weak. You need to stay strong for me," Dylan whispers.

"Why should I?" My anger flows freely, replacing my sorrows. "You were supposed to be there for me and you weren't. You left me again, just like you left me the first time. I hate you! Just leave me alone. I don't care about my soul. I don't even care that the alliance wants me dead. I care about the woman who gave up everything for me, and I can't even be there for her. Unlike you, it's because I can't!"

"You're wrong." Dylan cups my face in his hands. "I love you. I love you more than anything in this life or the next. I can't bear the thought that you're dealing with this without me. But I don't have a choice. Something happened to you last night. Something big. Whatever it was, it shifted your soul so far over, that you and I are no longer fighting for the same thing anymore."

My head spins. "What are you talking about?"

Dylan sighs, hugging me closely. "You're no longer teetering in Purgatory, Cami. You're Hell-bound."

My head feels like it's been slammed into the ground when I open my eyes. The cold room is dark with only a single pale line of light seeping in through under the door. My head rolls, the aching in my skull making it difficult to stay focused.

I'm disoriented, unable to think straight. I vaguely remember Dylan holding me and something red. I can't pinpoint what it is, but my heart pounds and my eyes prickle with tears. I try to move my arms, but they're fastened tightly to the back of the chair. Hard metal bites into my legs, and I can't move them either. I'm trapped in a room with damp air, almost like a basement. The only exit I see is the door, but I can't even move a limb to get to it.

I have no hope for escape.

I fall back into darkness.

"Cami, love, come back to me." Dylan's voice rings in my ears, and I feel his warm touch on my shoulder.

"I-I'm scared, Dylan. I don't know where I am." My voice is frail, weak, and I barely hear it myself.

"I'll find you, love."

"Dylan, help!"

A bright light shines in my eyes and I groan, unable to see past the intrusive light. It burns my eyes, and they sting with tears, the pressure of someone's fingernail holding them open.

"She's waking up," a smooth, melodious voice says.

The bright light blinks off, leaving dark shadows in my vision. My face is sore, and I have a neck ache from having nothing to support it.

The shadows clear from my vision, and Raya smiles at me, her face fully made up, looking like she's ready for a party.

I clear my throat, spitting, and she backs up behind a tall, wide man who's going bald. Four other faces appear, but I only recognize two, one being Clark and the other, Aston. My heart drops as I stare through heavy eyelids at the man who should be on my side.

"Ms. Anders, do you know why you're here?" Clark asks, stepping forward, trying to intimate me with his height towering over me.

"Because you're going to kill me just like you killed Alana!" I scream, rage boiling my blood.

"Where did you hear that?" Aston asks, speaking up. He draws close, staring deeply into my eyes.

"I saw your hunter slit her throat! Your daughter and mother were there to witness." My vision flashes red, my inner demon begging to be released. It slinks and coils in my mind, waiting for the perfect opportunity to strike.

Aston slaps me across the face. "You will *not* bring them into this."

I clench my fingers, twisting and wriggling them in their

bindings. My wrists sting with pain as I rub them raw. I need to get out of here.

"Ms. Anders, it's my duty to inform you that you've been found guilty of treason for dealing with demons and for undermining our authority by not completing your punishment as previously stated. Do you have anything to say for yourself?" Clark says, interjecting.

"Screw you!" I yell, jerking forward. "You can all go to Hell!"

"You're the one we're worried about ending up there, my dear," Raya says softly. "And that's why you're here. We can't let that happen."

I slump forward, unable to move or do anything to protect myself. I've been sentenced to death, and there's nothing I can do to save my own life. I regret never having the chance to say goodbye to the ones I love, and I hope Dylan can find my mother's soul to set her free.

Melanie flashes in my mind, and I envision her in this same chair, in this same predicament, but with different people. It's a vicious cycle, the ways of the Hunter's Alliance, and I wish there was something I could do about it.

But, I can't.

Not in this life, and I'm sure not in the next. Not if I'm Hell-bound like Dylan says. I'll never see anyone I love ever again.

It's the last thing that bothers me the most. Knowing that my soul has chosen the path of evil. I can feel my demonic blood slithering through my veins, tempting me to release it—to taste the power it'll give me. But I resist.

I jerk my head up when the door flies open and blink, unsure if what I'm seeing is real or something my mind is making up to comfort me.

Dylan stands in the doorway with his loose fitted jeans, plain black shirt, and his mess of curls and chocolate-brown eyes I've become so familiar with. His eyes widen in surprise upon seeing me, causing him to hesitate.

"Oh, God, Dylan save me," I beg through red-tinted tears. "Tell them I'm not evil. Tell them how I've saved three souls this week. Tell them anything."

I sigh, leaning my head back to look at the ceiling. Dylan doesn't move or even look at me. His eyes shift to the floor, studying the dirty tiles like they're some precious piece of art. He shoves his hands in his pockets, turning to the people that hold me hostage.

"You didn't say it was her," he says lowly, afraid I'll hear his words. "I won't do this."

"She doesn't deserve her soul and you know it," a man mutters, gripping Dylan's shoulder.

"Calm down, Monte. Can't you see the boy's in love with her," Aston says softly.

"Which he knows was never supposed to happen. He was assigned to monitor her, not fall for her demonic charms. He needs to do this, otherwise I'm afraid to think of the outcome," Monte argues.

Fire burns in my veins, and a deep crimson red coats the world around me. The alliance leaders discuss my life as if it were a simple matter, like I'm a rabid animal that needs to be put out of its misery. And they're using Dylan to help them.

I yank my hands hard against their bindings and feel a warm trickle of blood oozing down my hands, dripping from my fingertips. If I can get out of these ties, I'll still have a fighting chance.

Dylan pushes past the alliance members and strides to me, staring at me for the first time. His chocolate-brown eyes shine with tears, and he presses his lips against my forehead. "I'm so sorry, love. I wish there was some other way." He pets my hair, and his fingers stick in the tangles.

"There's always another way," I whisper. "Don't let them kill me."

"I don't have a choice, Cami. I have a duty as a demon watcher to save the souls of the lost, to help them find peace, and I've been assigned to you."

"You don't have to kill me to save my soul." I shake my head, refusing to believe what Dylan is saying. His angelic father was a demon watcher, not him. He's half human. He has a choice. "Just heal me."

"It's too late for that. You've chosen your side, and I can't risk the damage you are capable of doing," Dylan says, leaning forward, wrapping his arms around me.

I yank away, the crimson haze threatening to overpower my thoughts. The desire for death and blood becomes overwhelming as my inner demon slithers its way to the surface of my soul.

Nothing Dylan can say will change my mind. He's turned into one of *them*, my worst enemy. I've never felt so betrayed in my life, and I'm furious I let myself have feelings for him. His good looks and angelic charms disguised his true identity—he's a liar, a manipulator, and a fake. He doesn't deserve those glorious wings. He deserves the same fate as his fallen father.

"Cami, calm down," Aston says from behind Dylan. "You'll only hurt yourself."

"You think that's the worst of my problems?" My voice echoes through the room.

I tug my bleeding wrists against the wire ropes to keep myself stabilized. I close my eyes, concentrating, and for the first time in hours I find my blessed levitation ability. I pull against the binding, the chair squeaking as I force the bolts to break free.

I've lost control of my inner demon, and it's out for blood and death. My humanity doesn't hold my demonic side back any longer, and I'm unafraid of what will happen to me. I'm not going to sit back and let Dylan take my soul. I'm not going to let the alliance snuff out my life like they did to poor Melanie.

I release the power swirling inside of me and feel it pulsating through my bones.

Dylan presses his lips to my ears, his warm breath feeding my deepest, darkest desires. "I'm going to set you free, love," he whispers, slipping his arms behind my back.

I expect to feel light headed as Dylan squeezes my soul from my body, but all I feel are my hands breaking free from the wire digging into my wrists.

But he shouldn't have released me, because now it's too late. I've allowed my inner demon complete control, and all it wants is to destroy the alliance leaders.

A smile crosses my lips. Because now, as they stand there smugly waiting for my life to end, I'll be more alive than ever.

Now, they'll pay. They'll be the ones to die. And no one will save their souls.

CRUSHED

I PLOW INTO Dylan, knocking him into Raya and Clark who fall back into the others watching patiently. I levitate, hitting my back on the ceiling, devouring the fear pouring from the leaders.

"Dylan move!" I scream, carefully calculating the alliance leaders' next move.

Dylan scrambles to his feet, ducking out of my way in the corner. I fly at Monte, wrapping my small hands around his thick neck, squeezing as tightly as I can. I force him into the wall, cracking the drywall, and slowly lift him off his feet. He grips my hands, trying to pry them open, but the demon within me won't let him get the advantage.

"Cami, behind you," Dylan calls, and I blindly kick out, nailing Clark with the heel of my shoe, under his chin. His head jerks up, bones cracking, before crumbling to the floor.

Flashes of steel draw my attention away from Monte. The leaders finally realize that I'm not going to let them off easily.

Aston points his dagger at me, the sharp blade glinting in the fluorescent lighting. "Don't make me hurt you," he pleads. "I don't want to hurt you."

"You want to kill me!" I scream, the shrill sound making Aston wince.

Monte grabs my hair, yanking my head back, trying to disable me. I elbow him in the throat. His knees buckle, and he chokes and spits, unable to breathe, turning blue before he falls unconscious.

I'm not going to die without a fight. Aston charges me, and I side step, punching him in the elbow. The dagger flies from his fingers, and he grabs his injured arm, stepping back.

"Don't worry, Aston. I'm not going to kill you," I say sweetly, hot fire burning in my chest. "I'm just going to kill everything you stand for. Not for me or Cadence. But for Melanie. Because Melanie was fond of you, I'll save your soul."

Aston's eyes widen as he's taken aback. The alliance doesn't know that I know about Melanie, but I'm not going to let them forget.

"Cami, no!" Dylan yells. "Please. You don't have to do this. Let me help you."

"And then what? Let the leaders go so they can continue to hunt me like an animal? They sent hunters to kill Alana! They murdered Melanie! And now, they want to murder me!"

"You're letting your demonic blood carry you away. You're not a murderer. You can overcome the evil raging inside of you. Please, love, just stop. Stop!"

The dagger falls from my fingertips, clattering to the ground. I cross my arms over my chest, hugging myself. The leaders stare wild-eyed, but none of them attempt to move. Monte and Clark lie on the grimy tiled floor, hurt but still breathing.

My anger slowly dissipates, melting away as Dylan's words sink in. My soul might have shifted, but that doesn't make me a murderer—it doesn't make me evil. Demonic blood flows through my veins, but I still have my humanity. And it's my humanity that will save me.

My feet lightly touch the ground, and I walk across the room, reaching my hand out to Dylan. The moment our fingers meet, something plows into my side, and I crash to the floor. My head smacks the tiles, shadows bursting in my vision, and before I have a chance to move, Raya sits on my chest, pressing the air from my lungs.

"You're an abomination," she says, disgusted. "Did you really think we were going to let you out of here alive?"

I squeeze my eyes shut as Raya pulls her dagger back, aiming for a death blow straight to my heart. Fear slices through me deeper than any knife could ever reach, and I pray silently for a swift death.

The door bangs open, and I peek through my eyelashes expecting to see an army of demon hunters to guarantee my death. Raya hesitates, and I punch her in the nose, sending her reeling backwards. My breath catches in my throat, and I scramble on all fours to Dylan's side.

"A little birdie told me you were in trouble, Camilla," Malicevile drawls. "So I thought I'd pay you a visit."

My mouth runs dry. "You're why I'm here," I whisper hoarsely. "How are you even in this place?"

Malicevile beams a smile. "Does this look like a church to you? Or the academy? The alliance wouldn't dare murder someone on holy ground. With the help of your desperate friends, I've managed to break the blessed barrier."

I glance at Dylan, seeing fear lining his eyes, before looking back at Malicevile. "I'm not trading my soul for your help," I say.

"I'm not asking anything from you," he says. He saunters in from the doorway, dressed in his usual sophisticated suit, turning to the fallen and frightened alliance leaders. "I'm here to make a deal with *them*."

The leaders watch nervously from their places along the wall, shrinking as small as possible to avoid attention from Malicevile. He paces the length of the room, rubbing his smooth chin with his fingers.

He turns to Aston and a woman I've never met before. "You two are of no use to me, so you may leave."

Aston grabs the woman's hand, gazes at me for a split second, and rushes out the door. I sigh, relieved, that Aston didn't catch Malicevile's attention. I couldn't bear to tell Cadence that my demonic father murdered her dad.

Malicevile pauses, smiling wickedly. "Oh, how deliciously foul your soul is." He turns his eyes to Raya. "So young, yet so sinful. Greed, lust, wrath, and my favorite, pride. You'd make a fine asset to my collection." He licks his lips, standing before her, and she cowers when he glides his long fingers along her jaw line.

I try to yank my arm from Dylan, but he holds me against him. "No," he whispers. "You can't save her."

Raya cringes, biting her bloody lip. She squirms but visibly moves closer to Malicevile, trapped by his alluring gaze. She grabs his hands, falling to her knees to grovel. "Please, I'll do anything," she says.

Malicevile's smile dazzles me, and I can't help imagining him on the cover of a magazine. Raya releases her breath when he moves on to Monte still passed out on the floor. He taps his arm with the toe of his shiny designer shoe, and mumbles something to himself.

I watch in horror as he assesses the other alliance leaders. The longer he inspects their flaws, the more excited he grows. My stomach twists, and Dylan grips my arm, refusing to let me go. He's probably more afraid than I am, being so close to my demonic father for the first time.

Malicevile's eyes travel around the room before landing

back on mine. He looks between me and Dylan with a sharply raised eyebrow. "I should kill you, Nephilim," Malicevile says, his green eyes shining brightly.

Dylan gulps, and I lean over, half covering him behind me. "He saved my life," I say, praying Malicevile will take that into consideration.

"I didn't say I would. I said I should," Malicevile says. "But since he did save your life, I'll let him live...for now."

I close my eyes, swallowing hard in relief. Dylan's hands tremble, and he keeps glancing at the door, planning our escape.

"But as for the rest of you—let's just say, you'll make me a very happy demon. I've waited so long for this. You should've learned the first time around to never mess with my daughters."

Everything happens so fast. Malicevile flies across the room, grabs Raya by the head and swiftly breaks her neck. She crumbles to the floor lifelessly, and I know she's dead.

"We have to leave, now!" Dylan yells, yanking me to my feet.

I stumble, firmly placing my hand on the door frame to prevent Dylan from dragging me out. It was my inner demon who wanted them all to die—not me. I can't let Malicevile do this. I fly across the room and smash into his back, sending him into the wall. He growls, throwing me off him, and I narrowly miss landing on Monte's unmoving body.

Sparks erupt from Malicevile's hands, and he shoots them out, hitting the frightened alliance leaders trying to escape. I charge at Malicevile again, blood pounding in my head, and graze his shoulder with my fist.

He slaps my face hard, and my head jerks to the side, but I don't let the pain knock me off my feet. "Camilla, what do you think you're doing? These people sentenced you to death. Their wretched souls don't deserve to be saved."

As I stumble from the slap, I glance at the tile, seeing the precious glint of a dagger within my reach. I reach down, grabbing it before Malicevile notices me move. He's more focused on keeping the leaders in the room than on me. Bending my knees, I jump into the air and drive the dagger into his shoulder. The blade cleanly slices through his suit jacket, and he reaches out, grabbing my arm.

Yanking free, I reach for the dagger, but Malicevile's faster. He dislodges it from his shoulder, and before I have a chance to react, molten pain consumes my shoulder. The hilt of the weapon protrudes from my own shoulder where Malicevile has stabbed me.

I drop to my knees, tears leaking from my eyes, and hot blood drips from my shoulder. My fingers go numb, and my arm settles limply at my side.

Screaming, I slide the dagger free. Against my better judgment, I glide towards Malicevile again. He elbows me in the face, and my nose cracks, sending shooting pain through me. The pain is excruciating, hazing my vision with black spots, and I breathe heavily through my mouth to keep from passing out.

I'm severely outmatched. I don't know why I even bother.

To make a point? To show that I'm not my father's daughter? It's not like my point will matter in the end. I'm not the alliance leaders' savior. I'm just a demi-demon who is Hell-bound. And fighting Malicevile isn't going to be my redemption.

Through my tears, I watch in horror as Malicevile's head begins to twitch on his neck, the popping sound of a body shifting, deafening. His handsome face begins to contort, the bones in his forehead expanding as his skin tightens against the pressure. Blood spurts on my face as his skin rips, a crown of sharp, black horns pushing through.

My heart nearly explodes as Malicevile shifts into his true demonic form. He's the scariest creature I've ever laid eyes on, like a skinned human, just muscles, tendons, and bones. His underskin is the same crimson color as blood, but black liquid flows through his veins. Spikes made from bone jet up his arms, ripping through his sleeves. Fire burns in his emerald eyes.

He steps closer to me in all his demonic glory. "You will *not* interfere, Camilla. I have claim on these spoiled, rotten souls." Malicevile's voice reverberates through the small room, deep and thunderous, and my soul almost jumps from my body.

I take a deep breath, bend my knees, and launch at my father, who looks how I imagine Lucifer himself to look like. My foot snags, and I drop to the floor, peering behind me. Dylan grips my ankle, his golden wings flashing in and out of existence, and drags me away from my demonic father. My nails scratch the tiles, but I can't find anything deep enough to grasp onto.

"Cami, we have to go, now!" Dylan yells.

Thrashing, I resist him, punching him wherever I can make contact. He scoops me into his arms and holds me tightly to his chest. Screams erupt, piercing my ear drums. Blood splashes my face, the warm, coppery liquid coating the floors, walls, and everything in a sick, gut-wrenching blood bath.

"He's killing them," I cry helplessly into Dylan's ear. "You have to save their souls. Don't let him take them."

"I can't fight him. I'm only a nephilim," Dylan says. "It's too late, Cami. They're already gone. They were gone the moment he stepped in."

"Oh, God, no." The blood of the alliance leaders drips down my face, mixing with my tears.

Clutching me to him, Dylan races out, tears up a flight of stairs, and pushes open a door to the outside. We were in a cellar of some sort. I can't tell where we are by the surroundings, but it looks like we're in the middle of nowhere.

He speeds up, jumping into the air after a few feet, and we soar into the sky and away from Malicevile and the dead alliance leaders. The night sky glitters with stars and the moon is low in the sky, preparing to set.

The headlights of a parked car beam a line of light, illuminating a small, one lane road. Two figures wave at us, and I can tell they aren't ordinary humans.

"Dylan, look!" My heart races when the glow of the headlamps lights up Cadence's deep purple hair.

We drop suddenly, heading for the ground. Dylan carefully drags his feet on the road, bringing us to a stop, and I jump from his arms.

Evan and Cadence almost knock me over, hugging me and kissing my hair. It feels like I've been away from them forever, and I never want to let them go.

Cadence steps back, runs to Dylan, and squeezes him against her. I jump into Evan's arms, wrapping my legs around his hips, breathing in his amber and patchouli scent.

After the excitement dwindles, raw, sheer sadness overwhelms my soul. My smiles melt into tears, and I hiccup and sputter, trying to pull myself together. "Malicevile killed them," I cry. "And it's my fault."

Cadence gasps, covering her mouth with her hand. "My dad? That wasn't part of—"

Dylan squeezes her again. "He's okay. You're father's okay."

Cadence's panic shifts to relief but sadness still lines her eyes. She kicks the tire of the car and screams, covering her face with her hands. "He said he wouldn't kill anyone!" she yells.

Evan clears his throat, shifting his aquatic eyes to the ground. "He said he wouldn't kill any *innocent* leaders."

"We were so stupid," Cadence mutters. "He tricked us."

I study Evan, tracing my finger along his knitted brow. I use my good arm to lift his chin, making him look me in the eyes. He pulls me closer, pressing his lips to mine.

Dylan coughs behind me. "It's not over."

I push away from Evan, dropping to my feet. When I see Malicevile gliding toward us, slow, soul-shaking convulsions begin in my stomach and work their way through me. He's shifted back to his human form, but it doesn't disguise his torn, bloody clothing.

I stagger forward, blocking my friends from my demonic father. He smiles brilliantly, showing off his perfectly white teeth.

"Don't look so frightened, Camilla. I'm not going to hurt you. I've done you a favor by taking care of our enemies."

I open my mouth to argue, but I can't. I'd be lying if I said the alliance members were my friends, because they weren't. I just wish they didn't have to die like they did.

"Just leave," I mutter. "You've done enough damage."

"If you wish," he says smoothly, glancing at my friends behind me. "Now that I've held up my end of the bargain, it's your turn."

I stare between Malicevile, Evan, and Cadence, my heart slowly breaking in my chest. They've made a deal with a demon to save my life, but what did they give up for it?

No one moves.

No one breathes.

And then Evan steps forward.

It feels like the world shifts under my feet, and I lose my balance, landing hard on the ground. My palms scrape on the dirty pavement, and I can barely hold onto my consciousness.

"This can't be happening," I whisper, my throat burning

with a silent scream. "Evan, what have you done?"

Evan's sad eyes gaze at me lovingly. He bends down and kisses my head, the touch like the whisper of wings. "I love you, Cami. You know I'd do anything for you. I want you to fight the good fight for me, okay? You deserve a good life."

Numbness washes over me as his words sink in. "I—I...No. Evan, please. No. You deserve a good life. We'll figure this out."

Tears rim his eyes. "It's already done. I've traded my soul to save yours." He lets go of my hands.

"How could you?" My hands tremble.

"How could I not? It's the best decision I've ever made." He kisses my cheek. "Goodbye, Cami. Take care of the others for me. Live your life. Do it for me. It's why I did this. I hope you can forgive me one day."

I shake my head back and forth, my hair whipping my face, sticking to my wet cheeks. Words lodge in my throat, and I silently watch through my hot tears as Evan steps into the car before Malicevile. He presses his fingers to the window, saying goodbye one last time.

I dig my fingers into the ground, searching for anything to grab onto. I can't find the strength to stay together any longer. My heart breaks, and the pain is so overwhelming, it feels like I'm suffocating. Cadence and Dylan call my name, but I don't respond. I can only focus on the red taillights growing smaller as Evan is taken from me.

"Cami, we'll get him back," Cadence says, clutching my shoulders. "I swear to God. We'll get him back."

I'd love nothing more than to believe her, but in my heart I know there's nothing I can do. My father has won.

Dylan's warm, pure light encircles me, caressing and soothing my frail, tormented soul. I try to absorb his light, allowing him into my soul to take away this pain seizing my heart, but there's nothing he can do to stop the pain that blazes in my core.

It's too late. My soul's been crushed beyond repair.

MOVING ON

THE COOL BREEZE tangles my hair, playing with soft, dark tendrils that hang loosely down my back. Sunshine warms my face, and it feels like I'm trapped in one of Dylan's dream worlds.

The luscious, emerald green grass is soft under my bare feet, and I carefully bend down, leaning on my knees. Vases of flowers waft sweet scents around me. It seems too beautiful of a day to spend in a cemetery.

After all the death I've seen, it's strange that this is the first funeral I've ever been to. My heart beats with sorrow because the boy who gave his soul for mine couldn't be here with me to celebrate the life of the woman who spent almost all my life protecting me from my demonic father.

I trace the engraving of my mom's name with my fingertips, the smooth stone cool on this warm, sunny day. I pull the crystal cylinder vial from my small bag and dig my fingers into the grass to make a spot for it.

"You're home, Mom," I whisper, even though I know her soul has moved on to be with my dad. Dylan made sure of it. I can't help talking to the empty cylinder though. It's the only thing I have left that belonged to her, and I'm finally ready to let go.

I sit silently, remembering what she looked like. How her brown hair was the same shade as mine and how her eyes would crinkle when she laughed. I remember how she would tuck me in at night and how I would complain about the blankets being too tight. She'd laugh and say it was to keep me from floating away. It didn't make sense back then, but I can't help the smile forming on my lips when I think about it now.

"Say hi to Dad for me," I add, pressing into the grass to push myself up.

I turn from my mom's resting place and see Cadence, Alana, David, and Dylan waiting for me by the Jaguar. Alana smiles sadly, rubbing the rough scabs healing on her neck. The hunter who tried to break me by hurting Alana missed slicing important arteries by a hair, and luckily for her, our friends acted quickly to save her life.

Alana opens her arms for me, and I run to her, burying my

face in her shoulder. I sob silently, releasing all my sadness and grief.

"It's over, Cami," she whispers, soothing me. "It's time to move on."

Wiping tears from my eyes, I nod. Alana's right. The past isn't something I should hold on to when I have my entire future ahead of me. My parents are now together, somewhere in the beyond, and I've found the peace I've craved for so long since their deaths.

"There's one more soul I need to free, Alana. I made Evan a promise."

She nods without another word.

The boy I love most in the world traded his soul for mine, and I won't let him down. One way or another, I'll release him from his contract with my demon father. I won't waste a moment of my second chance at life.

I don't know how long I'll keep the demon within me at bay, or if I'll ever manage to teeter my soul back to the side of goodness, but right now, I need to pick up the pieces of my life and my soul, and fight on the side I want to be on. Right now, because of Evan, my soul is finally free.

To be continued...

ACKNOWLEDGMENTS

THIS PUBLICATION JOURNEY would not have been as much fun if it weren't for the team of awesome people who have put so much time and effort into this series. Without them, I'd be a crushed (hehe) mess. Thank you to Jamie for letting me tell you every single spoiler before you've even had a chance to read them. You're a great critique partner, and I'd be lost if I had no one to work plot points through with. Thank you to Jan for letting me pester you all hours of the day and night with questions, and for giving me your expertise when it comes to fragrance, flowers, and writing. And lastly, thanks to Katie Harder-Schauer for your proofreading expertise. To all three of you, I am sorry—wait, no—I'm NOT sorry if this book elicited some strong, angry emotions from you. It did the same to me as well!

Thanks to my BFF Jazmin Garcia for letting me use your name. I appreciate that you let me talk about my characters like they're old friends, and for giving me the inspiration to write a rather funny character interview with me, you, and oh-so-scarily-charming Malicevile.

As always, a big thanks to my family for your love and support through my publication journey. Thanks to my husband, who lets me spend countless amount of hours glued to my computer, and to my daughter, who hangs out with me while I write, and is ever so patience when I ask if I can finish just one more paragraph. To the rest of my friends and family, thanks!

Lastly, thank you to my readers—whether you're Team Evan, Team Dylan, Team Cami, or even Team Malicevile—I appreciate every single one of you. Without you, this journey wouldn't be as fun.

ABOUT GINNA MORAN

GINNA MORAN IS A WRITER from sunny Southern California. She started writing poetry as a teenager in a spiral notebook that she still has tucked away on her desk today. Her love of writing grew after she graduated high school, and she completed her first unpublished manuscript at age eighteen.

When she realized her love of writing was her life's passion, she studied literature at Mira Costa College in Northern San Diego. Besides writing novels, she was senior editor, content manager, and image coordinator for Crescent House Publishing Inc. for four years.

Aside from Ginna's professional life, she enjoys binge watching television shows, playing pretend with her daughter, and cuddling with her dogs. Some of her favorite things include chocolate, anything that glitters, cheesy jokes, and organizing her bookshelf.

Ginna Moran loves to hear from her readers so visit her online at www.GinnaMoran.com. You can also find her on her Facebook page or Group, Twitter, Instagram, and Snapchat. To stay up-to-date on new releases, sign up to her newsletter. You'll not only get a FREE book, but you'll be able to participate in monthly giveaways!

Ginna Moran is currently hard at work on her next novel.

MORE BY GINNA MORAN

PARANORMAL

Destined for Dreams Series
Demon Within Series
Finding Nate Series
Going Ghostly Series
Spark of Life Series
When Souls Collide Series
Demon Watcher Series
Call of the Ocean Series

CONTEMPORARY

Falling into Fame Series

STANDALONES

Life After Lila